HEKATE'S
DAUGHTER

HEKATE'S DAUGHTER

a novel by
Mirjam Dikken

Stonehouse Publishing Inc. is an independent
publishing house, incorporated in 2014.

Cover design and layout by Elizabeth Friesen.
Printed in Canada

Stonehouse Publishing would like to thank and acknowledge
the support of the Alberta Government funding for the arts,
through the Alberta Media Fund.

Government

National Library of Canada Cataloguing in Publication Data
Mirjam Dikken
Hekate's Daughter
Novel
ISBN 978-1-988754-58-1
First edition

For my parents, Gerhard and Rija,
who taught me the love for language

CHAPTER ONE

The complicated lacy bras on the second floor of De Bijenkorf, Rotterdam's largest department store, lure my gaze—as they're supposed to, I guess. Should I try one for a change? Must be six years since I tied myself up in something fancy. When I'd finally figured out where the numerous black straps were supposed to go, I resembled a netted ham instead of a seductive lingerie model.

I march past the frilly display. With a non-existent love life, there's no point in lacing up and have wires puncture my skin. Besides, having just quit my fourth job in as many years since university is change enough for now. I grab my usual comfy sports bra and join the line at the cashier.

A lady with a bulging bag leaves, and the man in front of me steps forward. The cashier's emotions spike, and her thoughts jump at me—*What a creep.* She holds up crimson red lacy panties between forefinger and thumb.

The man hunches in his black coat. His worries worm their way into my mind—*Wish he could come earlier. Hate it when he makes me hold on to the merchandise for hours.* The cashier wraps the lingerie in thin paper. The man pictures the garment on a young girl. *He'll pay the raised price once he sees her in this.*

What? What's going on? And that girl, why does she seem familiar?

I concentrate on his mind, where the girl's face is distorted with fear, brown eyes crying, dark blonde hair disheveled.

I've seen that face before, recently. Closing my eyes, I review the past few days.

Yes! The Amber Alert Bert showed me this morning at work. A

girl went missing on her way to school. In the photo, those sweet brown eyes smiled, but it's the same girl alright. Does this man have her? As 'merchandise'?

Someone taps my shoulder. "Miss? It's your turn." A woman behind me gestures to the now empty counter.

"Sorry, I... forgot something." I step aside to let her pass and scout the floor. The man steps onto the escalator, clutching a small bag. His balding head descends out of view. I dump my unpaid underwear on a rack with white sports socks and run to the escalator.

As I step on, the man steps off below. I jump down the metal steps. A young mother frowns, but pulls her toddler aside to let me pass. The man scuttles through the perfume department towards an exit.

A girl in a navy-blue dress with a name tag steps out of her booth, a strip of white cardboard in her hand. "Would you like to try our newest fragrance?"

I shake my head, not even making eye contact, and suppress a fleeting feeling of guilt. She's probably been brushed off in worse ways.

I push through the revolving door he just disappeared through. Among the many pedestrians huddling in their coats, several wear a dark one. *No, no, no, I can't have lost him already!* I scan the area. A balding head unlocks a rusty bike in a disarray of parked bicycles along the wall, a bag hanging on the left handle. He starts pedaling, swerves around a few shoppers and enters the bike path towards the crossing with the Coolsingel.

I take off, my backpack bumping into my spine. The traffic light changes to orange, and he speeds up. Red. I sprint across the busy street. A car pulls up and brakes hard, the bumper halting two inches from my knees. I feel the adrenaline surging through the driver, followed by anger. He honks and I hold up a hand in apology.

The man in the black coat zigzags through a group of teenagers and takes a left. After a few minutes, he rounds a corner to the right and crosses a canal. I pant and sweat trickles down my back. What was I thinking? I can't keep this up for long.

The girl's face swims before my eyes. Smiling in the picture, crying in the man's memory. I grit my teeth and ignore my burning quads.

In a street with identical, brown-bricked townhouses, he slows down and dismounts. Wheezing, I drop my pace to a firm walk. He places the bike against a tree and locks it. He gazes around and focuses on me. *Who's that?*

I walk to a bus stop across the street from him and lean against the sign. Still panting, I attempt to yawn, grab my phone, and make scrolling movements.

Just waiting for the bus. No one watching me. Buyer should be here in half an hour. He enters a house.

From his direction, an intense terror washes over me, knocking the new air from my lungs. *The door! Who's there? Mommy... I wanna go home...* The little girl's emotions are so strong, it's as if she's standing next to me. She collapses, her knees grazing a rough concrete floor, fright shaking her entire body. I bend over, hands on my knees, nursing pain that isn't mine.

He has the Amber Alert girl. And she needs to be rescued within half an hour. I glance at the house. A door and two windows on the ground floor. Possible other entry points at the back, but getting there takes time and exposes me to neighbours. Breaking a window? Draws too much attention. Forcing a way in through the door? Equally low chance of success.

There's just one way. I clench my fists. I'd promised to protect myself, to keep my nose out of everybody's business. Never again do I want to sit across the table from a row of accusing, scrutinizing faces, and lose my job and reputation. I vowed to live like everyone else, like everyone who passes by criminals every day, in blissful ignorance.

But that's the thing. There's no blissful ignorance for me. My fingernails drive into my palms. This is about the devastation of a young girl's life versus my oath to protect myself—that doesn't even qualify as a choice.

I yank the old sim-card for emergencies out of my wallet and slide it into my work phone. While the phone boots up, I rehearse a short and precise message. I call the emergency number and tell them where to find the Amber Alert girl. The operator asks me how I know.

"Just hurry, she'll be moved in half an hour!" I hang up and take the sim-card out.

How long would it take the police to get here? We're close to the main police station and they're on high alert for the girl. Five, ten minutes max. It might help to stall and distract the man. But how? I contemplate throwing a stone through his window, until a movement to the left of the man's house alerts me to a neighbour watching me through her purple curtains. Breaking something won't help.

I cross the street and grab an envelope sticking out from the mailbox of his neighbour to the right, take a deep breath, ring the man's doorbell and search for his thoughts inside.

Can't be him already? Better check. He unlocks the door and peers through a small gap.

Bile rises in my throat. "Hello, sir, I work for the municipality. I'm checking in on your recent complaint."

"What complaint?"

I look down at the envelope as if to check notes. "You complained a few weeks ago about the trash collection, right?"

He shakes his head and retreats.

I place a hand on the door and peek through the gap. In the dark hallway, I can make out a staircase and two doors. I shiver. "Excuse me, sir. I need to follow-up. Can I come in?"

The man shakes his head. "I'll withdraw the complaint."

"I would still need your signature for that, sir. Could you let me in?"

We stare at each other, both pressing our hands at opposite sides of the door.

Blaring sirens pierce the cold air. I release the pressure on my side of the door and the man hurls it shut.

I stuff the envelope back in the neighbour's mailbox and watch screeching police cars speeding past me. Several neighbours now hold their curtains aside and peek out.

Police officers ring the bell twice and then force themselves in, leaving two cops outside to guard the door.

People emerge from their houses and form a small crowd on the street. Nobody pays attention when I join them.

I concentrate on the people inside the man's house. The girl's terrified thoughts stand out among the thoughts of three cops searching, focused, driven by adrenaline. I close my eyes to focus and find the kidnapper's mind. His unease ebbs away until he almost sings his thoughts. *I knew it! Such a clever idea.* He pictures his ingenuous cover up of the entrance to his cellar.

My shoulders tense. I tune into the thoughts of the guarding cops. One scans the crowd, bored. The other rehearses answers for a job interview to become a detective. She's ambitious, driven. More likely to act straight away.

Casual but loud, I remark to a woman next to me, "These houses have cellars, with a trapdoor in the closet under the stairs, right?"

The ambitious cop perks up and disappears into the house, thinking, *A cellar!*

I stay in her mind while she asks her superior for permission to check under the stairs. She opens the closet door, removes the vacuum cleaner, the carpet, and grabs the ring of the trapdoor.

The intense fear of the little girl merges with unbelief, when she sees a female police officer coming down the ladder.

With a long sigh, tension disperses from my body, leaving fatigue and trembling muscles behind. It's over.

An intense thought penetrates through the curious minds of the crowd. *That one's acting strange.* The male cop outside studies me. *Got her on the body cam. Need to check her out. The guilty ones often hide amongst the sensation seekers.*

I jerk my head up, right into his fixed stare. Then another cop emerges from the house, and his attention shifts.

My stomach sinks, and I slink away.

Did I just lead the police to discover a lot more than the little girl?

CHAPTER TWO

In half an hour, the tranquil streets of Rotterdam will fill with the continuous roar of car engines gearing up and down, drowning out most other sounds. But for now, I pedal in relative peace past trees where chirping birds announce a new day, under a sky transforming from a pitch black to a deep blue.

My legs complain, still tired from the chase three days ago. Physically, the metro is an easier, and certainly warmer, mode of transport. Psychologically, it's exhausting. A metro is big enough to carry a fair number of people, and small enough to hear most of their thoughts. Or worse, feel them. Emotions are contagious. I don't want to end up at the office being angry or sad for someone else.

From my loft in the city centre, I bike past a mix of old houses, modern architecture, and concrete apartment buildings. As if a kid built this city from different toy construction sets. Near the Erasmus University, the roads widen and the space between buildings increases. The tall office blocks east of the highway A16 loom closer for the last time. When I gave notice last Monday, Ted wasn't amused and summoned me to hand everything over by today.

Bert's already at his desk. "Good morning, Kathy." He wrings his hands. "I heard you discouraged Ted from firing Mark?" *Secretary says they yelled at each other.*

I shrug. An HR manager shouldn't talk behind her boss's back. Besides, people apparently know anyway.

Bert grins. "You're considered a hero. The general opinion is, Ted wants to get rid of the best manager in his team, just to fix his own insecurity." He swallows. "I'm really sorry to see you go."

I sigh. "Yeah. Me too." For a year, I hadn't abruptly left meetings because the man sitting next to me thought about hitting his wife. Nor did I call anyone a hypocrite because they were sucking up to a colleague they despised. But when Ted pictured me naked and fantasised about how he'd like me to obey, I'd blurted out my resignation. Someone else's emotions became too hard to handle, and I'd taken a rash decision. Again.

Three hours later, I hug Bert in the lobby. I walk towards the exit and turn around one last time to wave. His shoulders sag with the work I just handed over. Both our smiles don't reach our eyes. The sliding office doors click to a close behind me.

My backpack feels weightless without the company laptop, now on the desk of IT. I retrieve my bike from the rack at the back of the office building.

I steer south towards the Nieuwe Maas for a soothing dose of ever-flowing water. I reach the river, inhale the water's wet dog smell and turn right towards the city centre. Today, the surface of the river is smooth, but it conceals the powerful force underneath. A plastic bottle bobs up and down, going faster than I can keep up with.

I cross under the Van Brienenoord bridge and park my bike against one of the colossal pillars. The other side of the river is far away. This immense body of water separates the city into two unique halves. Several striking, robust bridges patch the city to a whole again, traffic crossing, mingling between north and south.

I look up. A massive amount of concrete spans the river, carrying a rumbling twelve lanes of traffic.

Will I ever find a bridge with two-way traffic between me and the world on the other side? Once I come closer to others, I'm hit with the cruelty of understanding them in a way no one will ever understand me. And I withdraw to my side of the river. Burning the bridges.

Why is she here? Almost missed her leaving work.

I glance around. The only person in sight is a man walking his dog. The thoughts don't belong to him, his mind is on his home renovation. His style of thinking is different, anyway.

They say her mother worked for the Syndicate. Only with Bernard.

No clue why we need to follow her daughter now.

Squinting, I scan a larger perimeter. The thoughts seem to come from several cars parked along the road a few hundred metres away. But it can't be about me. My mother died, just before I turned four.

Her face swims before my eyes. Devoid of expression, its whiteness accentuated by trickles of dried blood, her beautiful eyes closed. A persistent second-hand image, handed down through my dad. I shiver and shrug deeper into my coat.

As usual, I try to push the awful vision away by replacing it with nicer memories, although those are few and vague. The safety of her warm hug. Her reassuring hand on my head. Fragments of a happy infancy, bringing along their unwelcome companions, yearning and sorrow.

Did my mother work? I don't even know that about her. What would she have said about me quitting a job again?

I walk to the edge, the cold water luring below me. What would it feel like to jump? Cold, no doubt, but at least the water would embrace me, carry me, engulf me.

CHAPTER THREE

The woman establishes her seniority without a doubt, standing firmly upright, positioned in front of her male colleague. She holds her badge to my face to confirm she is indeed Cecilia Yong, a detective with the Rotterdam police department.

Simultaneously with her authoritative, "Kathy van der Laan, may we come in?" she takes a step forward, confident to be granted access. Although her advantage in height is just a few centimetres, her personality towers over me and her stern eyes stare me down.

I step aside and close the door behind them. The cops must have finally figured me out. My stomach sinks. Shivering, I tune into their minds.

Cecilia walks around to assess my compact loft apartment. *Functional, small living room. Clean kitchen. Clearly single. No visible sign of pets. No clutter, except memorial cube. Tea still steaming, next to laptop on dining table. Job search website open.*

Her matter-of-fact staccato observations contrast her state of mind. I feel guardedness, a professional keen interest, and an overall suspicion towards me.

Arms crossed, I remain at the door. They're in *my* personal space, where nobody enters uninvited. Or to be precise, where nobody enters at all.

I glimpse at the river, a silver ever-present force behind the building across the street, and straighten my shoulders. If they're here to expose me, they can do so standing up, thirsty. No need to dust off my rusty host-playing skills.

Unperturbed, Cecilia gestures to the chair I obviously just sat in, seating herself on the opposite. Somehow, she blends in, as if she's been here countless times before. After a brief hesitation, the male cop, although not invited by Cecilia, sits down next to her.

Fine. I plunk down in my chair, seat still warm, and snap my laptop shut. Those cops have no business glancing at the screen. Even if it just shows a legitimate job search.

Cecilia observes me, not in a hurry to start, arranging her thoughts before getting to the purpose of their visit. *See if she's the babbling type, who can't stand silence.*

So they're not here for my mind-reading. I release my breath.

Cecilia's gaze intensifies. *There's something about those eyes... Make her look way older than twenty-seven. Have to nail her on the sim-card. To know why she called in tips. Especially for the Amber Alert.*

Shit, they caught on to the sim-card. Heat crawls up in my face.

Cecilia notices. *She feels uncomfortable. Good. More likely to tell the truth.* She leans forward and locks her almond-shaped, dark eyes onto mine. "When you called in the tip on the girl from the Amber Alert, why did you use your work phone with a different sim-card?"

She likes the direct attack. No surprise there. I shift in my chair. How can they know it was my work phone? I scan their thoughts, but both just look at me, trying to read my behaviour.

"I bought this sim-card for private calls."

Wrong answer. Their anticipation of being onto something flares up. Cecilia's eyes narrow. *Bullshit! First call in a year with that sim-card. Plenty private calls on her work number.* She asks, "In the past, you've called in several anonymous tips. Some very useful. How come?"

I wince. The absolute truth would explain it all. 'Oh, you see, I'm a mind-reader. I can tell when people are about to commit a crime, or where they've hidden the evidence, or when they're about to sell a little girl.' But they'll come after me like a pack of wolves chasing elk. Life as I know it will be over. I need to lie. Convincingly.

Cecilia barks, "Well?" Her fierce face reminds me of the scary three-women-statue at my mother's farmhouse. Cecilia would be the one holding up a knife, ready to point it at my throat.

I shiver. "I don't understand. Just called in this one. I bought the sim-card that afternoon for private calls."

"Which shop? You have a receipt?"

"No... I just wanted a cheap prepaid sim. Let me write down the name of the shop." I stand up and pretend to search for a piece of paper. What was the name of that shop I passed a few weeks ago? Someone had walked out, congratulating himself on buying a non-traceable sim. I rumble through a few drawers. 'Cheap calls', that's it. I jot it down on a yellow sticky-note.

"You realise we'll check this?" Cecilia pushes a strand of sleek black hair behind her ear and scans the paper. *Know that shop. Shady. Won't admit to selling it, even if they did. Dead end.*

My shoulders relax. "Of course."

Cecilia's eyes fixate mine again. "Take us through how you knew where to find the girl from the Amber Alert, step by step."

I swallow. Better stay as close to the truth as possible. "Monday morning at work, my colleague showed me the Amber Alert. He has an eight-month-old son, and ever since he became a father, this kind of news is personal to him."

A rush of angry adrenaline surges through the male cop. *So true. I thought being a cop would harden me to these situations. But ever since Julia was born... In six months, she'll go to the same school as that girl! So glad we got this lowlife off the streets.*

I continue, "I'd taken the afternoon off and went to De Bijenkorf to buy clothes." Oops, need to include my earlier lie. "That is, I first bought the sim-card, then went to De Bijenkorf. When I waited in line, I noticed the cashier responding oddly to the customer before me. She held up crimson red lacy panties for scanning. The garment didn't seem to fit an adult woman."

Cecilia's eyes widen. "You would suspect any man buying small-sized lingerie?"

My cheeks burn. Maybe I should think through my answers. I grab my tea mug, ready to take a sip.

The male cop watches us with interest, suppressing a chuckle.

Cecilia has met her match. She probably lives in a similar singles apartment, bare of personal stuff. Personality twins. Both direct, no-nonsense, straightforward. Like to give it right between the eyes.

I want to kick him under the table. I take pride in the traits he just summed up. Traits, however, that turn Cecilia into a pain in the ass.

"And then?" Cecilia raps her fingers on the table, then stops. *Shouldn't show impatience. Hate it how she stalls.*

I slurp some tea and take my time to swallow. "He… seemed to be hiding something. I decided to follow him. When he arrived at his house, he scanned his surroundings. Nobody does that, coming home." A stone settles in my stomach. "I… had such a strong feeling about this. I'd put the new sim-card in my work phone to try it, so I guess I called the emergency number with that sim."

"We checked the body cams of the cops waiting outside the house. You were there. Mentioning something about a cellar." *She knows more. Why doesn't she tell us?*

"Right. I started to walk away but couldn't leave and turned back. I thought some of these houses had a cellar, so I asked another bystander." My hand trembles and I put my mug down. "How's the girl? Is she alright? She must have been terrified."

Cecilia softens a bit. "The girl is quite shaken, but unharmed." *Thanks to you. Still, doesn't add up.* She looks at me.

I smile at both. See how they deal with their own technique of silence.

Cecilia stands up. *Need to dig deeper. She knows more. I will get at the truth.* "We might ask you more questions at a later time."

They nod and leave. I close the door behind them, leaning my forehead against the cool surface. I really should stop calling in tips anonymously. People won't understand my abilities. How can they? Even I don't.

CHAPTER FOUR

"You quit your job again?" Dad tries to hide the desperation in his voice.

It's a good thing we're on the phone. I don't want to hear the critical thoughts he chooses not to say out loud. My own father should have the opportunity to communicate just the things he *wants* to share with me. Not the rest, too.

I mumble, "I didn't like my boss." Even without reading his mind, I know he thinks, *Kathy, there are difficult bosses everywhere.*

"Right." Dad sighs. "Will you look for another job in Human Resources? Or are you looking for something else all together?"

"Probably another job in HR. I like the field."

"I'd hoped it would suit you. As a teenager, you were quite withdrawn. People were unnerved by you. The way you observed the world, with eyes that they felt saw right through them. I thought it might be an asset in HR."

My stomach knots. What if he knew about my real asset... The first time I tried to tell him he laughed, stated the impossibility of mind-reading, and stroked my head. The second time, eight-year-old me wanted to show off and told him what he was thinking. For a few seconds, he contemplated it, his fear and confusion building. Then he pushed those emotions to the back, stated again it wasn't possible, and locked it up in his mind. Indignant, I thought of better ways to raise the topic with him. Then he fell in love again and became too engrossed in his own thoughts. Thoughts that confused and embarrassed me... He attributed my withdrawal to resentment towards my stepmother, and I left it at that.

Meandering through my living room, I pick up the memorial

cube with some of my mother's ashes Dad gave me. I squeeze my fingers around the cube. "Did my mother have a job?"

He inhales audibly. "Yes... yes, she did. Although she had no formal education after high school, she worked a few years as a personal assistant. For an organisation that had something to do with the European Union." He pauses. "Why do you ask?"

"Oh, just wondering. Did she not want to study after high school?"

"Well, she always thought she would continue the farm she grew up on. But times were bad for small farmers, so her parents sold the animals and most of the land just before they died. Your mother got offered a job by someone at a party. That was before we met. She liked the job at first. After you were born, the care for you became hard to manage with her irregular hours. We were talking about her giving up her job, when..." He halts.

I rush in to save him from the most horrible flashbacks I have seen entering his mind when thinking about my mother. "I see. Thanks, I was just wondering. Uhm, gotta go. Tell Alida I said hi. Love you Dad."

I place the memorial cube back on the windowsill. Dad and I never talk much about my mother. Brings back painful memories. They never found the hit-and-run driver who left her dying on the side of the road late in the evening. I would love to know more about her, but Dad won't be able to answer my most burning question anyway—could she read minds as well?

A few months after she died, I went to kindergarten. I was just learning to distinguish other people's thoughts and emotions from my own. A girl named Pamela bullied a boy in our class, with a knack for timing, as she always managed to harass him when the teacher didn't notice. Pamela contemplated tearing up his drawing, so I hit her. She screamed, the teacher came over, and I adamantly recounted what Pamela had been thinking.

'You can't know what she's thinking,' the teacher said. 'And we never hit someone else, now do we, Kathy?'

Dutifully, I shook my head.

I glanced at Pamela, expecting a triumphant look for being pro-tected by the teacher. Instead, fear sparked in her eyes. From then on, she avoided me.

Children learn by discovery how to make friends and be loved—be nice; share; decide together on what to play; let others go first sometimes. I learned to add one more to that list: don't expose peo-ple's unspoken thoughts.

I walk over to a drawer and open it. At the back lies a picture of my mother, me on her lap, both smiling at the camera. A lovely picture. I push it back again and slam the drawer shut.

Without a warning, my mother was gone, and all I had left were my dad's horrifying memories of her lifeless body when he had to identify her.

Well, technically, she left me more. I inherited the farmhouse she grew up in with her adoptive parents. She'd stipulated not to sell before I turned twenty-five, so Dad sublet on my behalf. It's beyond me why my mother loved that farmhouse in an agricultural area south-west of Rotterdam, an impractical location inaccessible by public transport. Although I just have a few memories of the house, according to my father, she took me there often. A few weeks before she died, she showed me a statue in the garden. 'One day, it's yours. You will understand why.'

I don't. The unsettling sculpture shows three women standing back-to-back, representing the three sides of the Greek goddess Hekate. One woman holds up two torches, another a torch and an impressive knife, and the third has a snake curling around her arm while holding a key in the other. The goddess of crossroads, of spac-es in between. The goddess my mother had named me after.

After she died, we never went back there. I didn't want the house. Nor the statue.

I just wanted my mother.

CHAPTER FIVE

"Have you been to one of her sessions before?" asks the woman sitting next to me. Her eyes shine, full of expectation.

I shake my head, unable to speak in the middle of this mass of people. The air is heavy with their desperate hope for a miracle, resulting in a wholehearted devotion to the healer who is about to materialise on stage.

"It's my third session! When I heard she would grace us with her presence during this Festival of the Paranormal, I jumped at the opportunity to see her once more. She hasn't appeared publicly since she was accused of fraud." With her hand to her heart, she continues, "*Sooo* unfair! If people don't believe in her healing, why don't they just stay away?"

I shrug. "Well, she charged people for infusing normal bottles of water with her healing power, claiming it would help cure serious diseases."

"Worth every penny!" the woman replies with sincere indignation, before turning away from me. *If she doesn't believe Brigit delivers on her promises, what is she doing here?*

Indeed. What was I thinking?

Ever since I earned money, I travelled to find people like me. With eight billion people inhabiting our beautiful planet, there must be others who can read minds. Isn't there some statistical law stating the impossibility of being the only one with a brain irregularity? If not, there should be.

But then, so far, I found no one. I travelled extensively, chasing every hopeful story, and spent a week with two South-American shamans, a month learning from Indigenous people in Australia, seeking out special gurus all over India for three weeks.

I even tried fortune tellers. Like the one in New Delhi. The streets were full of human sounds, not unlike the excited audience in this hall. With eyes closed, I am transported back to Janpath about a year ago.

A friendly face under a bright blue turban had put itself into my path. I stepped to the right to skirt around him, he stepped to his left. I stepped to the left, he to his right. A dance performed by people the world over, when trying to get out of each other's way, only to find themselves blocking each other with every move.

Then he stepped to the left, just a tiny bit later than I stepped to my right. This was not one of those serendipitous dances. There was no avoiding this man.

"Madam, I can see you are a very special person. You have a beautiful future awaiting you. Let me tell you about it."

His thoughts, in one of the Indian languages, were not clear. Oh well, there couldn't be harm in trying him out.

"Let me first tell you about yourself." The energetic fortune teller took my hand, put a crumbled piece of paper in it, and pressed his fingers against mine to fold them shut. "I will prove I know about you and your future. Now, tell me why you're here."

Because I desperately want to find people like me. "Uhm, holiday."

He proceeded to ask me the name of my father and my year of birth. I humoured him, though grudgingly. He put both his hands around my fist again.

"Madam, could you now open the piece of paper and tell me what it says?"

I opened my hand and smoothed out the paper. It said 'holiday,' 'Gary' and '1993'. What?? How… I looked up at him. He beamed with pride.

"You see, Madam? I knew all this before we even talked! Now, I will tell you your future." He opened a folder. "Could you kindly please put some money here? To help the process."

I looked again at the paper with his scribblings on it. After we talked, he must have swiftly changed the papers. Clairvoyance played no role here. He'd been very skillful, I had to give him that.

He inched his folder into my view. With a little bow, he said, "Madam, please?"

I fumbled in my purse for some money and put fifty rupees in the folder.

He laughed. "You have seen what I am capable of, madam. Please, a little more. It works better with the power of several bills."

I rolled my eyes. But then again, most people work better when paid sufficiently, so I put in two more bills. He closed the folder. "Now, about your work. You are in a managerial position, right?"

I nodded.

"Yes, you have a great mind. And you enjoy your job, I can see that."

I didn't want to enlighten him I'd just quit my third job.

"I see there will be a big promotion for you in the future."

A snort escaped my mouth.

He pushed on. "Oh yes, a big promotion, within six months. I promise you that, Madam."

Sensing my lack of enthusiasm, he changed topic.

"This year you will meet your husband. If you could give me another bill, I will tell you about it." He opened the folder again.

I laughed.

The fortune teller looked upset. "I am very serious Madam. Very serious! Marriage is important."

This man needed a lesson. "Now it is my turn, sir. You are married, and have kids."

Involuntarily, he pictured a woman, a young boy, a younger girl, and a baby.

Eyes closed, I held my hands in front of his face. "Yes… yes, I can see them. A beautiful wife, a boy, a girl and a baby."

Irritation surged through his mind, feeding his determination to prove this foreign woman wrong. He pictured his glowing wife, telling him something, and an older man and woman being very happy. He narrowed his eyes. "You are not completely correct, madam."

Taking my chances, I responded in a dismissive tone, "Well, I didn't count the unborn baby. Your parents are very happy with another grandchild, right?"

His eyes grew wide with surprise, and he froze.

I grabbed the money and walked away.

Suddenly, the murmur of the audience explodes in wild applause. I open my eyes, and for an unsettling moment still seem to be in India. A woman with a dark blue gown resembling a sari, trimmed with silver lace and a matching headscarf, studded with sparkling stones, has centred herself on the stage. For effect, she raises her arms slowly. When her hands are fully in the air, the crowd goes silent, apart from a few people sobbing.

Poor lambs. I've still got it. Time to arrange a few bigger sessions. Time to make serious money off these innocents again.

I get up and leave, disgusted.

CHAPTER SIX

For half an hour I stroll around the stands of healing stones, crystals, tarot cards and psychic readers, before the next session starts. A workshop by a man who claims to be a psychic, teaching others how to stimulate their paranormal gifts. Although sceptical, once in a while I still cling to the idea there must be people like me. If the chance of finding someone takes spending an otherwise empty Saturday attending sessions at a dubious Festival for the Paranormal, so be it.

Five minutes before the start, I head to the corridor with small rooms in the exhibition centre. A thin man with white fluffy hair, smiling serenely, palms together in front of his heart, bows to participants giddily entering the room. I bow my head a little in response. In the room, nine chairs form a circle, of which five are occupied. A pair of women, faces so alike they must be sisters, are chatting. Another pair of women is going through a brochure together, to decide what they will do afterwards. A fifth woman appears to be alone, like me.

"Welcome, welcome," the man says after two more participants have come in and are settling themselves. First, he moves graciously to a corner, demonstrating his mindfulness by taking his sweet time to light two incense sticks. Their sickly pervading smell occupies the space almost immediately. I inspect the ceiling for conveniently located sprinklers, hoping they'll douse out the culprits. Alas, he placed his pollution sticks well.

The man floats to the last empty chair and lowers himself carefully. He surveys the circle. *All women, prefer it that way. More susceptible. The one next to Cherry seems sceptical. Need to be careful with that one.*

I glance at the name stickers he asked us to stick on our clothes upon entry. Cherry is the woman next to me. Given the faithful adoration on the face of Cherry's other neighbour, that makes me the sceptic. At least he got that right.

"As a child, I had paranormal visions. Unfortunately, my gift wasn't recognised as such in my social circle." He closes his eyes for a moment, raking up feelings of being lonely and misunderstood.

That makes two of us... Maybe I could warm up to this guy.

"To this day, I am filled with gratitude that the universe graciously allowed me to develop my gift when I was about twenty years old. I felt an inner fire growing in me."

He holds his fist against his chest and pauses. Six fixated, mesmerised faces are absorbing every word. Only Cherry looks bored.

"There are so many people out there like the little boy I once was, blessed with insights but not knowing how to make sense of them. I made it my personal mission to guide other people on their wonderful journey of discovering what they already have, re-establishing their connection to the spiritual world." He pauses again to look around the circle. His ethereal choice of words, thickening the already heavily incensed atmosphere, completely dampens my sympathetic feelings. "Who has had paranormal sensations before?"

Two women hold up their hands. They tell stories about 'knowing' a loved one was sick before he got the test results, and feeling their friend shouldn't go to a party and then the friend got into a car accident on the way.

The psychic nods solemnly. "You see, we need to take those signals seriously. The universe and spirit world are presenting them to us every day. We just need to become more open to receive the divine messages." From a folder at his feet, he produces a picture. "One way to practice your gift is to look at photographs and see what you can read from them." He holds it up to one of the two women claiming to have had a premonition about her friend having a car accident. "What can you tell me about who this guy was?"

Excited, she bends forward. For a minute, she concentrates intently on the picture. "Uhm. I think he is a salesman, about forty to forty-five years old."

The man nods, hiding his disappointment with an encouraging smile.

I feel a sharp exasperation from Cherry. *How did she miss that little cue 'was'? Most people pick up on that. Not quite the sensitive type.*

The first woman continues, "He's probably married. I think... two kids."

The other woman, the one knowing a loved one was sick, interrupts. "He died, didn't he?"

The man nods, his face drawn in the grave compassionate expression usually reserved for funerals. "He did. Very good. Excellent reading." *Bingo. A little more encouragement and she'll sign up for my weekend course.* "Now, does anyone else have a picture we could have a look at?"

One woman yells, "I do!" She waves her phone in the air.

The man shakes his head sadly. "For a good reading, we need an actual photograph. I'm afraid the magnetic radiation of the phone interferes with the vibrations of the spiritual world."

Cherry sits up, alert. "As a matter of fact, I have a photograph with me." She fumbles in her handbag, takes out her wallet, and produces a black-and-white photograph of a man. His hair style and military clothing suggest the picture was taken somewhere in the fifties.

"Who wants to try reading this photograph?" The workshop leader looks at the woman who 'read' the man in his picture was dead. *Reel her in.*

In a serious tone, she says, "This man died a long time ago. He... might have fought in the Second World War?"

Cherry gasps theatrically. "Yes! It is my great grandfather, he indeed was in the army."

Encouraged, the woman continues. "He had children. But...I sense he was sad. He might have lost his wife?"

Cherry brings her hand to her heart. "Wow, spot on! My great grandmother died young."

"Very good," the man chirps. "Now you can develop that gift. You can find out remarkable details from someone's life if you concentrate. Let me demonstrate." He closes his eyes and circles his hands slowly over the photo. A rhythm comes to his lightweight voice, as if reciting a mantra. "She didn't die a normal death. She lost her life…in an accident. An unusual accident."

Cherry produces a tear. "She helped a farming neighbour and got crushed under his tractor."

I swallow twice to keep myself from laughing. No one else seems to find it odd Cherry carries a photograph of a great grandfather who died decades ago, and still cries over someone deceased decades before she came into the world.

The man opens his eyes. "My apologies, unfortunately we are endowed with a limited amount of time today. You are a fantastic group. I am sensing a huge potential in many of you. If you would like to explore and develop your naturally given abilities, to strengthen your intuitive ability to spiritually connect with the amazing world around you, I would be humbled to continue working with each and every one of you in one of my workshops."

He retrieves a stack of slender brochures from his coat pocket and starts handing them out. *Should have at least one customer out of this.* Before he can turn to me, I rush out.

In the main hall of the exhibition centre, drowning in the bombardment of voices and thoughts of hundreds of visitors, my knees buckle. Each hopeful but useless attempt to find a fellow mind-reader feeds the hollowness inside. I sit down next to a serene dark grey statue of Buddha, slightly bowed in prayer towards a cute little fountain humming the luscious sound of tumbling water.

Should I give up hope to find someone like me and resign to hide who I am forever? Or face growing despair and disillusionment every time I unsuccessfully try to find someone like me? Maybe I should first decide which one is worse.

CHAPTER SEVEN

The whole day rain kept drizzling down, and the wetness of the passengers has accumulated on the metro's interior. The droplet pattern of the fine condensation on the inside of the windows morphs the view into a Van Gogh-like painting.

To be gentle to my suit, I'd chosen the metro over biking. Not that showing up in a dry, pristine suit would have made a difference. The job interview didn't go well. When they thought *her motivation is not strong enough*, I had to agree. My heart wasn't into it. The four jobs I'd held so far ended because I allowed my mind-reading to get me in trouble. Why would it be different next time?

Hello Kathy.

Surprised, I look around. Did someone say my name out loud?

I am the man with the greyish hair, sitting two rows in front of you, on the right. Don't say anything to me, I don't want other people to know we are chatting. Well, that I am chatting to you. In case you wonder, I can't hear your thoughts. But I know you can hear mine.

Shocked, I sit up straight. *What the hell?* Does someone know I can read minds? How is that even possible, if he doesn't read minds himself? It must be my imagination.

Just in case, I check. Two rows in front of me, to the right, are two people. As the person on the window seat is a woman cradling a snivelling baby, I turn my attention to the man next to her. He wears a long beige raincoat, with the collar turned up. His hair is silvery, with still some dark strands. He fits the description.

No, impossible. No one knows about me.

Your mother used to call this 'mind-talking'. We used to work to-

gether. We developed the habit that I would think, and she would talk out loud.

My mother comes to life in his mind—sitting at a table, relaxed, talking and laughing. His memories are vivid, I feel his concentration and intent to give me the best viewing he is capable of. Shock paralyses my doubts.

My mother... My mother! I don't know whether to scream, cry, or run. To steady myself, I clutch my backpack, eyes closed, bracing against an overwhelming longing to feel her, talk to her, be held by her.

We need to talk, but not here. We are probably watched. Come to your favourite coffee shop tonight, at 7 P.M., order something to go. I will communicate with you there.

He gets up, and through the foggy windows, a beige blur quickly walks out of sight.

What just happened? My mind must be playing tricks. It has been an intense week...being interviewed by the police, quitting my job, talking about my mother yesterday with Dad.

Could someone really know I can read minds? Or am I finally losing it?

At 7 P.M., I'll know.

CHAPTER EIGHT

Most mornings, I get my shot in this coffee shop, among other minds fixated on the workday ahead. This is my first visit in the evening. There's no line, and the atmosphere is more relaxed, now that people are winding down.

Too agitated to wait any longer, I got here ten minutes early. I order a double espresso and follow the process of producing the black liquid through the barista's mind. By now, I can probably squeeze a decent drink out of that impressive, hissing machine, knowing all the barista's moves by heart.

Tonight, the barista seems curious towards me. He places the coffee on the counter and, with an awkward gesture, places a card on top of it. He leans towards me, and says, "Hold on to it" thinking, *Such a strange request.*

Through his eyes, I see myself walking away and taking a seat. I always stomp straight past the arrangement of non-matching, worn chairs, almost always occupied, regardless of their uninviting look. But hesitation over the smudgy, frayed green velvet disappears once I sink back in the soft, deep chair.

Something feels off. Has the square clock always been on the wall between the windows? Why did I never notice the view outside before? That's why we like routines. Deviation feels awkward. I grab a magazine from a table and flip through it, searching for an interesting article. But none of the words make sense today.

I had almost convinced myself not to come. During the past hours, my left brain came up with reasonable doubts whether the incident in the metro was for real. 'Of course, no one knows I'm mind-reading.' 'If my mother would have been able to mind-read,

Dad would have known, wouldn't he?'

But would he have told me? I never asked... I stopped asking even little things about my mother, because every time that terrible image of her—eyes closed, dried blood—would flash through Dad's mind. Even now, my memory refuses to come up with anything else. I flip my wallet open to the picture of my mother, face intact and alive. But today, the creased image doesn't deliver comfort. I want the glorious video clips metro-man showed me. She was so alive, so real. Happy, beautiful. Her warm eyes open, smiling. No trace of dried blood.

And that's why I'm here, and have lowered myself into this faded but cozy monstrosity. Yes, the incident in the metro might very well just be a product of my fantasy. However, no matter how illogical the man's existence is, I would never forgive myself for not going. For not having another chance to see my mother as happy and alive, even if just through another person's memory.

I pick up my cup. Damn it. Half of the exquisite black liquid is already gone. I peek at the clock again. A few minutes past seven.

Did I imagine the man in the metro?

Seven past seven.

Shame and disappointment fight for first place, observed by Left Brain sitting back with arms crossed, pursed lips, saying, 'I told you so.' In a reasonable tone, Left Brain continues, 'Go home, take a bath, go to sleep early.'

The episode in the metro just can't have been real.

Studying Psychology, I learned how people go through experiences that feel as tangible to them as the chair I sit on, but are as fake as the Gucci handbag of the girl opposite of me.

If even a normal mind can trick the owner, my unusual brain certainly must be capable of deception. Being different eats away at you, a small bite every day, leaving a strain of inviting crumbs for insanity to catch up.

Is mind-reading finally compromising the rest of my brain? Am I losing it altogether?

I wrestle myself out of the chair's embrace, zip up my jacket, place my empty cup on the counter, and leave.

Outside, the wildfire of my chaotic thoughts gets doused by a welcome gust of cold air. See, that proves I'm weird. Cherishing the strong, chilling wind, while everyone in sight huddles together in the bus stop shelter.

Hello, Kathy. I'm glad you came. Keep walking. Go to the Blaak hotel. The card the barista gave you is the access key card. Take the elevator up to suite 1411. Let yourself in. I will join you in about twenty minutes.

Adrenaline pumping, I turn my head around to scan the area with such force, a muscle in my neck flinches.

Apart from the bus shelter, there's no one.

With tired groaning brakes, a bus pulls up to the stop. Among the throng of people boarding, one wears a long beige raincoat, with the collar turned up.

CHAPTER NINE

Halting outside the door of suite 1411, I scan for thoughts. There seems to be no one in the room. My throat tightens. So here I am. Entering a hotel suite to wait for someone I never officially met. I've never been so foolish before.

But then again, I've never met someone who knows about my mind-reading before.

The obedient lock buzzes when I hold the key card close. I push the door open to reveal a room furnished in oversized green and orange flower prints. Seriously? Do they expect anyone to appreciate this attempt at Dutch-tulip-themed cheerfulness?

From the doorway, I take a minute to get acquainted with the oppressive room. Two comfortable armchairs stand opposite a couch with a smoked glass coffee table in between. To the right of the couch is a door. A cupboard on the left wall contains a sink, microwave and a coffee machine. Closer to the windows is a dark wooden dresser that seems to be standard issue for hotel rooms worldwide, with a wide-screen tv on top.

I take a deep breath. Let's do this. I walk over to the large windows, framed by curtains with the same huge flower print. What a magnificent view. Down there are the grey, pointy roofs of the cube houses, and the few that have lights on show modern interiors. I pass the cube houses on the street all the time, but viewing them from above is a rare treat.

To the left, the vast arc of the Markthal is lit from the inside, exposing its colourful murals. Inside, this modern version of a market hall must be busy, as the shops close late on Fridays, at 9 P.M.. From this high viewpoint, the apartments plastered to the arc's outside look like a protective layer of the vast space within. If I didn't need several walls between me and others, I would love to live among the hip in the Markthal, or a cube house.

The view further showcases modern office towers, guarding the occasional older building that survived the severe bombing in World War II. Although the builds from the fifties are like huge scars, making almost every other Dutch city centre more beautiful and historic than Rotterdam, the city has risen to the challenge and reinvented itself. Rotterdam belongs to the workers, to down-to-earth citizens, from very diverse backgrounds. The bustling city breathes at night, its lights giving away the activity hotspots.

I take another deep breath and turn to face the door. Ready to assess the situation as soon as somebody shows up. A ping announces the elevator's arrival. I feel a presence and tune into the thoughts of whomever just exited the elevator into the hallway. *Here we go. I hope she's here.*

A buzz signals the unlocking of the door. The man in the beige raincoat halts in the doorway. His jovial, weathered face has a pronounced nose, small, keen eyes and a warm smile, matching his friendly and curious thoughts towards me. He scans my face, comparing it to my mother's, to find similarities. I know he won't find many.

"Hello, Kathy. Thank you for coming." He walks in and extends his hand. "I am Bernard. I realise it must have been a shock when I contacted you this afternoon."

I shake his hand. "It was." I shift my weight onto my toes and then rock back on my heels, as if to physically curb the urge to fire questions at him right away.

Bernard hangs his coat on a hook and gestures for me to sit down. "Would you like anything to drink? Water? Or tea, coffee?"

"Water, please. Thanks." I sit down in the armchair closest to the door. He seems trustworthy, but still, if needed, I want to be able to make a quick getaway.

Bernard sits down on the opposite couch and places the bottles on the table. "My apologies for the indirect approach. Certain people watch my movements, and I don't want to alert them to our meeting." He smiles. "You must have a lot of questions. Where would you like me to start?"

"How do you know I can mind-read? How do you even *know* me? And how did you know my mother?" Other questions tumble through my mind, like clothes in a dryer.

His mind contracts into the concentration of someone finally performing on stage the piece practised for so long. "Your mother started working for me before she became pregnant. She didn't come to the office often, so we could keep her pregnancy a secret. This was, of course, the era before social media. I am the only one in our organisation who knows about your existence." He smiles and shrugs. "As for your ability, I suspected it. I kept track of you. You may not look much like your mother, but your eyes..." He gazes into mine, comparing them to hers. "To be more specific, the *expression* in your eyes. The way you look at people. The way you look away from people. The way you look around for people, to check where thoughts are coming from. And," he clears his throat, "your behaviour. The way you keep a distance. The detached way you observe others. As if..." *you are from a different world, studying humans on earth.* He holds up his hand in apology. "Sorry. I didn't mean to say, think, anything upsetting."

"Right." I shift in my chair. He kept track of me for years? His intentions might have been friendly, but it's suffocating, nonetheless. I swallow. "How did you know about my mother?"

"A fortunate coincidence. I went to a New Year's Eve party at my nephew's house. He invited several neighbours. Your mother's parents had died in the previous year, and he felt she needed to meet people again. At one point, my nephew's son snuck up on her. She turned around to tickle him before he made a noise. Despite being shy, she intervened when two men were about to start a fight. And in conversations, she was extremely understanding." He smiles at the memory. "At first, I just thought she was highly perceptive. I could use those skills in my organisation. After a few weeks of working together, she told me."

Fascinated, I follow the conversation both through his words and thoughts. I see my mother, with long, dark hair, tied in a ponytail. She keeps smoothing imaginary wrinkles from her green dress. From Bernard's viewpoint, she's much smaller than I remember her as a three-year-old. She's not moving around much, rather stays with one group once she's made contact. Her green eyes and smile are adorable—shy but genuine.

Bernard generously treats me to his memories. He shows me how she tickles the nephew, the way I'd forgotten she tickled me. How she observes the room, the way I do. How she wrings her hands when she tells him she can mind-read. Tears run down my cheeks, but I don't care. Bernard's kind eyes tell me he understands.

I swallow. "Even my father doesn't know she could mind-read. Why did she tell you, and not him?"

"She loved your father dearly. But she wasn't sure how he'd react. I suspect she wanted to tell him but kept postponing. She became pregnant with you soon. She didn't want to scare him away." He studies me and thinks, *Has she told her father?*

It doesn't seem Bernard's intention to ask me, but I answer anyway. "No, I didn't tell my father. I tried to, but he didn't believe me, and it scared him. He chose not to believe me. Maybe he reacted to my mother in the same way."

Possibly. My apologies, it has been a while, communicating with a mind-reader. I'm not used to someone reading my mind anymore.

I rub my temples. "It's so weird… I've been hiding my mind-reading all my life, and suddenly there's someone who knows…"

He smiles. *How does that feel?*

"Well… shocking. A bit of a relief at the same time. I've always been scared what would happen when people find out."

Bernard leans back. *It's good to be careful. But it must be hard.*

I sigh. "Why contact me now?"

I would like to offer you a job.

CHAPTER TEN

I stare at Bernard. "A *job?* Doing what?"

I head an organisation called the Syndicate. In short, we facilitate processes within the European Union. We smooth potential political difficulties, remove barriers. Bernard sits up. I feel his passion growing, and he starts talking out loud again. "The European Union enters the next phase of its existence, its purpose. For decades, the USA acted as the informal political leader of the world. They led in many areas—trade, technological developments, sports, establishing order in unstable geopolitical regions. The world, rivals included, admired them. Unfortunately, similar to market leader businesses just before their downfall, they became too complacent, too confident in their dominance and superiority. Their leadership role crumbled, upsetting a delicate balance." His eyes sparkle. "The void left behind by the US has to be filled. We believe the EU should take on a leading role in world politics."

I let out a cynical laugh. "The EU isn't even popular in its own countries. For years, several European countries talked about decreasing EU interference. Not to mention the long-lasting soap of Brexit."

Bernard's forgiving smile reduces me to a child who has not quite understood. "People focus on futile hiccups of the EU, the bickering on the surface, but a true democracy is like a family—siblings fight each other all the time but form a front to outsiders. Nothing solidifies cohesion more than a crisis, or a common enemy. In recent years, the EU had both: Brexit causing a crisis in the family, a war close to the EU border, and a US president insulting EU family members."

"Still, doesn't the complexity of the EU's organisation hinder its effectiveness?"

Bernard nods reluctantly. "Sometimes. In recent years, ideas have sprung up to combine the roles of the President of the European Council and the President of the European Commission. The benefits of having two different organisations, next to the European Parliament, dried up. They overlap and need to be streamlined, simplified, become more efficient." Bernard bores his eyes into mine. "This is still confidential. I would appreciate if you keep this to yourself."

I grin. "I believe I've built up an impressive track record in keeping things to myself."

Bernard scans my face, and I feel he's unsure whether he should laugh or feel sorry for me. Instead, he lets his passion overtake him again and continues with the sales pitch. "Did you know the EU is the largest development and humanitarian aid donor? Or the largest trade power?"

I shake my head, then frown. "You make it sound like the EU is one country. But all European countries still insist on sovereignty, and resist EU influence in their own politics."

Bernard's passion intensifies. "And that is *exactly* the reason why the EU has the potential to coordinate world politics. Nobody wants one dominant, patronising country anymore. Countries like China and Russia might want the position the US once held, but they are pursuing an obsolete dream. The era for one dominant country as world leader is over. Increasing globalisation necessitates better cooperation between countries from all continents. The EU has decades-long experience of delicately traversing cultural realms and negotiating between a colourful range of various needs. Therefore, they are a much less threatening, and a much more capable candidate to take centre stage in world politics."

Bernard sinks back into the couch, his voice a little hoarse from talking. He looks at me, pleading. "The momentum to take the EU a step forward is now. To succeed, I need you in the role your mother fulfilled for the Syndicate years ago."

"So what did she do? My dad told me she was a personal assistant."

"In a way, yes. I had just started working for the Syndicate in 1992. The European Union officially started a year after. Although the key European countries had worked together for a while by then, politicians first and foremost had to answer to their national electorate. Careers and images had to be protected. Certain things couldn't be said out loud. The Syndicate was formed to let certain negotiations take place out of the public's sight. We needed to build trust between countries, to stimulate leaders to collaborate on shared goals while we had cultural differences to reckon with."

I nod. Very much like HR trying to build trust between people. "Right. And a simple word in one language can mean something different in another language when translated. That doesn't make things easier."

"Exactly. Such incidents caused days of delay to smooth the misunderstanding. We needed to know the genuine feelings and hidden agendas of the political leaders. To know straight away when to take action, before problems would simmer for days and cause more delays."

Bernard pauses to see whether I still follow, now that we have come to the crucial part. I nod in encouragement. "You see, your mother read their minds for me. For that, she needed to be in the same room, of course. Posing as my personal assistant made that possible."

I frown. She needed to be in the same room? One wall, and sometimes even two, is not an obstacle for me. Although I do prefer to see the body language as well for a complete picture.

Oblivious, Bernard continues. "She was quick in learning languages. After a year, next to English, Dutch and German, she understood French, Danish, Spanish, Italian and Portuguese." He jerks his head up, realising something. "That is, I assume your mind-reading is like your mother's. How are you with languages?"

"I speak English, Dutch and German, and have an understanding of French and Spanish, thanks to studying with several exchange students. I'd have a hard time with the other languages."

Bernard rubs his chin. "Good enough to start with. Hopefully, you'll learn as quick as your mother."

"Sure, no pressure."

Startled, Bernard pauses. Then he decides to ignore my mocking tone. "The original purpose of the Syndicate is not known to many. Officially, we are consultants, but certain negotiations still take place out of sight." His eyes become misty. "You know, you can be proud of your mother. Without her, the start of the EU would have been less smooth. We wouldn't even be where we are now. Although no one will ever know." He holds his hands up and shrugs in an apology. "That is important to understand. We keep your ability a secret, which also means you won't get any credit."

"Why do you need me at all? Isn't the cooperation in the EU established enough by now to conduct negotiations without a mind-reader?"

"Right now, we're entering the next crucial phase. Several countries are discussing how to keep the EU's unique model of collaboration between sovereign countries, while improving the fabric of the organisation. Word is getting out on combining and streamlining two of the EU's institutions—the European Council and European Commission. As usual, change feels threatening to at least part of the establishment. The terrain is rocky, if not booby-trapped. We could use a mind-reader, to know people's unspoken fears, goals, irritations. As my personal assistant, I can bring you into the room to advise me the way your mother did."

Bernard exudes confidence and energy from every pore of his body. Was that why my mother felt at ease with him and thought him worthy of her secret? It does feel good to talk to someone who, despite knowing about my mind-reading, seems to accept me. Am I ready to put the same level of trust in him as my mother did?

I massage my temples. So much information... I can deal with my brain being flooded with stimuli, with other people's emotions or thoughts whirling through my head. Like Bernard said, I just detach myself from the situation and observe. But this is different.

This concerns *me*. This afternoon, I knew little about my mother, not even whether she was a mind-reader. Now, I talk to the man who was her boss for a few years. Who is offering me the job she held.

"Uhm, could I use the bathroom?" I don't wait for his answer, lift myself onto shaky legs, and enter the door next to the couch.

"Through the bedroom, door to the right," Bernard yells after me.

The bedroom has the same smothering, exuberant flower print on the curtains and bed cover. I flee to the bathroom, gasping for air. My reflection in the mirror above the washbasin smirks at me. Sure, Kath, blame the flower print.

It's just so much to take in… So my mom could read minds. My hands clench into fists. Not only did that hit-and-run coward rob me of a loving mother, he or she also killed the only person in the world with whom I could have been myself. Who could have taught me how to deal with this gift. This curse. Who would have known me, in that all-encompassing way I know others.

I push my fists against my closed eyes, to press back tears I fear will keep streaming once I allow them to enter the stage. I focus on Bernard. He thinks about my mother. It would be prudent to give him some privacy. As my mother couldn't mind-read through walls, he probably expects I can't read his mind from the bathroom two doors away.

But he's streaming memories of my mother… His mind is as close as I will ever get to her.

Y must have known I was jealous of her capabilities. And insecure. I had always been good at reading people. Facial expressions, body language, subtlety in tones or a change of words, nothing escaped me. It's why they asked me to lead the Syndicate in the first place, and to conduct the majority of the negotiations that had to be done out of the spotlight. Then Y came along, making me feel junior, like an intern just starting to learn the skill. Although her insights improved my abilities, too.

Y was discreet. And gentle. Told me my thoughts in general were normal. According to Y, I had nothing to be ashamed of. Such a loss when she was gone...

There's no guarantee that working with Kathy will be like working with her mother. Was it smart to involve Kathy? She seems different from Y. I did a good job without a mind-reader, but I'm getting old. And this has to go right. The entire world will benefit if we get the EU to the next level. Let them be a model for future global politics.

He sure believes in the EU. Did my mother share his passion? I sure don't... Would it be fair to take the job, even though I couldn't care less about the future of global politics?

I run cold water over my wrists and join Bernard again.

CHAPTER ELEVEN

I pull the duvet cover over my head, grumpy at the inevitability of having to leave the warm safety of my bed to go to work. Wait, it's Saturday. Not to mention, there's no job to go to.

Unless I accept Bernard's offer. In my cozy, down-filled cocoon, I list the pros and cons.

Cons: chances of being exposed increase. I'm leaving my beloved HR field for a job I'm not trained for. I know next to nothing about the EU. I hate politics. And detest the way politicians talk—seriously, are they all required to complete 'How to speak a lot but say nothing 101'?

Pros: getting to know more about my mother. Contributing to the world with my ability. Working with someone who knows my secret and is okay with it.

I throw the warmth and safety of the duvet aside. Who am I kidding. Of course I'll accept. Just getting to know more about my mother outweighs all the cons I will be able to come up with.

After lunch, the mail arrives, with the letter from the recruitment agency Bernard told me would come. He wants to hire me in a legitimate way, so no one suspects we already know each other. He had taken the liberty of writing my application and had given it to a recruitment agency to process. They now confirm the official interview for Tuesday.

Another letter is from Dad, a stack of documents with a note. 'Kathy, you need to decide about the farmhouse. The current lease ends in a month. Would you want us to find other tenants? Love, Dad.' I frown. Why doesn't he mention the other option? I've always wanted to sell. Why would I need an entire house for myself?

As if I'm ever going to be in a long-lasting relationship. Besides, the area has no public transport and I don't have a car. Not to mention I just don't want the responsibility of owning a house. Nor the painful memories. I don't want the questions, the guessing why my mother wanted me to have that stupid bunch of bricks.

Or the awful statue… The freakish Hekate sculpture in the garden. The three terrifying women my mother was so fond of. She sometimes pictured the sculpture in her mind, looking at me. I felt her love for it. What possessed her to name me after that spooky goddess? I bang my fist on the table. Another question I will never find the answer to. I grab my phone, search among my recently dialed numbers and punch redial. Dad picks up after one ring.

"Hi, sweetheart. Got the papers?"

"Yes. You talked to the broker not only about selling but also about leasing it out again, I see." Even to my own ears, my voice sounds a tad accusing.

"I did. Because the decision to sell, or rent it out, is entirely yours."

I sigh. He knows my decision. I've spent years trying to get him to go against my mother's wishes and get rid of it early. He always heard me out, but stuck to my mother's stipulation not to sell before I was twenty-five. And when my twenty-fifth birthday came, he pointed out the rudeness and legal difficulties of throwing out existing lessees. And now he discussed leasing again with the broker. Is this his passive-aggressive way of asking me to reconsider?

Even worse, is it working? I sigh. Now that I've met Bernard, or more specifically, met his memories of my mother, I wonder. Why did she love that house so much? Why did she leave it to me? Do I want to let go without knowing?

Dad reads my silence for what it is—indecision. "Sweetheart, why don't we go and check after the tenants moved out? You don't have to decide until then."

I close my eyes. Wouldn't selling without having seen it again be unfair to my mother? Or even to myself? I respond, "Sure. Doesn't hurt to see the place." Hopefully, Dad thinks I couldn't care less.

CHAPTER TWELVE

Next to the dark blue bowl of yoghurt (to match the colour of blueberries I like to mix in) I smooth out the application letter Bernard gave me. As the supposed author, I'd better read it before attending the interview.

'With this letter I express my strong interest in the esteemed position of Personal Assistant.'

Rolling my eyes, I take a spoonful of yoghurt and start chewing on the delicious blueberries. Oh, that lovely moment when my teeth sink into the fleshy little fruit ball, making it pop.

'As I have always pursued the highest level of serving my superiors, I trust I will be able to fulfill the requirements of this position.'

For a desperate micro-second, I try to swallow the yoghurt-berry mix. Then, the inevitable snort comes and droopy white-purple spray elbows its way out through my pursed lips, splattering all over 'my' application letter.

I crumple the letter up. Let's just hope no one but Bernard will attend the interview. The process is bogus, so why bother about the details anyway?

***

At the agency, a receptionist tells me to take a seat in the waiting area. I suppose she means the arrangement of three low, uncomfortable looking, beige lounge benches. Why do people choose esthetics over comfort when deciding on furniture? But I guess people waiting here are not comfortable even if they can sink into a comfy, cushioned sofa. When waiting for a job interview, better sit upright and alert, than slump down and doze off.

Two of the benches are occupied. A woman goes over a company brochure she pretends to read, flipping the pages with manicured nails, the understated soft lacquer gloss aimed to stress her nails' perfection. She wears a dark blue jacket and skirt, over a white embroidered shirt. Crossing her long, slim legs, she sits at a slight angle and stretches further upright, working hard to come across as both professional and attractive.

On the second bench, a man picks up his coffee, then puts it down again without taking a sip. He strokes his red tie. *Should I have chosen a less aggressive colour?*

Just when his nervousness starts fuelling mine, he's collected by a recruitment consultant. The recruiter takes one look at him and tries to hide her sigh. *Too nervous. Trying too hard. Not confident enough. Won't be able to explain the two gaps in his CV. No, not going to make it.*

Poor guy, failing at the infamous first impression. Involuntarily, first impressions influence us all, even though most of us know we need to give people a fair second chance. I've seen many candidates make a great first impression and then disappoint in the interview. Or candidates too nervous to make a favourable first impression, and once thawed, turned out to be the perfect person for the job.

Easy for me to say. Reading someone's mind beats any first impression.

When the next consultant comes, I check into her thoughts. She's not too pleased. *Hate it when the client picks candidates for the short list. Would never have invited this one. No experience with the political arena at all.*

She looks the grilling type, someone to rapidly fire questions to confuse and fluster the candidate. Despite my extensive interviewing experience, I don't enjoy sitting at the other side of the table. Especially not on the other side of her table.

When she passes reception, she puts on a fake smile. She surveys the waiting room and decides the other woman looks the type. Aiming her words to Miss Lacquer Perfection, she calls, "Kathy van der Laan?"

I cough in acknowledgement and get up, enjoying the flicker of surprise in her mind.

She extends her hand. "Hi, I'm Suzanne. The recruitment consultant for this application process. Let me lead the way to the interview room." She sashays past reception to enter a hallway with several doors on each side. Looking back, she asks disinterestedly, "You found your way here okay?"

I smile. I've asked this question hundreds of times. Silly, because when the candidate is on time, they obviously found the place okay, but I appreciate she follows one of the unwritten recruitment rules. Ask an innocent question to break the ice, to enable the candidate to get a little accustomed, before you spend a minimum of forty-five minutes well within each other's personal space.

To perform my part, I respond, "Yes, no problem at all."

Just before we enter one of the rooms, I feel Bernard's thoughts. And then Suzanne's, irritated, *Hate it when the client wants to do interviews on his own. As if dismissing my expertise.*

Relieved for not having to keep up job interview appearances with her, I walk through the door she opened. She introduces us, leaves the room, and shows her disapproval by closing the door a little louder than necessary.

"Hello Kathy."

"Hi."

I take in the depressing, clinical room, with the obligatory copy of a modern artwork on the wall behind Bernard, a fake yucca in a corner, condiments for coffee and tea on the table between us. A reluctance settles in my chest.

CHAPTER THIRTEEN

Bernard senses my hesitation and smiles. "How was your weekend? I realise our meeting Friday night must have been quite a shock. You had plenty to contemplate this weekend." *I should have been more cautious. I went too fast. Oh, she...* "Sorry," he continues out loud. "I'm still not used to sitting opposite a mind-reader again."

I shrug. "That's okay. I'm still not used to someone knowing I can...mind-read." The words hesitate to come out. After all, I've been hiding the essential element of who I am, for, well, forever. "It's strange to know you worked with my mother. And although I'm not sure what I am getting myself into, I accept." No point in letting him spend energy on courting me, while I'm pretending to think about it. I want to know more about my mother. Therefore, I want the job.

"Great. Why don't I tell you more about the basics of the Syndicate. We might have started as a small organisation, but we've grown over the years."

I snigger. Every organisation, political or not, will mushroom if given half the chance. As soon as you put a few people together, they keep hiring more to perform tasks they don't want to do themselves. Or because they feel the importance of the organisation increases with its size.

Bernard produces an organisation chart of the Syndicate and slides it across the table.

Chagrined, I lean forward. Whenever HR produces one of those bloody schematics, all hell breaks loose. There's indignation—'This person might officially report to A, but he also reports to me. You should at least draw a dotted line between him and me!' There's whining—'In this chart it looks as if I'm on a lower level than B, but we're in the same paygrade.' There's hurt pride—'As project manager, I know I don't have anyone report to me directly, but now it looks as if I have no reports. That's not true! I have to lead many people on a daily basis.'

Managers fight for hours to see their importance bumped up on a sheet of paper. Why do people think their spatial location in a diagram of boxes and lines affects the content of their jobs? Inevitably, the discussion escalates to the highest echelons of the organisation. You can tell a lot about an organisation's culture and CEO's personality by looking at the org chart—does s/he go along consoling hurt egos by allowing an org chart so complicated, everybody stops using it? Or does s/he take a firm stand and not waste valuable time on geometrical shapes, lines and the way they are spaced relative to one another?

The Syndicate's org chart is a fine specimen of the complex variety. Spread over several pages, to allow for deep dives into parts of the organisation, not only the lines and boxes are shown, but also an intricate crisscrossing of dotted lines, abundant use of asterisks and footnotes, and even colours requiring explanation in a separate caption in the lower right-hand corner. Bernard clearly gave leeway to self-conscious managers to present their version of reality.

The executive team consists of 'Directors,' except for the head of the department 'Operations and Research,' who features prominently as 'Vice President.'

Bernard points to the box of the VP. "Kurt is my deputy. Second in command. In the coming two years, I will remain President of the Syndicate until the restructuring of the EU is completed. At that point, Kurt is destined to take over. Therefore, even though you will work for me, Kurt is an important part of the Syndicate and I would like you to meet him. We use the four-eyes principle for my hires. He's here waiting, just in case you would accept the job."

"What does his department do?"

"He oversees several negotiations himself. Especially when there are…sensitivities."

I sense Bernard's unease. He then represses it, by thinking of

Kurt's accomplishments. Does Bernard do that for my benefit? Or does he hide his unease from himself? Wait a minute—I can't be sure why Bernard thinks certain things. That's a new one for me. When I read other people's minds, I look into a naked, unpolished version of their thought process. As Bernard is aware, I know what he thinks and feels, so he might repress thoughts he otherwise allows to flow freely.

To get more on how Bernard sees Kurt, I ask, "What kind of sensitivities?"

Bernard clears his throat. "Kurt handles…potentially explosive situations. Sometimes politicians find themselves in dire circumstances. Circumstances that should not matter, but could show them in a less favourable light. These unrelated issues could upset an ongoing negotiation, or lead to the disgrace of a leading politician essential to the process. Given the confidential nature of the issues Kurt's dealing with, he's running his department independently. That way, we contain sensitive information to a small group of people on a need-to-know basis."

Wow, isn't he being political all of a sudden. I raise an eyebrow. "Too flowery for me. Is that code for 'Kurt makes potential explosive situations go away, without informing me, so I can deny knowing about any unethical actions?'"

A pained expression crosses Bernard's face. "That would be an excessively crude translation. I know the Dutch like saying things right between the eyes. Most other cultures prefer to present facts in a more…pleasant way. You will have to learn to be a little less direct, I'm afraid. Given your mother's roots, she understood. But you have been raised differently, I realise."

I lean forward, hungry. "My mother's roots?"

Bernard shakes his head. "Sorry, Kathy, that will have to wait. I'll tell you everything I know about your mother. But first, I want you to meet Kurt. He doesn't know about your mind-reading. He won't have to, so don't worry about that."

Before I can protest, Bernard gets up and leaves the room.

CHAPTER FOURTEEN

A man in his fifties opens the door and nods curtly. He seats himself and leaves Bernard to close the door. His hair shines an unnatural pitch-black. A glimpse of dark purple skin shows just above one ear. The telltale sign of a recent hair dye.

I love how most people above a certain age carry their personality visibly on their face. Day after day, patient but relentless, favourite facial expressions sculpt their evidence into a skin born flawless.

Kurt is an interesting case in point. Lines curve the corners of his mouth downwards. A deep, vertical ravine settled as an eternal frown between his eyebrows, emphasizing the absence of laugh lines around his eyes. A prominent arched line above his left eyebrow suggests he often raises that eyebrow in a demanding question. He has chosen to complete his image with dark-rimmed glasses of a well-known expensive brand.

The perfect illustration of a vain man. Difficult to please, easy to dissatisfy.

Again, first impressions can be wrong. I like to complete my assessment by shamelessly mind-reading, to get a better insight into someone's personality.

And that's where I draw an unsettling blank. I tune in beyond his face, only to find a mind equally non-inviting. A strong wall, normally present when people concentrate on one thing, bounces me back. He doesn't seem to have thoughts, other than an intense focus on me. I shiver.

Bernard introduces us and then lets Kurt take over. Surprised, I watch their dynamic. In most situations, you can tell who's the boss by identifying the dominant force in the room. In this case, that's Kurt. When a subordinate owns the room while the boss is present, it means one of two things—either Bernard is weak and Kurt actually runs the show, or Bernard's leadership position is so established, he feels no need to assert it.

I hope for the latter.

"Welcome to the Syndicate." Kurt's sorry attempt at a smile confirms my hypothesis—he is inexperienced when it comes to smiling.

"Thanks."

Bernard tells Kurt, "I explained to Kathy how the Syndicate facilitates the political processes within the European Union." Bernard sits up, excited. "The competencies built up within the EU are unique and the basis of our future world. No other country or group of countries has learnt so well to coordinate between different countries, different ideologies, different religions."

Now that I've had a few days to mull it over, I counter, "What about the United Nations?"

Kurt waves his hand dismissively in the air. "The UN has a different focus. They try to stay out of national politics. Their set-up is for non-political goals, such as health-related topics, addressing poverty, or providing relief in the aftermath of war or natural disasters. But to *prevent* wars, set up trade agreements, protect countries from their invasive neighbours, the UN lacks the mandate and unity between members to take the lead."

"Well, I don't know much about politics, but the EU doesn't seem to deserve the first prize in swift and pro-active decision-making either."

Kurt nods. "We need to improve on that. And by structuring the political organisation of the European Union more like a company, we are ready to take up the role of world leader."

I laugh incredulously. "The EU will never be as united as the US."

Bernard smiles at me in his forgiving way, taking on the tone of a patient teacher spelling out the obvious. "And that, my child, is their strength. The EU's decades' long experience of building one economic and political force while maintaining individual national identities is what the world needs, going forward."

Kurt raises his left eyebrow. "We are done with one country being patronising and condescending towards the rest of the world."

Bernard's smile is thin, probably to hide the irritation I feel on his mind. "You might be right, but we have to be careful not to become patronising and condescending ourselves. We can still learn from the US."

Kurt crosses his arms. "Look what the US political system does with their society... A choice between two parties is not a choice at all. If you're a conservative person, you don't vote for the Democrats. If you're a liberal, you wouldn't dream of electing a Republican."

Bernard sighs. "It is unfortunate for a democracy to have just two dominant parties."

Kurt snorts. "Exactly. Like in sports, they always have one winner and one loser. That ups the stakes enormously. Look at the grim way elections dominate the news in the US preceding Election Day. People aggressively cheer on their party. Their *team*. In the process, they've created a deep-rooted division in society."

Bernard coughs. "That might be a bit of an overstatement. But yes, in most European countries, citizens can choose between several parties of similar size, decreasing the feeling of Us versus Them. Parties have to work closely together to form a government. Building bridges, negotiating, trying to reach an agreement in the middle—European politicians handle these strategies on a daily basis. In the US, one party can approve legislation without having to negotiate much. At most, they just have to convince *a few* members of another party. That type of negotiation is essentially different from when several minority parties govern a country together."

Bernard's warm passion provides a comical contrast to the statue of resistance next to him. Kurt's mouth sits rigid in grim disapproval, the deepening lines curving his mouth downward even further. "The EU is being too nice to the US. We should already assert our dominance."

Is he irritated? Or does he just disagree with Bernard? His mind remains impenetrable. I search for his emotions, his thoughts, but I get nothing, apart from intense concentration. How is that possible? I have never met a mind I couldn't read before. Well, apart from people who are unconscious. Even animals, who don't think in words, have emotions, or I see what they see through their eyes. With Kurt, I don't even get that. My stomach cramps. Am I losing my mind-reading skills?

But Bernard's thoughts are loud and clear. *He's getting increasingly stubborn. He's good at his job, but is he still in for the right reasons?*

Bernard wags his finger towards Kurt, shaking his head. "I respectfully disagree. These processes need time. Asserting dominance turns others against the aggressor."

I try to sense what Kurt thinks about the statement, if not gentle rebuke, by Bernard, but again, I don't feel any thoughts or emotions, just a cold, intense concentration.

Bernard turns to me and smiles. "As you can see, we touched upon one of the differences between Kurt and me," he jabs his finger at the table, "which demonstrates the strength of the EU. We include people with different views, and we make sure we arrive at agreements a big majority can live with. We need to bring the cooperative style of the European Union to the foreground of global politics."

CHAPTER FIFTEEN

The waiter leads me to a table in a private corner. Bernard appears from the corridor leading to the washrooms. He'd sent me a text only an hour after our meeting this morning, to propose discussing the contract over dinner.

"Thank you for coming." Bernard sits down and signals the waiter.

After the waiter has taken our orders and is out of earshot, I ask, "Why the secrecy to meet each other the first time?"

Bernard places his fingertips together. "For a few weeks now, I suspect I'm being followed. As Head of the think tank brainstorming the EU organisation, many stakeholders would like to know what I'm up to." He waves his hand. "It doesn't concern you. I just didn't want anyone to know about you until you officially joined the Syndicate. Now that you've accepted the role as my PA, people won't read anything into our meeting."

The waiter places a bowl of delicious smelling Thai coconut soup in front of me, and a broccoli cream soup in front of Bernard.

Bernard meticulously spreads out his napkin on his lap. "What did you think of this morning's interview?"

I roam the spoon around in the soup and fish out the hard pieces of lemon grass. "You and Kurt are quite different types."

Bernard laughs. "Indeed. In many respects, opposites usually work quite well together." *Competent guy. Although…*

I inhale the delicious scent of the soup. "What are your doubts about Kurt?"

Bernard drops his spoon on the floor. He leans forward, murmuring, "I still have to get used to you reading my mind." He sits up and continues at a subdued volume. "I wouldn't say *doubts*. But

I do have, let's say…hesitations, about the way he works. He has a way of getting people to cooperate which isn't always, well, to their liking. But when my type of friendly diplomacy proves ineffective, I involve Kurt, and he gets it done. He has been running his department for the last fifteen years and has always delivered. So, I guess you could say we complement each other well."

"Right." With closed eyes, I cherish the sour, spicy taste of the soup by rolling it around in my mouth for a second before swallowing. "I'm not sure I'd like to work for Kurt."

"You don't have to. You report to me, and only to me. However, I always involve my second man in recruitment decisions. He would've been suspicious if I hadn't this time." *Should tell her, though.* Bernard coughs. "In two or three years, I may retire. Kurt's the most likely candidate to take over. By then, you'll know whether or not you want to work with him."

"That's fine. Two to three years would be a record for me, anyway." I bite my tongue. Not what a new boss wants to hear.

Funny, would have expected her to be more like her mother.

I look up at Bernard, eyebrows raised.

He holds his hands up in an apologetic gesture. "Right, you got that. Well, you are quite…" *direct? Rude…* "Straightforward. Your mother was a little more soft-spoken."

I grin. "Right. Well, at a certain point, I figured it's only fair. I can read people's minds and know everything they're thinking, including their ugly thoughts. I decided to be upfront with them as well for most of the time. To get the balance right."

"But they don't know you read their minds. Including the less well-meaning thoughts."

"True. Still, I see all the time what miscommunication leads to. The world would be a better place if we'd all be brutally honest with each other. That's why I try to be. Even if it doesn't earn me brownie points." I put my spoon down, having finished every single drop. "I'm quite different from my mother? Tell me more about her."

Bernard smiles. "She was a little shy. She told me when she grew up, she preferred animals to humans. At least they didn't lie. Nor did they blame anyone." He sighs. "I think she regretted telling me about the mind-reading."

"Why?"

"Bad experiences. She was intensely afraid of being hunted down."

No kidding. I nod, then frown. "So, why *did* she tell you?"

"Once she said, '*If you've got a unique talent, you like to show it off. Like top athletes, who are admired for something no one else can do.*'" He searches my face. "Don't you feel like that?"

I shrug. "As a teenager, yes. Everybody enjoys being admired. As a child, I tried to show off. Always resulting in a rejection or misunderstanding." I mull over my mother's words and frown. "I'd say this unique ability is nothing like being a top athlete. They can do something *better* than others. Other people also run, or swim. Athletes are just faster, because of intense training and sheer dedication, and we admire *that*. Being able to mind-read is more like being a unique acrobat that can fold himself in knots because of a bone deformity. People don't admire such a freak show. They feel a mix of fascination and disgust. Since I realised that, I don't feel the urge to show off at all."

Bernard strokes his chin. "You might be right." *Intelligent girl. Different personality from Y.*

The familiarity he feels about her warms and stings me at the same time. "You called her Y?"

"Yes. We liked the feeling of it. Like a code word." He submerges himself in memories.

I tune in. This is why I took the job. In his memories, she's so lovely, so attractive. A stark contrast to Dad's memories of the time he had to identify her. Cold, expressionless, hair messy, a crust of dried blood on her right cheek and ear. Even though I never saw her body myself, I can't get rid of that horrifying image.

The way Bernard remembers her, walking, talking, laughing... views of a gentle, grown-up woman, just a few years older than I am now.

Bernard notices the concentration on my face, and he snaps out of his trip down memory lane. He leans forward. "Would you consider yourself lucky for being able to read minds?"

I swallow. I want him to keep remembering, to keep her alive, even if for only a few moments longer. Be patient, Kath, there'll be plenty time. I force a smile. "No…not really. As a teenager, I wished I couldn't, until I watched my stepmother's favourite soap series with her and became fascinated by the way people communicate with just words. They have to rely on what others say or do, instead of what they think or feel. All those misunderstandings, misinterpretations, miscommunications. I felt incredibly sorry for people, having to go through that."

Bernard throws his head back and laughs. *She's right. But…how difficult it must have been, going through this on her own.* He abruptly stops laughing. "I hope you've experienced that soaps are not reflective of how most people manage to interact and communicate with each other."

I wink. "I wouldn't be too sure about that. Social media gives me the same feeling. People show you their polished version, their bright and sunny side. They share their good fortunes, or jokes, or epic moments. But you don't know what they're really thinking."

Bernard grimaces. "We are a sad species."

We eat our main course in silence, Bernard thinking of my mother, so I can see her. He shows her seated at a table, concentrating on the thoughts around her. He shows her to me pregnant, with her glowing soft face, hand on her belly. He shows her cuddling me as a baby on her lap, her eyes full of love.

A thought bursts through the surface. Holding a baby, walking, agonising over what to do, how to keep him safe.

What? Whose memory is this? I zoom in, but the memory fades, leaving a residue of fear. I concentrate on Bernard again. But the grateful ecstasy of being immersed in her presence doesn't come back. Why did I have to grow up without her? I missed her so much… To see the loving mother I had to do without is like winning the lottery but then realising you've lost the ticket and can't claim the money.

Two waiters are murmuring to each other and glance our way. I quickly check their thoughts. *Weird combination. Old man, young woman. Not talking, but she's smiling at him so much. Hey, is that a tear? What is going on here?*

I dab my eyes with the napkin. With a whiff of regret, I notice half of my food is left uneaten. Usually, I seize every opportunity to eat a proper dinner, to justify skipping cooking the next day. Cooking for only yourself is such a massive waste of time.

After dessert, Bernard briefly discusses the employment contract and says, "I'd like you to start soon. What about tomorrow?"

My cheeks burn. Earlier today, Detective Yong left a short voice message requesting my presence tomorrow. "Uhm, well, I need to attend to something tomorrow. Why don't I start the day after?"

"Thursday it is, then," Bernard says.

I ignore the shudder of dread surging through my body.

CHAPTER SIXTEEN

The tall, slender frame of Detective Cecilia Yong appears in the hallway of the police station. Picking me up herself? Oh my, this must be important.

Agile and gracious, she leads the way to the interview room.

No small-talk. Her mind is focused on the walk, so I can't tell whether she skips the niceties on purpose, or because she's just not the type to bother with it.

For the second day in a row, I'm trudging behind someone, past anonymous multi-purpose rooms, for an interview where I'm not in control. The type of apprehension differs from when I walked behind the consultant for the interview yesterday, but it's apprehension nonetheless.

Cecilia Yong enters one of the rooms and gestures to a chair.

"Please take a seat."

She doesn't smile. On the upside, her face doesn't impersonate a dog on a promising scent, like two weeks ago.

She seats herself opposite of me. Behind her is a camera, and there's one above the door too. A proper interrogation room. I can't sense any thoughts outside of this room, but I'm not sure whether that means no one is watching us, or whether the walls contain some other barrier I can't read minds through.

She spotted the cameras. Unsettles her. Good. Let her think there's someone watching.

Ha, thanks for clearing that up.

"I would like to ask you a couple of follow-up questions."

I feel like saying 'Yes, thank you, I'm well. How are you?' Gee, could she be any more to the point? How annoying, to be on the receiving, intimidating end of the direct approach I master so well myself.

Cecilia doesn't seem to notice my irritation. "When the house was searched, you were part of the thrill-seeking crowd in front of the house. You mentioned many houses in the area had a cellar that could be accessed through the trapdoor in the closet under the stairs."

She stares me down, eager for my confirmation.

"Uhm, I guess so."

"How did you get to know the houses in that area?" The determined look in her eyes betrays her casual tone.

"I visited once. Don't remember why. I think a friend of a friend in college lived there."

"In that street, most houses don't even have a cellar. Let alone a trapdoor."

"Oh, well, I don't know." Why is the explanation so important? I've done nothing wrong. I have every right to pose as a slightly confused but honest and helpful citizen.

Still doesn't make sense. Especially not considering those other tips. She's hiding something. Why? Just want the truth. "During our first chat at your house, you mentioned you just got your sim-card. We pulled your phone records and found some interesting coincidences." *Shame we couldn't trace two of her work phones. Too much job switching, this girl.*

I try to get more thoughts, but goal-oriented people like Cecilia don't allow their brain to wander much. They use a structured approach, in which they go from one step in the deduction process to the next. To get useful information, I will have to lead her thought process. "What coincidences?"

"Such as your work phone being at the same place as where the anonymous tip was called in from." *For three of the eight tips we can pin her on the spot. Too few for Roel to get warrants. Still, too much of a coincidence.*

So Cecilia is more or less on a quest of her own. Admittedly, three occasions are a bit of an unusual coincidence. Depending on which ones. Some calls were from public places, or festivals, even the Marathon of Rotterdam. Being at roughly the same place could be justified. "Really? Which places?"

"In one case, the call came from a petrol station along the highway."

I suck in air, involuntarily. That must be the one about the truck smuggling people. The collective despair of twenty-six people gasping in an air-sealed container was so strong, I had almost run myself off the road when I passed the damned coffin on wheels. I'd been debating what to do when it pulled into a parking lot at a petrol station. I called it in from my car and waited until the first police car came on site. "Well, in one job as consultant I was on the road a lot." I shrug. "It's really hard for me to answer your questions if you don't tell me specifics."

Cecilia sighs. *Not budging. Need to use another tactic.* She makes an effort to display her sympathetic face and smiles. "Listen Kathy. It would be okay to tell us it was you. We would be thankful. Several of those tips led to important busts. Saved people's lives even." *But we also need to know how you know so much about organised crime. You must have a source of information. I want those criminals behind bars!*

I fight the urge to shift in my chair. "I really don't know anything." Lying to the police is not something to be proud of, but I can't even begin to imagine what this fierce, determined hunter will do if I tell her the truth.

"You do know." She gets up. "My apologies, I need to get my other notes, will be right back." *Let her simmer for half an hour. See what that does to her composure.*

She walks out. After a few minutes, I sense her thoughts, watching me on the closed-circuit cameras. Good to know the observation room isn't too far from here and empty, apart from Cecilia.

Needed that coffee. Now let's see what she does. Roel won't let me spend time on her as a lead if I don't get anything soon.

After having studied the room to show her how relaxed I am, I yawn and get out my phone, pretending to check messages. Cecilia keeps her eyes on me, but her thoughts start to wander. *Hope Gin-*

ger eats better today. Otherwise, I'll have to take her to the vet again. She'll hate me for weeks. After a few more minutes, her presence is gone. She must have left.

I sense another cop stepping into the observation room. His thinking pattern resembles that of the male cop who accompanied Cecilia to my house.

The door opens and Cecilia steps in empty-handed. I open my mouth to joke about not bringing the extra notes she told me she would get. But no, I'd better not get on her bad side.

Need to pressure her more. "Kathy. I don't think you realise the danger you are putting yourself in. You obviously have a source for criminal information. You call in tips based on that information. When, and I mean *when*, not *if*, those people find out you're tipping off the police, you're in *deep* trouble. And I won't be able to protect you. I can only provide you with protection when you come clean." She pauses for dramatic effect, and then adds, "I think we both want to protect innocent people. So why not tell me everything?"

Admirable approach. She might mean it. Would she be able to handle the truth? Nah, she'd think I'm mad. Or she'll use me to solve her cases. Wouldn't that be fun, to testify in court: 'It was in his thoughts, your honour.' Yeah, right. There's no way telling her would end well. I seek her intelligent dark eyes. "I really have no clue what you mean."

Cecilia holds my gaze. "I think you do. I'm patient, but don't try me too hard."

The person in the observation room chuckles in his mind. *Patient…sure. More like, won't let go, like a bulldog. Hardly patient with people. Can't stand anyone around her for too long, anyway. Except for that moody stray she picked up from the dumpster. Typical. She can only stand another extremely independent soul around her.*

CHAPTER SEVENTEEN

The office building of the Syndicate in The Hague gives nothing away on the outside. I had pictured an older property, full of character, with an interesting history, like many buildings in The Hague. But given the discretionary nature of the Syndicate's activities, a non-descript red-brick building in an inconspicuous park of similar buildings probably fits. The absence of a logo on the building and entrance confirms the Syndicate is not exactly advertising its existence.

What would the Syndicate's headquarters in Brussels, Belgium, look like? Next week, Bernard will give me a proper induction there. Since he's in the Netherlands this week, he thought it'd be easier to have my first day here. In Kurt's domain. I shiver.

I push through the glass revolving door and swirl into the building's belly. A floor-to-ceiling metal gate divides the huge and strangely empty entrance hall in two. A reception desk sits on the right end of the gate, next to a turnstile. To the left behind the gate is a set of elevators, and to the right several doors. No plants. No works of art even. No chairs or comfortable couches with stacks of magazines for visitors awaiting their appointment. Either very few visitors come here, or the waiting is done somewhere out of sight. My footsteps echo off the walls.

An older woman with blond-grey hair curled on top of her head sits at the reception desk. Four dark grey pins stick out of her bun. The colour suits her mood.

"Are you Kathy van der Laan?"

I nod.

"Could I see your ID please?" She studies my passport, taking her time. *Picture—shape of ears—yes. Shape of eyes—yes.* She fiddles with my passport behind a white screen, and through her eyes I see a flash of blue light. *Doesn't light up. Genuine.*

Wow. Not quite the obligatory glance I spend on new hires' IDs.

She returns my passport and hands me a plastic card on a key-cord. "Here's your visitor pass. Hold it against the black square to go through the turnstile and use it at the elevators as well to go up to the third floor." Her smile doesn't reach her eyes. *Poor thing. Bad day to start.*

Poor thing? Bad day?

The turnstile swallows me, concluding my entry with a solemn 'click.' I hold my card in front of the black square featured by all doors and exits. The elevator zooms discreetly. It seems that without a key card, no one makes it past the receptionist's desk, or anywhere else in the building.

At the second floor, the elevator's doors slide open without a sound. A young woman in a white lab coat widens her eyes. *Shit, somebody's in. Should have taken the back elevator.* After a split second, she enters. *Might as well get in now.*

As social norms dictate when strangers share a small space, we both step away into opposite corners. Through the closing doors, the unforgiving metal of another floor-to-ceiling turnstile glimmers. Do all the floors have another checkpoint? The security firm setting this up must have thought they'd died and woke up in heaven.

Aaron was so excited this morning. New work! Experiments never done before. Might finally get him his PhD. Stupid asshole. Being kicked out of university for plagiarizing. He's so keen now…

Experiments? There must be another organisation in this building.

When the doors open on the third floor, the girl waves to let me go first. *I hope there's no one in the hallway. Don't wanna be caught for using the main elevator.*

I step out, not sure where to go next. The girl slips past me and vanishes into a corridor.

"Kathy, right?" a voice from the left asks. I turn around and nod. A man in his thirties flashes a brief, uninviting smile. "Welcome. Let me bring you to Kurt's office. He's expecting you." *Why didn't Kurt cancel her contract straight away? He actually seems pleased she's coming onboard. Hope it won't affect my job. Or that Kurt moves to the Brussels office.*

What a weird organisation. Everyone's mind is apprehensive, tense. I sure hope I won't have to spend a lot of time here.

Kurt's office is fairly small and has no windows. I'd assessed Kurt to be the type to claim the biggest and brightest office, only accessible through a secretary's room, to impress visitors by the sheer physical evidence of his importance. I search for pictures or any other personal touches such as postcards with mottos or little knick-knacks revealing Kurt's personality. Nothing. This colourless, sterile office reflects the void I feel while trying to read his mind.

"Hello, Kathy. Please take a seat." Kurt gestures towards a chair opposite his desk.

"Thanks. Is Bernard not joining us?"

Kurt takes off his glasses, inspects their cleanliness, then puts them back on. "I'm afraid I have disturbing news. Bernard was found dead early this morning."

The office's bare walls close in, leaving me gasping for air. Bernard, dead? What the hell?

After waiting a few seconds, Kurt adds, "Drowned. In the Nieuwe Maas, close to his hotel in Rotterdam. Police say he bumped his head and fell into the water. They are investigating." Kurt studies my face. "It doesn't change anything. Now that I take over Bernard's major negotiations, I will need an additional personal assistant, for the…type of work Bernard had in mind. You've just met Jason, who will continue to be my primary PA." He pauses. His mind shows nothing but concentration on my response. Maybe he interprets my silence as non-comprehension, as he continues with deliberate emphasis, "Your role will be the same as it would have been under Bernard's supervision."

In what feels like a herculean effort, I lower my eyebrows from my hairline into their neutral position. Bernard dead... And with him, the memories of my mother, laughing, talking, working. I was so close to getting to know her better... A lump forms in my throat.

I dig my nails into my palms. Come on, Kath, get a grip. How selfish, to mourn the death of a mind more than the death of its owner.

But it hurts so much. He was the only person who *truly* knew her. I'd wanted him to rewind his memories over and over again, like an old projector showing long forgotten clips. I swallow. What would Kurt think if I cry over the death of a future boss I officially met only twice for recruitment purposes?

Kurt watches me with interest. "Bernard will be dearly missed. We'll need to reorganise the Syndicate. I could use your help, given your HR background. I hope you're still interested in the job." He attempts to smile, the corners of his mouth straining to go upwards, instead of the disapproving downward curve they seem so used to.

Suddenly I'm freezing. Not only does Kurt's intense focus on me chill me to the bone, but I also just lost my mother yet again.

I look down. The carpet is grey, with light and dark blue curling lines weaving through it. Like flowing rivers. As I've already jumped into this river by signing a contract, I might as well go with the flow. I look up at Kurt and straighten my shoulders. "Yes, I'm still interested in the job."

Kurt seems satisfied, even though my voice is completely lacking the enthusiasm a new boss usually likes to hear.

"Great. I have a couple of meetings this afternoon. I'd like you to join me, it will be the quickest way to learn about the Syndicate and what we do."

CHAPTER EIGHTEEN

During the third consecutive meeting that afternoon, all the unfamiliar words, and even the familiar words in unfamiliar combinations, punch my skull from the inside. Politicians shouldn't be surprised the average citizen couldn't care less about politics. You've got to know a huge amount of context to even try to understand the political arena.

In addition, there are too many new minds to read. Many suspicious of what my arrival will do to their jobs and status. Maybe this wasn't such a great idea... With Bernard as boss, at least someone would have understood me. And I would've been able to see my mother, to get closer to her, even if just in spirit.

With renewed reluctance, I tune into the discussion between Jason and Kurt. They're discussing a strategy to help the opposition leader of a French pro-EU party maintain his sound position for the election later this year. Why are they concerned about national politics? Or would this be one of Kurt's 'sensitive matters?'

At the start of the meeting, Kurt sat down next to me. Probably to send the subconscious message 'we're on the same side.' An HR technique I'm too familiar with. Suddenly, he leans towards me. I shrink back. "Would you like to contribute anything, Kathy? Feel free to give us your thoughts. A fresh look on the matter always helps."

Which fresh look? I feel far from fresh. Physically and mentally wrung out, maybe. "Er, I'm afraid the topics are quite new to me. I...would've thought the Syndicate would be involved in the EU, less so in national politics."

"We're involved in everything that ultimately affects the processes in the EU. Mediating negotiations within the European Council as well as European Commission are indeed our primary activities. Bernard focused mainly on those. I was in charge of ironing out any wrinkles in the path towards the main negotiations."

"Where does this French politician fit in?"

"He's the leader of the opposition, and in favour of an important pact we want to close early next year. French elections take place soon, and the winning party will influence France's vote. His chances are good, but there's a certain indiscretion in his recent past that might hurt his election prospects. We help him…contain that indiscretion."

Jason chuckles. *Sucker. Having a former model as a wife, you'd think he'd be able to keep his hands off of other women. Or at least smart enough not to get one pregnant.*

I rub my forehead. "You're saying, he did something that could cost him the election, so you're helping him hide the truth?"

Jason rolls his eyes.

"More or less." Kurt studies my disapproving frown, and adds in a soothing tone, "Listen, he didn't do anything illegal. Just a moment of weakness he earnestly regrets."

Jason snorts. *Only thing he regrets is the blackmail. Idiot couldn't keep zipped up, or at the very least rubbered up, if his life depended on it.*

Kurt frowns at Jason, then turns to me. "He's an excellent politician. Such minor, private things shouldn't even affect public opinion. Unfortunately, it does. We're just ensuring the election focuses on the right issues. On the rational, political matters, not irrelevant personal matters that influence the constituency emotionally."

"On the surface, that sounds reasonable. Still, isn't that exactly why people stopped believing in politicians? Because they don't tell the truth when they're afraid it harms their goals? Isn't the essence of integrity that the end does *not* justify the means?"

Jason's increasing irritation reaches his personal threshold, and he bursts out, "Come on, Kathy, don't be so naïve. We're not talking some minor goals here. If the end goal is a pact benefiting all Europeans, it's certainly justifiable to curb a few nationalistic leeches that'll swoop down on anything in a man's past to disrupt the process."

Kurt holds up his hand to Jason. "It's understandable a new person needs time to appreciate what we do. It's a very specific job. Kathy won't be involved much in these matters, but it's important she knows about them." He turns to me. "I just wanted you to be aware of what we do. Tomorrow, we'll attend a few meetings in Brussels. Those will be of a very different nature." He retrieves his phone from his pocket. *Write notes [...].*

Hey! Those weren't Jason's thoughts. They must have been Kurt's... I scramble to read more, but his mind has taken on the infinity of outer space again.

Kurt shifts in his chair and his phone falls from his pant's pocket. While I bend to pick it up, Kurt swiftly puts something in his other pocket. Puzzled, I stare at the phone. I'd swear I saw him type on it, just when it fell to the ground from his pants.

Kurt clears his throat. "Keep in mind, all of our meetings need to be kept secret. To that effect, you'll need to sign a confidentiality agreement." Kurt raises his hand when I open my mouth to protest. "Yes, I know, you signed one with your employment contract, but I prefer a more elaborate one. The departments here deal with even more sensitive information than the Brussels office. Since you'll primarily work here, I need you to sign the other one. Jason will hand it to you now, so we can finish the paperwork before you join me tomorrow."

Jason scowls. *'Primarily work here'? Not if I can help it. Will make her life miserable.*

I sink deeper into my chair. Great. Instead of working with the soft-spoken Bernard, airing delightful clips of my mother's life, I'm stuck with a couple of drooling hyenas.

CHAPTER NINETEEN

The Brussels Syndicate office is surprisingly small, compared to the one in The Hague. In the elevator, Kurt explains. "Employees mostly work in the European Commission's offices, or from home. Besides, in The Hague we've got the Research Department."

Would that be the second floor? "What's the Research department for?"

Kurt stiffens, and when the elevator opens, marches to the office of Bernard's secretary. An older woman stands sobbing in a neat and structured room. Through a door, a spacious office is visible. Apparently, Bernard needed an office to match his self-importance.

The woman dabs her eyes with a tissue. *There he is. Doesn't look disturbed at all.*

Kurt doesn't waste time offering consolation. "Marie, this is Kathy van der Laan. Kathy, this is Marie Verbeeck." He picks up a pile of mail from her desk, addressed to Bernard.

Marie swallows. *That's it? Nothing about Bernard?* "Have you heard from the police? They released information about their investigation. The alcohol level in Bernard's blood was quite high. They think Bernard had become very drunk, fell and hit his head, and then stumbled over the edge." She balls her fist. "I don't believe that for a minute."

"Right. Well, we have to let the police do their work. Marie, since Kathy is Bernard's hire, she will now work for me. I expect you to fully cooperate with each other." He opens an envelope and starts reading.

I shrug in an apology. She'd probably like to do just the opposite of the order he just barked out, given the finality in his tone and the rudeness of not looking her in the eyes.

Marie grimaces at me, and with the tiniest curl of her lips, says, "Of course, sir. I *am* looking forward to work with *Kathy*."

Kurt, still absorbed in the mail of his deceased boss, nods absently.

He doesn't even pick up on my insult? Well, even if he had, he wouldn't care. Such an awful boss to work for... Bernard made me work hard, but also made me feel like a human being. To Kurt, we're just servants. Poor Kathy.

Kurt proceeds to justify Marie's opinion of him, by holding a cold five-minute meeting with all staff present, establishing himself as the successor of Bernard. The strong hypocrisy lies like a blanket over the room. Dislike and even fear towards Kurt seem to be the general sentiment, while outwardly, everyone shows nothing but respect for the person now responsible for their salary increase. Except for Marie. She stands in a corner, her back towards Kurt, and stares at a tree on the square outside. *Only two more years to retirement.*

The politicians we meet that afternoon at the European Council have widely different attitudes towards Kurt.

That leech! Need to get rid of him ASAP!

Heard he can take care of things. When you're prepared to pay the cost of eternal loyalty.

I wish I didn't owe him. I linger on the thoughts of this man. He seems to feel subdued gratefulness towards Kurt, with that mix of relief when someone saves you from a difficult situation, combined with fearing what they'll make you do to pay back your debt.

The passing thought of one of the senior leaders strikes me the most. *A shame Bernard died. He was the only one that could reign in 'The Eraser.'*

CHAPTER TWENTY

The rest of the afternoon proves to be an enlightening view into a world I didn't know, and never cared about. I'm glad Kurt keeps his mouth shut while we drive back.

The stroboscopic effect of the lights along the highway intensifies my headache, one flash at a time. Every five minutes, I check Kurt's mind for thoughts. But he focuses on the steering wheel and the road ahead, his mind echoing the shooting lights, further amplifying the pulses in my brain. I close my eyes and lean back. Was staying in this job after Bernard's death a good idea? My new boss is known as 'The Eraser,' for crying out loud. He 'can take care' of things, claiming it's of world importance to sweep unsavoury incidents under the rug.

I'm so unfamiliar with this work and this world. I'm clearly not qualified. And on top of it all, I've lost the chance to get more information about my mother. I lean over to adjust the air flow from the vents to have it bounce off the windows instead of my body. This is not what I signed up for. It can only end in disaster. There won't be a single person sorry to see me go. Including me. Once again, I'll be writing my resignation.

Kurt relaxes, his focus less intense now that we have left the busy ring road of Antwerp behind. "What did you think of the meeting at the European Council?"

"Long and windy." Like this highway.

Kurt snorts. "This was one of the shorter meetings. I guess you'll need to get used to the delay the translations cause." His hands grip the wheel tighter. "Did you feel any reluctance from the Portuguese delegate?"

The Portuguese delegate? Does he expect me to remember everyone we met?

Rapping his fingers on the wheel, Kurt clarifies, "The one with the ridiculous red shark tie."

Ah, the shark tie. A shimmer of cheerful resistance in an otherwise boring group, all dressed to the same innocuous template, trying to fit in. I do remember him. "He seemed engaged. Taking part actively." Actually, he'd been admirably patient, given his strong irritations. I didn't understand most of his rapid Portuguese thoughts, but his feelings were clear.

"But what did you feel in his thoughts?"

I freeze. "What did I…think about him, you mean?" I try to read Kurt's mind but get nothing, apart from his focus on the road.

Kurt snaps, "No, what did you read in his mind. Bernard told me you can read minds. Like your mother."

Bernard told him? The throbbing pain in my head intensifies to hammer blows. Bernard had promised no one knew about my mother, or me. Not even his deputy Kurt. For twenty-seven years, I managed to keep my ability a secret. And now two people know, in as many weeks.

Frantically, I search Kurt's mind again. I have to know what he knows. This could be one of those situations people try to trick the truth out of someone by pretending they already know it. Like when employees ask me, after a colleague had an intense meeting with her boss, 'Now that she's fired, who will get her job?' They hope I'll answer, 'How do you know such and so was fired?' or, 'Such and so will not be fired, she's just being disciplined.' Good thing I have an excellent poker face. I will certainly not admit anything to Kurt.

With the hint of a carnivorous smile in his voice, Kurt says, "Didn't Bernard tell you? My apologies for springing this on you. I know the real reason for hiring you is your ability to read minds, enabling him to address unspoken issues before they become a problem. And that your mother did this for him in the past."

Whaaatt?? "Really? When did he tell you?"

"Tuesday, after we interviewed you. Although you're a competent person, I didn't quite understand why he hired somebody with your background. Until he explained your special abilities."

"Right." Shit. Years of self-protection reflexes just flushed down the drain.

"Apart from me, nobody knows. I intend to keep this a secret as much as you do."

He'd better keep that promise. But if he knows this, what more does he know? I clear my throat. "Did Bernard tell you anything else about my mother?"

"A little. About her abilities, and how she helped him."

"I...had hoped to know more about her through Bernard."

Shit, shouldn't have confessed that... Kurt's mind flashes, like a predator pouncing.

"I might be able to help. Bernard might've kept a file on your mother, outside of the regular personnel system. I've ordered Marie to give me access to all his notes and files. I'll keep an eye out for you."

"Thanks." I stare out the side window.

After a few minutes, Kurt breaks the awkward silence. Or at least, awkward for me. Kurt's probably not even capable of those feelings. "I joined the Syndicate before your mother died. We hardly knew her, but her accident was investigated by people from the Syndicate. There was a suspicion of foul play. But they could never prove it."

"Foul play?" I bite my tongue when I hear how squeaky that came out. Great, Kath, show 'The Eraser' how badly you want to know more about your mother. Very smart.

"Although no one knew about your mother's mind-reading ability, everyone knew she was important to Bernard. Strongly influenced his decisions. People were jealous. Some were unhappy with the progress they made together. Her death might not have been an accident."

Is he suggesting...she might've been hit *on purpose?*

Kurt taps the steering wheel. "More about that later. Listen, you'll go on your first assignment on Monday. Jason has arranged for you to stay two nights in The Hague. Rent a bike, and follow the

Dutch Prime Minister from his house to the parliament buildings and back. Just two days, we don't want it to become too obvious."

"I beg your pardon?" He must be joking.

Kurt raises his eyebrows. "Just a training exercise. To get a reading on the Dutch Prime Minister. A chance to get to know one of the key politicians."

"There are plenty of other ways to get to know them."

Kurt snorts. "This'll be quicker. Everyone knows the PM often bikes to work alone. Will be an easy job, to follow him and read thoughts in Dutch. Arranging to meet him will take ages."

"Not quite the ethical assignment!" I can't believe my ears. Maybe they're plugged, given that my heartbeat is up there. Loud and clear.

"You don't have to get so worked up about it. I don't have time to get you set up early next week, anyway. I need two days to transition Bernard's files from Brussels to The Hague, and to wrap up issues around Bernard's death. This is just a training exercise. The PM leaves his house around 7:30 A.M. Wait about two blocks away, and then just fall in behind him. You're competent enough not to screw that up."

I snort. Does he really expect me to spy on the Dutch PM?

"It's a straightforward assignment." The intensity of his mind strengthens, his knuckles turn white from grappling the steering wheel hard. "I'm the only one that knows about you. We should keep it that way. You know, someone with your abilities should be really careful." He looks sideways at me. "As long as you work for me, I'll be able to protect you."

My brain wants to hear the comforting words. But my sinking stomach recognises the carefully veiled threat.

"So, can I count on you?"

My eyes burn. He's threatening me. But two can play the manipulation game. I can follow the PM, but I don't have to tell Kurt his real thoughts.

I nod. I guess I won't quit the job just yet.

CHAPTER TWENTY-ONE

I close the dark-blue door behind me with a soft click. The bed-and-breakfast stands proud in this old The Hague street, shouldered by an Indian restaurant and an upscale furniture store. The window of the latter features a single large black ribbed vase, against the backdrop of a cobalt blue rectangle on a wooden easel. What would that look like in my unassuming, functional apartment? Probably as ridiculous as my assignment today.

I stroll past buildings that house shops and restaurants as well as the eclectic mix of people you'll find living in every city centre in The Netherlands—families, retirees, students, hip couples. Only a few houses are fully residential, owned by the lucky ones who can afford it. The others feature shops or restaurants on street level and living quarters upstairs, roughly falling into two categories: decent sized hyper-modern apartments owned or rented by retirees or career couples, exteriors beaming with a fresh coat of paint, windows framing stylish renovated wooden beams contrasted by simple, steel furniture; or small rooms, rented mostly by students, with smudgy windows, paint peeling off and shabby curtains still closed.

Dutch city centres are beautiful blends of old and new buildings, of business and pleasure, of prosperity and poverty. Because so many people call the cores of Dutch cities home, streets are never deserted. Even now, at 7 A.M., several people hurry along past the closed shops.

On the corner, the rented bike is still chained to the bike rack where I left it last night. A small miracle. The inhabited nature of Dutch city centres does not make them less prone to theft than foreign, business-dominated downtown areas. Would've been the first time I'd have been happy to see a bike gone. A great excuse to not fulfill the task ahead.

Unhurried, I pat myself down to check which pocket contains the key. After retrieving it from my left jeans front pocket, I unlock the bike and pedal towards the north of the city.

Thinking of the task ahead, my hands become slippery on the handlebars. I respect Paul Schipper. He got elected over a decade ago as one of the youngest PMs The Netherlands ever had. Since then, he led the country through several crises, despite a few inevitable scratches on his reputation. His effort to come across as a down-to-earth, regular guy that could be anyone's neighbour or friend is a little too much for my taste, but I like his directness. Most important of all, I believe he has a genuine motivation to do what's best for the country, instead of prioritising the upkeep of his alpha-male position. I coloured the box next to this guy's name twice.

And now I have to spy on him.

I cycle around and pick a street corner providing the best chance of spotting him on time. A girl is standing there, drumming her fingers on the handlebars of her bike. Through her mind, I enjoy the pumping music coming from her earbuds. Occasionally, she checks the street to the right to see whether her classmates are coming. She doesn't notice me, even though I feel completely out of place. Everyone is going somewhere—people leave their houses to get into cars parked along the street, walk to a bus or metro stop, or zoom past on their scooters.

There. Someone with the stocky silhouette of Paul Schipper approaches. My fingers cramp around the handlebars, my heart rate perks up. The bald head, the face—yeah, it's him. Until now, at a deep level, my mind apparently believed this wouldn't happen. Not for real. I blow up my cheeks and exhale through pursed lips.

Then, the moment to casually fall in behind him is gone. I jump on my bike and peddle fiercely to catch up. Any moment now, bodyguards will ambush me for sure.

But in this morning rush, haste is not the exception. Nothing happens. Not even when I close the gap with Schipper to a mere five metres. His thoughts come across clearly.

When meeting someone new, I first need time figuring out their thought process. Some people are quite visual, others think almost entirely in sentences. Some are structured, others jump from one unfinished train of thought to another. Some people's minds are a bunch of emotions, others consist of rational thoughts. Within a person, it also varies, depending on the situation or their mood. Especially with booze or drugs, thought patterns can dramatically alter.

You'd think, with all the scientists and psychologists in the world, there would be much more accurate knowledge about the thinking process. It's amusing to read books about how people's brains work. Scientists rely on their own thinking experiences, and what others *tell* them about their thought processes. But so far, I've not read correct descriptions about what's really happening when people think.

Tuning into Schipper's thoughts is easy. He's a structured thinker, using sentences together with visuals, and hardly has distracting emotions. Understanding the content of his thinking is much harder though. He has the speedy thought train of the intelligent. On top of that, I'm not familiar with the topics he is thinking about.

After ten minutes of pedaling behind him, a pattern emerges. Schipper's thoughts often revolve around others. *Will compliment Iris today for her excellent report summary. Discuss with Bert today that great remark Frank had about improving the relations between our parties. Prepare for press conference tomorrow. Emphasise John's role, such a great job he did.*

For most leaders I've met, political or not, at least half their thoughts revolve around themselves. 'What will the board think of me? How can I convince Tom to see it my way? I should demand that promotion.' But Schipper seems to be a proper, nice human being, with genuine interest in others, and an inner drive to make things right. Someone ethical, like I used to be myself. But here I am, spying on an experienced, well-respected Prime Minister.

When he turns left towards the parliament buildings, I keep biking straight and take the next left. I need a strong coffee.

CHAPTER TWENTY-TWO

"… report states it has failed miserably. Could you deny or confirm this?"

"Thank you for your question. I sincerely appreciate your concern. We have studied the report in detail, including all the underlying data, and see rays of hope in their conclusions." The minister's voice drones on, with just the right frequency to numb my brain.

If only it would numb the rest of my body. I roll my shoulders and wiggle on my butt, lean forward and back. Still uncomfortable. The visitor area looks like the grandstand of a sports arena and is certainly just as comfortable. Not.

Two hours of debating, and they've not even covered half the agenda. Jason must've known this would take ages. 'Go follow a Dutch parliament session live,' he said. 'It'll be useful to learn about politics in general.' Asshole.

From the visitor's area, it's impossible to follow Schipper's thoughts. In the crowd of parliament members participating, reading specific thoughts is like trying to follow a sea lion diving under the surface for long stretches.

Okay, after three minutes I might've stopped trying. These people weigh every word as if picking the right tool, find complex ways to hide a message in long sentences, or to score points in a verbal battle. They probably don't realise normal people give up trying to follow their cocky monologues. Or they don't care.

Some people in the circus arena down there seem to feel the same, though. And they can't just tune out like me. They have to say something smart and to the point when it's their turn. Brave.

"…therefore, we feel it isn't expedient to relate the height of the recycling deposit to the size of a particular bottle, according to the classification proposed."

The eyes of the speaking member of parliament shine. As if he genuinely cares about the changes to the regulations around recyclable drink packaging.

Maybe I should, too. He puts me to shame. As a citizen committed to the environment, I dutifully sort waste into the applicable bins, use public transport to minimise my carbon footprint and recycle all re-usable items and materials. This is an important decision. I should care.

But I don't.

"… close this deliberation and move on to the next topic."

Excellent timing to sneak out. I tiptoe to the exit, ashamed. I turn around and bow, to salute the people who have the stamina to get such things right. Who can discuss one detail for two hours and then still have energy for the next, equally tenacious, debate.

Outside of the parliament building, I take a few deep breaths. Following Schipper by bike, sitting in on a parliamentary debate–these two days were easily the two weirdest in my working life so far. I walk through the gate of the Binnenhof square towards my bike.

"Hello Kathy." Cecilia leans against one of the bike racks. Her arms are crossed in front of her chest, the wind blows through her long black hair. She'd look relaxed, if it weren't for her dark, inquisitive eyes, not needing make-up to be intense.

She notices my surprise with satisfaction. *Good first step to push her off-balance.*

Careful lady, I just watched the best of the best in debating. Maybe it rubbed off.

Last week in both Syndicate buildings. This week attending a parliamentary session. Doesn't make sense at all. She smiles. "How was the session in the Tweede Kamer? Interesting?"

"No." At least this I can answer with the truth, and nothing but the truth.

"Why are you here?"

I clear my throat. Would Kurt be okay if I tell others about working for the Syndicate? It's not a secret. And since Cecilia seems to know already, I better come across as cooperative. "I started in a new job last week. Assisting someone who deals with the European Union, so as a way of getting trained, they thought it would be good to learn how governments work."

"Who will you be working for?" *For Kurt directly?*

I drop the smile. My cheeks feel cramped for trying, anyway. If she knows so much, there's no point in asking me. She shows up here and knows where I've been the past week. A familiar obstinate lump grows in my chest, and my shoulder muscles tighten. Once, at a parent-teacher conference, my father was told, 'Kathy does not respond well to leading questions.' For weeks, Dad had reveled in describing the teacher's acrid expression when he'd answered 'Good for her'.

In the spirit of the debaters in the building behind me, I settle for an exaggerated explanatory tone. "The organisation I am now working for goes under the name 'the Syndicate.'"

Cecilia frowns. *Is she slow in understanding? Or does she play me?* "I meant, who is your boss? Just wondering. Odd timing. The President of the Syndicate happens to have died last week." Cecilia's jaw tightens. *Damn! Shouldn't have said that. Wish I could break through that impenetrable face.*

I blink a few times and nod. "I was supposed to start working for the President. It was quite a shock when I turned up Thursday morning and heard he was dead."

"Had you met him before?"

"A week ago, on Tuesday. Job interview."

"You only met him once before you accepted the job?" *Doesn't strike me as the impulsive type. Besides, the Syndicate's elaborate screening procedures usually take weeks.*

"Well, twice on that Tuesday. We also discussed the contract later that day." Given the efforts Bernard went through to keep the first meeting secret, I better keep it that way.

"So now you work for..." Cecilia stops abruptly. *Shit, almost mentioned his name. Shouldn't let her know our interest in the Syndicate.*

"For the deputy, who's taking over." I smile innocently at Cecilia, who, to her credit, doesn't buy it.

You know I wanted a name. Stubborn as hell. "Quite a different job than your previous ones. Your fifth job, I believe? Remarkable list, for someone who's only twenty-seven." Cecilia bites her lower lip. *Now, now, careful Cecil. You're letting her get to you. You want to know where she gets her info from, not push her into defensive mode.*

I shrug. "My track record isn't great for holding jobs. Have you never considered another career?"

Cecilia's jaw sets. She thinks of her parents, sweating away in an industrial kitchen. *They're still hoping I'll take over the restaurant one day. No way.*

She narrows her eyes, steps forward and brushes imaginary dirt from where she leaned against the rack. "Listen. I don't believe for a minute you just got involved with the Syndicate. They're shady. You know things about crimes. The head suddenly dies, and then you officially start working for them. What do you think that sounds like?"

I shrug again. I honestly have no clue what someone could read into that.

Wait. The Syndicate, 'shady'?

Cecilia takes a long look at me. *Remarkable girl. I can't seem to throw her off balance. Or would she know I am out of my jurisdiction here? Need to wait for results on Bernard's autopsy. After that, hopefully I'll have a reason to interrogate her.*

Cecilia nods. "'Til next time, Kathy." She shields her inquisitive eyes by sliding mirrored sunglasses on, which leaves me looking at myself.

CHAPTER TWENTY-THREE

The diverse landscape between Rotterdam to The Hague flashes by on the 'ka-dunk-a-dunk' rhythm of the tracks. Water-regulating creeks divide the agricultural land in small patches, each with its own type of vegetation or roaming cattle. The outskirts of Delft announce themselves by a sudden increase in building density, and the train slows down for the Delft Campus stop.

After that stop, the train dives into the new tunnel, enclosing us in the dark instead of treating us to views of the beautiful old inner city. The city centre itself has improved, but the train ride, not so much. Old buildings stimulate my imagination. What have those walls seen inside? Who lived there? What role did they play in Delft's rich history? So much we don't know, so much left to our imagination.

Whereas with people...

Hope the professor gives me another day for turning in the assignment.

What a selfish asshole. Plunking his backpack on the seat next to him. Trying to force others to keep standing while he sits alone.

Why did I drink so much yesterday... Does that witch talk so loud on purpose, or what?

That chick's spicy... I could give you a great time, babe. First, I'll rip that top off and then...

I get up and walk to the next carriage, where a myriad of new thoughts tumble over each other into my head. I should buy a car. Or work from home.

The train ascends into the light, coming up for air next to the industrial complex in the north of Delft. A few images of houses, a highway and then we go underground again and slow down. Rijswijk station. I jump out and linger on the platform until most people are gone. A few minutes of much-needed silence. I trudge up the stairs, out of the station, into the street where the building of the Syndicate looms in the distance.

The receptionist nods. "Hello again!" She places a different type of key card on the counter. "This is your employee key card. It grants you access to the elevators and the floors and rooms you have clearance for."

"Thank you. Which floors are the Syndicate's?"

She raises her eyebrows. "The entire building is occupied by the Syndicate. You just don't have access to all areas."

"Oh? Which parts do I have access to?"

She scowls. "I don't know. The key cards are set up by security." *That awful Jason. I'm the receptionist, for crying out loud. It's my job to know who is allowed access to what.*

"Okay, no problem." I smile, warmed by the feeling of two strangers bonding over a shared dislike. Except, I'm the only one who knows we both dislike Jason.

I hold my key card against the black square by the elevator. The doors open, I step in and press the button for the third floor. The elevator obeys. Half disappointed, I get out at the third floor, ignore Jason, and barge into Kurt's office.

Kurt stares at his computer screen. *I should feed it to her in bits and pieces. Keep her hungry.* He notices my presence and sits up, startled. His mind switches to his usual thought-less void. As if he's blocking his thoughts from me. Impressive.

He barks out, "Kathy. Next time you report to Jason first."

I nod, fighting the desire to click my heels and salute him.

Kurt casually puts a hand over one of two identical phones on his desk. *Ah, he does have two phones.* I wasn't imagining one phone dropping out of his pocket while he checked another one.

Jason appears in the door opening with a smug face. *Yes, hon, you heard the boss, better report to me first. Don't undermine me.* "Kurt? Shall I bring Kathy to the waiting room first?"

Kurt shakes his head. "Thanks, Jason, but it's okay for now. I'd like a latte, please. Kathy, would you like something to drink?"

I yearn for a strong espresso. Or even a weak substitute, as long as there's a hint of caffeine. "A bottle of water, please." It's easy to see whether the cap of a bottle is tampered with. Wouldn't put it past him to spit in my coffee. I prefer additives of my own choice.

Kurt turns off his computer and pulls out two cables below his desk. He mumbles, "Need to reset the damned thing."

Jason re-enters, placing a diluted, sickly beige coloured coffee in front of Kurt. Almost as an afterthought, he hands me a bottle of water, cap still sealed.

The door clicks to a close after him, and Kurt asks, "How did the assignment go?"

Better answer short and quick, get it over with. "I was able to tail Paul Schipper on Monday and Tuesday morning. I missed him going home both days." Not really a lie. I just wasn't there to try. "I also attended the parliament session Tuesday afternoon."

"Good. What did you think of Paul Schipper?"

"It was easy to follow him. No security, as far as I noticed."

Kurt frowns. "It's a shame you didn't manage to follow him home in the evenings." He sighs. "But, given it's your first time, you did well."

For a micro-second, the compliment pleases me. Jeez, I'm pathetic. A compliment for my first improper job, from the unethical boss of a strange organisation, is nothing to be proud of.

Kurt leans back. "Were his thoughts mainly on the job? Or also his private life?"

Here we go…the immoral part of the assignment. I inhale. I practiced this. Show some cooperation without giving anything away. "His thoughts were on the job. Names of politicians, colleagues, debates they were going to have that day. Preparing for the press conference."

"Nothing on his private life? What he did this weekend? Whom he spent time with?"

I shake my head, leaning back as well. "But I wasn't to listen for anything specific anyway, was I? Just a training exercise, right?"

"Of course, of course." Kurt attempts to distort his lips into a reassuring smile. He'd be a great scare clown at Halloween.

I clear my throat. "On Tuesday afternoon, when I came out of the parliament building, a police detective approached me. A few weeks ago, I called in an anonymous tip to save a girl from a pedophile. She discovered I'd made that call and came to my house to ask me how I knew."

Kurt's thoughts flash. *Shit, police.* Followed by an intensified concentration on me. "She first came to your house? Where does she work?"

"Rotterdam."

Kurt frowns. "Why did she confront you in The Hague?"

"I have no clue."

"She has no jurisdiction in The Hague. I will check with a connection what is going on."

"Thanks." I could do with one less shark on my tail.

Kurt sits up. "The past two days, I started to go through Bernard's files. From a few written notes, I understand your mother was adopted."

I nod. I know that much.

"Bernard got information from the adoption agency. Your mother was found in a little village in the southeast of the Netherlands. She claimed to be seven years old and said her parents had left her on a road leading to that village. She spoke German. Child services put her in foster care. After a year, she'd gone through two different foster families, who claimed she was a difficult and strange child. Then a farmer couple, with no children of their own, adopted her."

I stare at the floor. Her parents left her? Going through two foster families before she was adopted? That must've been horrible. To be deliberately abandoned by your parents at the age of seven… only to be recycled through a couple of foster families. Does Dad know?

And then the memory of walking around with a little baby boy forces itself into my head. The pattern of the carpet blurs as the image of the baby boy comes into focus. But it wasn't a memory. It was a dream. A nightmare. I'd run to my mother to tell her. She'd freaked out.

Kurt studies me. "Didn't you know?"

I shake my head and force myself to act calmly. "Not all the details." According to my dad, she'd been happy with her adoptive parents on their dairy farm. In her spare time, she'd helped with the cows and other animals. The few times she'd taken me to the farmhouse, her love and gratitude for the farm, her adoptive parents, and the animals had shone through.

"I hope I'll find more information. I'll keep you posted." He gets up.

Apparently, the meeting ended. Just when it was getting interesting. Sighing, I get up as well and follow Kurt into the hallway.

"Jason, give her a laptop, phone and several case files to get acquainted with." Without waiting for Jason's answer, Kurt strides back to his office and bangs the door shut.

Lips pursed, Jason shows me the way to an empty office. *Will put you as far away from everyone as possible. You won't make friends here if I can help it.*

I concentrate beyond the walls. Apart from Jason's, I don't hear anyone's thoughts.

Jason frowns. *Why is she smiling?*

Because hostility sometimes works out well. All I need right now is a nice, quiet space.

CHAPTER TWENTY-FOUR

Late morning, the door swings open immediately after someone knocks. To my surprise, Kurt steps in. I'd judged him as the type to assert his power by commanding his employees to his office for every meeting, instead of making the effort to walk over to one of his subordinates.

He seats himself. "Catching up on the EU?"

"Yes. The white paper on the EU's future is an impressive read. I never knew the EU is the largest single market. Or that European firms hold 40% of the world's patents for renewable energy technologies."

Kurt's mouth curves downwards. "Right. It's embarrassing how few EU citizens know where the EU excels. Most only criticize the slow decision-making. However, the negotiations and long discussions also ensure decisions are accepted by many stakeholders. It keeps the EU sharp and in tune with many viewpoints."

"Hence the EU's motto I guess, 'Unity in diversity.' I like that, but I still think the organisation is too complex and the processes not transparent enough."

Kurt slams his fist on the table. "Absolutely. That is exactly what I'm going to improve. And I hope you will help me." He leans forward, his eyes intense. "You know, your mother was part of the start. She helped the EU become what it is today. And you can follow in her footsteps, to take the EU to the next level."

My heart swells. A great way to honour her, by playing an instrumental role in the growth of the EU like she did.

Kurt sinks back. "I talked to a senior police official in Rotterdam. Cecilia's boss doesn't seem to think you're an interesting lead.

He hasn't given her permission to investigate you. She seems just a low-ranking detective who wants to prove herself." He studies the wall behind me. "You know, it could be interesting to string her along for a little while and find out what she knows about the Syndicate. If she approaches you again, get as much information from her as you can. If she bothers you too much, I'll make sure her bosses keep her on a leash."

I narrow my eyes. I never told him she asked about the Syndicate, so why does he think she knows anything? And if he has a contact in the police force, he could find out himself.

Kurt coughs. "I also read more of Bernard's notes." *I understand he communicated with your mother this way. Bernard thinking, your mother talking.*

I freeze. The guy that's somehow blocking his thoughts from me is now communicating through his mind on purpose?

Just wanted to try how it works. But remember, no mentioning of your mind-reading skills out loud, you never know who's listening.

Listening?

Out loud, he continues, "Tomorrow we will go to Brussels again, for two days of meetings. Sara, one of my talented young negotiators, will join us. Sara used to be a member of a German political party. She had to give that up, of course, when she started here." *Oh, wait, I started talking out loud. This is difficult, it feels quite unnatural to think instead of talk.*

Not being able to connect with Kurt's mind surprised me, and now that he lets me in, it still feels unnatural. He doesn't have the free flow of thoughts I'm used to with others.

"We'll go by car with the three of us." Kurt shrugs apologetically. *Talking out loud again. Anyway, Sara has been in touch with her previous party colleagues. We can't be sure of her loyalty. Could you check on her thoughts? I need to be sure I can fully trust her, that her ambitions lie with the Syndicate and not her previous party.*

"Right." I rub my forehead.

"Great." Kurt pushes his chair back from the table. "Oh, I found several pictures of your mother. Will give them to you tomorrow."

He strides out of the room.

I stare after him. My chest tightens at the thought of another spy job. Of course, I can hardly claim innocence, having read other people's minds my whole life. But I never shared that information with others, except anonymously tipping the police off when it concerned criminal information. I've always been ethical. Or so I've been telling myself...

In this case, if Sara spies on the Syndicate for a foreign political party, that might be considered a crime. Something that undermines the stability of the EU. The EU that my mother helped set up.

How did she deal with walking this fine ethical line? My mother seemed to have been good at this. Maybe I'm just not as good a person as she was.

CHAPTER TWENTY-FIVE

My stepmom waits outside the building, car engine running. Her cheerful face is not at all in line with the gloomy, apprehensive feeling clouding her mind.

I open the passenger door and ask, "Would you prefer me to drive?"

"No, it's okay. I prefer to focus on the road right now."

I get in and wait until she's pulled into the traffic. "You haven't heard anything about the test results yet?"

She hits the brakes for a traffic light with a little too much force.

"No. I called, but they won't say anything. That means bad news, right?" She blinks her eyes.

"Not necessarily. The person on the phone probably hasn't the authority to disclose the results."

She sighs. *She's right. Of course. But if it was okay, they could've said so over the phone, right? Good thing I asked Kathy to come along. Gary would've stressed even more than me. I hope he doesn't have to lose a wife again...*

I clear my throat. "Alida, did you tell Dad you got tested?"

She takes a turn, hands gripping the wheel. "No, I didn't tell him. You know him. He wouldn't have slept one single night after."

"Probably. But Dad loves you and he deserves to know." My cheeks burn. Yeah, Kath, brilliant advice. Coming from someone who doesn't want to tell her dad about the essence of her being.

Alida sobs. "Oh, I know. But even if I get bad news today, I can't imagine going home tonight and telling him."

For a few minutes, we drive in silence. Then she pulls into the parking lot, stops in front of a red-and-white turnstile and opens the window to press the button for a ticket. Before she retrieves it, she turns to me. "If it is bad news, could you come home with me? Your dad will need you."

I swallow. "Sure. We'll tell him together."

We park the car and walk into the hospital.

"It's the end of this corridor on the left," Alida points. Last week, with the test, she went alone. I'd offered to go with her, but she declined, bravely stating it wasn't a big deal, anyway. Honestly, I was relieved. Hospitals are horrible places. Not because of the smell of frequent disinfection, not because of personal terrible experiences, not even because I don't like sickness or death. I just hate reading the minds of worried patients, mourning relatives and, most of all, doctors.

For one thing, healthcare professionals are people, just like you and me. While you want them to focus on your health problem, in your opinion *the* most pressing issue in the world, they focus on things like 'oh, forgot to buy a present for that party tonight,' or 'this patient seems just as arrogant as my ex, the asshole.' Very understandable, but a little scary if they measure the right dose of your medication or try to make sense of an abnormality on your X-ray.

Once, a colleague had asked me to come with her. She'd recently moved to Rotterdam, and she hadn't wanted to ask relatives to make a long journey for a short meeting with the doctor. Still, she wanted a second pair of ears. She'd had a pap smear test with irregularities, gotten a second one, and the doctor wanted to talk through the results.

When she checked in with the assistant, I knew. *So young. Doctor will suggest treatment, but at this age the cells multiply so quickly. Need to see if I can book her for additional tests next week.*

My colleague remained optimistic during the ten minutes we had to wait for the doctor. The longest ten minutes of my life.

Today, the experienced assistant is mentally ticking off a to-do list for a party she is organising in the coming weekend. Good. It feels fairer to have to go through the same agonizing wait as my stepmother.

Alida sighs. "You know what's weird? When you don't feel 100%, you go to the doctor and you want them to take it seriously. You want them to do tests. You want them to find something, so you can explain why you feel pain, or feel sick. But then, when they do find something, you wish they hadn't…" She shakes her head. I squeeze her arm.

The efficient assistant, satisfied with her meticulous to-do list, calls for my stepmother and we follow her to a room.

When the doctor enters, his cheerful optimism lights up the room. This is not someone about to deliver bad news. A funny wheeze escapes my mouth, releasing the breath I didn't know I was holding.

"Mrs. Van der Laan, the tumor is benign. We can perform a surgery in three weeks. We will be able to remove everything, and although you'll need some physical therapy, you'll recover completely."

Alida bursts into tears, smiling at the same time. "Oh, thank you. Thank you so much! That is great news." *So glad Gary doesn't have to go through this again.*

I tear up too and hug her. We were never very close, but I've always respected her admirable control of her jealousy towards me and my relationship with my father. Besides, she gave my dad so much, often putting his needs before her own. And I always admired their relationship, full of love and respect despite not truly understanding each other's minds.

The sun seems brighter and warmer when we retrieve the car from the parking lot.

"Let me drop you off at home."

I protest, because it means she'll have to drive back from Rotterdam during rush hour. But she won't budge.

So glad Kathy agreed to come with me. Gary is a wonderful man, but he's not the solid rock his daughter is. It's like nothing can vex her. She's always calm, even during crises.

I squeeze her arm affectionately. "Thanks. You will tell Dad about the surgery, won't you?"

"Of course. He'll still worry, but he won't lose me just yet."

"Right." I twist my fingers. "Talking about loss, there's something I'd like to ask. Something I don't want to bother Dad with. You know how badly he deals with loss."

Alida snorts.

"You see, as a child, when my mother was still alive, I once had a nightmare about walking around with a little baby. When I described the nightmare to my parents, my mother dropped the plate she was holding and ran away. Would you know whether she had a miscarriage? Or maybe they lost a baby? Either before or after my birth?"

Alida frowns. "No… No, I can't imagine. Your dad never said anything about a miscarriage or losing a baby. I'm sure he would've told me."

"Yeah, I guess." I wave it away. "It's so long ago, I'm probably remembering it wrong."

But I know I don't.

CHAPTER TWENTY-SIX

Kurt's dark blue BMW pulls into the carpool parking in front of the metro station. Presumably, the brown-haired woman next to him in the front is Sara, who lives in The Hague, like Kurt.

"Would you like to sit in the front?" she asks.

I grab the back door handle. "No, that's okay." To cut short her opportunity to insist, I slide onto the soft, dark leather seat in the back.

Kurt touches the gas pedal lightly, and the car shoots forward. Last time we drove to Brussels, Kurt said he was entitled to a driver, but he decided to save the Syndicate that kind of money. Sure. Instead, they just had to cough up a mere 120k for these excessive wheels.

Kurt introduces Sara and me, and shoots me a meaningful look via the rear-view mirror. In a conversational tone, he asks, "Do you go back home often, Sara?"

I would've sworn Kurt was incapable of small talk, which I'd consider one of his scarce virtues.

Sara shifts in her seat. *None of your business.* "I visited my parents twice since I moved to The Hague." *I'm sure you'd like to know about the other two meetings with my boss at the BND.*

Her thoughts are a mix of English and her native German, like most people who work in a language other than their native tongue.

"What do you miss most about Germany?"

My, Kurt is going all friendly on her. I'd never have guessed he had it in him.

Sara grunts, "My friends. Family." *Where are you going with this?* Both are tense. Interesting dynamic. I lean back into the soft leather. This conversation doesn't involve me, anyway.

Or does it? Kurt seems to think differently. He throws me another intense look by way of the mirror. "How do you like the job so far? Is it very different from your previous role?"

Ha! If you only knew. "The setting is different. The type of work is quite similar." *Doesn't matter whether I build up a file about a political party, or an organisation like the Syndicate.*

Ah… I slide my hands under my legs, so I won't slap myself. Kurt isn't making innocent small talk. He leads her thoughts with questions, so I can read her mind as per his request.

What a deplorable trio we are… All hiding something from the others, pursuing our own hidden agendas. I only got in the car for the pictures of my mother he promised me.

Sara stares out of the passenger window. *I'm glad Kathy joined us. Kurt makes me uncomfortable. A bit odd why the new political leader of the CDU has taken a personal interest in Kurt. And the BND's worried, now that he took over from Bernard. He's not the political type. But, I guess when both of your parents are politicians, you don't really have a choice. Especially with a mom like that. She was much smarter than his father. Could have had a much better shot at becoming a top politician for Belgium. Probably resented her husband for her sacrifice, especially after he got kicked out. Parents both projected their own failed ambitions on their only child. They must have been proud when he became one of the youngest members of parliament. And so angry, when only three years later he got kicked out as well…*

"You idiot!" Kurt slams the brakes.

Sara and I launch forward, strained by our seatbelts. An SUV cut in front of Kurt.

"Bitch," mutters Kurt.

I sink back, rubbing my right shoulder where the seatbelt cut in. Kurt never told me he'd been in national politics first. His motivation for the EU might have less to do with genuine passion than with thwarted ambitions.

CHAPTER TWENTY-SEVEN

"Come with me." Kurt grabs my elbow and pulls me away from the water cooler. "I have an assignment for you."

"Anything's better than just sitting around," I blurt out. After five hours of boring meetings, whatever Kurt wants me to do surely will be more appealing than attending another one.

"I just heard the Dutch Prime Minister and the German Chancellor arranged to meet on short notice. A bit of a surprise. We need to know whether they're concocting something we need to be aware of."

"Won't they meet in private? And be surrounded by security?"

"Everyone needs a drink once in a while. You worked in a café during university, right?"

Stunned, I nod. It was just a few months. I never put it on my resume. How does Kurt know?

Thirty minutes later in a bathroom, I whisper to my unfamiliar reflection in the mirror, "You should've remembered, be careful what you wish for." I can't believe I'm dressed in black and white to deliver tea, coffee, water or anything else of their liking, to two heads of state. How does Kurt have the connections to insert me as stand-in waitress, in an upscale hotel, with security on high alert? Not to mention, provide me with fake eyeglasses and a wig on short notice? That requires an entirely different skill set than mediating, negotiating and brokering information between political parties.

A rap on the door jerks me into action. I close the tap, feeling calmer after holding my wrists under cold running water for a minute.

"You're on." Kurt pushes me towards the bar. "They asked for coffee and water. Remember, you ask them if they'd like anything else to drink, and possibly eat, and you take your sweet time arranging their drinks on the table."

He points at a tray with four small bottles of water and a thermos of coffee. Not quite what I expected for high-level politicians, filter coffee in a thermos, but both heads of state are known for their down-to-earth, 'act normal' attitudes.

I pick up the tray, and Kurt frowns. "Get me Schipper's thoughts. I'm depending on you."

I step into the hallway. Even if Kurt hadn't told me which room they're in, I would've known by the number of people waiting outside. The ones wearing security uniforms scan the hallway to both sides. Others murmur to each other. They seem to be aides to the heads of state, waiting in case they're needed.

The security guard closest to the door glances at my tray and opens the door.

Concentrating, I enter the room balancing the tray. Paul Schipper and the German Chancellor, Greta Beck, stand chatting with each other. Greta Beck, always coming across on TV as a formidable character, is much smaller than I expected. Her head reaches just above Schipper's shoulders.

My hands feel moist. Don't let the tray slip. Not while you're in one room with two people who've led their countries for more than a decade, impressing friend and foe with their competent, empathic and calm leadership. I slow down to half my usual pace, not because Kurt wants me to 'take my sweet time,' but because I'll drop the tray for sure if I speed up.

They're joking with each other and stand close. Both are in a good mood, alert but respectful and appreciative of each other.

Finally, I make it to the table without embarrassing myself. I arrange the bottles, cups and thermos on the table, and listen in on Greta Beck's mind. She thinks in staccato thoughts, like Cecilia, but at rocket speed, and with several thought-processes running simultaneously. *Stubborn. Best candidate. Upsetting the others by voting against stipulation. Prefers leading his country. Need him in Europe more. Don't want French egotist. Appeal to strong sense of duty.* And that's just half of her thoughts, the rest is lost on me. Paul Schipper's thought process shows his intelligence too, but Greta Beck belongs in another category altogether. Not surprising, given the fact that she holds a PhD in quantum physics.

Oops, my hand must be hanging in midair for a while now with the last water bottle. *Jeez Kath, if you want them to think you're spying on them, you're doing a great job.* I lower the bottle to the table.

I clear my throat. "Madam, Sir, would you like me to bring you anything else?"

They turn towards me. Beck shakes her head, and Schipper says with a friendly smile, "No, thank you so much."

Still trembling, I make my way to the door, concentrating on getting out. I don't want to spy, but unfortunately, that's not how our brains work. When you tell your brain to not think of something, the stubborn bugger does just the opposite. And Schipper's thoughts are so structured and clear, they flow into my mind without me even trying to read them.

I don't want to leave the Dutch government. But she will make it hard for me to keep saying no... I would like to make much needed changes to the European Commission and Council. Too much politics, though. Especially now, with the weasel involved. Why is he here?

I grab the door handle and almost pull myself through. Outside, the same people stand absorbed in thoughts or their phones, and with a sigh of relief, I let their sea of murmuring thoughts flush over me.

"And?" Kurt demands, when he pulls me into another conference room two doors down.

"It was short. I'm not sure about what I heard. Didn't make sense after what you told me. Greta Beck wanted to convince Paul Schipper. And he was reluctant. That's all I got."

"Convince him about what?" His fingers dig deeper into my elbow.

"No clue." I yank my painful elbow away from Kurt. I want to piss him off, the way he pisses me off. "Beck thinks highly of Schipper. She wants him to play an important role in the EU."

Kurt's mind flashes. He waves his hand dismissively. "You probably heard that wrong. With the translation from German, I'm sure you've misunderstood."

I open my mouth to protest, to tell this pedantic ass that Schipper's thoughts were in line with Beck's. Besides, my German is quite good, thank you very much.

But no, if he wants to believe he's right, he can choke on it. I push the tray into his hands and walk out.

CHAPTER TWENTY-EIGHT

The next morning, Kurt, Sara and I sit for breakfast together, hotel buffet-style. Having breakfast with multiple others I can handle. Having dinner, not so much. At breakfast, people rush to chomp down the meal that gets them started. Or they're having their introvert moment, battling their morning crankiness. At dinner, people relax because the hard part of the day is over, and they're exhausting with their useless conversation and drawn-out thoughts.

Downside of hotel breakfast: the pungent smell of the suspiciously yellow scrambled eggs under heat lamps. Thankfully, Sara chose a trendy, strong, herbal tea. A bold rose-hip fragrance curls up from her mug.

We both chose to sit opposite of Kurt instead of next to him. Isn't it interesting how people just know instinctively who they need to keep an eye on at all times.

Sara rips the crusts off her toast. *Why were Kurt and Kathy at the meeting of Frau Beck and Paul Schipper last night? Does Kurt know about the plans to let Schipper run that new committee? Kathy must be one of his confidants, being in on his covert operations. Need to check her file again. Must have it in my desk.* She pictures a desk with a wildly yellow and purple painted wall behind it. Must be her house. Not quite office standard. Definitely not the Syndicate, and probably not the BND either, whatever that may be.

Kurt focuses on eating his custom-made omelet. He'd instructed the waitress—three eggs, no salt, mushrooms and onions but no peppers, and a touch of parsley. No 'would it be possible,' or 'please.' And yes, it's true what they say, you better be nice to whomever serves you. I could entertain many a bar night with friends, if I had any, by sharing thoughts I've picked up from affronted servers over the years.

The green tufts in Kurt's omelet don't look like parsley to me. Apparently, Kurt doesn't trust them either, as he meticulously picks them out, his mind fully engaged with the task. Amazing how someone can concentrate so hard on what he does. Unlike anyone I've ever met before.

Sara picks up her mug, the movement emitting another whiff of rosehip. *Ouch, tea still hot. Must get Kathy to talk, but not at the creepy building with ears.* She pictures the Syndicate's office in The Hague, has a memory of Jason sneaking up on her, and shivers, despite holding her warm mug with both hands.

I put my spoon down. "Excuse me, I'll finish packing."

The elevator doors open and two guests step out. I get in, push the button for my floor and turn around to find Kurt stepping in as well. I shrug into a corner.

"Did I startle you?" he asks, grinning.

"Just didn't expect you right behind me."

Sara strides towards us, her eyes squinting. *They're ditching me again! On purpose?*

Kurt stands with arms crossed, clearly not intending to hold the elevator. The doors close.

"Did you get anything from Sara?"

I look down at my hands. What would the hands of a spy look like? Probably not much different from anyone else's.

"Oh, I meant to give you these yesterday, but with our little excursion last night, I forgot." Kurt takes an envelope from his pocket, fishes out one picture, and holds it up for me to see.

I stretch out my hand towards my mother's smiling face, like a toddler reaching to be picked up.

"About Sara?" Kurt inquires.

I want those pictures. I swallow, and a whisper makes it past the lump in my throat. "Could it be Sara has another job? Does the name BND ring a bell?"

Kurt jerks back. "That's the German intelligence agency."

His anger bounces around in the elevator and I bite my tongue. If I keep tattling to Kurt like this, I soon won't have any tongue left.

He shoves the picture of my mother back into the envelope and thrusts the package at me.

I hold it close to my chest and stare at my feet. Damn it. Should've gotten myself better acquainted with the vast number of governmental organisations. With more context, I can filter the information I feed Kurt. Although when it comes to information about my mother, I'm afraid I'd still be a blabbermouth. Like the junkies on the streets of Rotterdam, I'm desperate to please my dealer to get my fix.

In my room, I take a few deep breaths. Who, and what, is wrong and right in this snake pit? Maybe following in my mother's footsteps is not the right choice.

"And then, Kathy?" I ask out loud. "Quit? That would be a record, even for you. To quit after one week."

I drop onto the bed and spread out the six pictures of my mother. In two of them, she looks straight into the camera, smiling. I bury my face in a pillow.

Fifteen minutes later, I'm about to step into the elevator going down, backpack slung over my shoulder. I prefer to travel light. I'm carrying enough baggage, anyway.

Three men stand in the elevator. I look up, directly into the eyes of Paul Schipper. The others seem to be security. Schipper notices my hesitation to get in, and he nods invitingly. His piercing blue eyes stay locked onto mine. Heat rises in my face. Does he recognise me from last night? Or biking behind him? Or both?

It's worse.

Didn't I see her before? Those eyes. That guarded, wary look in her eyes... A weathered soul in a young body. Only trusts herself. Reserved. She's got that shielded and...vigilant look from always having to be careful. From being alone in carrying the world on her shoulders. Do I know her? Or do I just recognise myself in her...

By the time we get out of the elevator, Schipper has brushed away his thoughts by joking to one of the guards.

I, on the other hand, feel my cheeks burning the rest of the day. So that's what it feels like when someone reads what you're trying to hide…

CHAPTER TWENTY-NINE

Without looking up from his phone, Kurt asks, "Can you shut the door behind you?" I hesitate, but push the door shut. Apparently, Kurt doesn't expect anyone else for this meeting. Intent on his phone, Kurt flicks his hand at a chair. I sit down.

"You're about to meet a Spanish cabinet minister, one of the more senior members of the European Council. We need to know how reliable he is. You understand Spanish, right?"

Kurt's eyes are still on his phone. Maybe he expects his virtual assistant to answer that question? Her Spanish will be better than mine, for sure. He looks up, frowning. "Well?"

I widen my eyes. "Oooh, you're talking to me, not to your phone. Right. It's been a while. I'll probably be able to understand bits and pieces. What do you expect of me?"

Kurt checks his watch. "No time to explain. Listen in, you just have to pay attention to Juan."

There's a knock on the door. A man enters. His jovial greeting to Kurt is in stark contrast to his thoughts. *Careful. [...] snake. Wish he had died instead of Bernard.*

I glance at Kurt. The vibes of Juan's intense emotion are strong, almost bouncing off the walls. Kurt can't be oblivious to that, but he greets the man back, claps him on the shoulder. Both inwardly recoil at the physical contact, their moods in a comical, brief synchrony.

Juan thinks in a Spanish accent I'm not used to, but he's so emotionally charged that his thoughts are fairly easy to follow.

Kurt offers him coffee. While serving Juan, he asks, "How are your wife and children?"

Exchanging pleasantries? Just as surprising as Kurt small talking with Sara yesterday. Meaning, he must want something important from this conversation.

Juan's smile shows his hesitation. "Great, thanks." *No [...] asking him [...]. Never married. Not surprising.*

Kurt pours himself a glass of water. "How's your daughter? Marguerite, right?"

With a strained nod, Juan answers, "Doing well, thank you."

"I heard her marble business is doing well?"

Juan sips his coffee, his body tensed.

"She sells quality materials from local quarries, mostly to construction companies, right?"

Juan's growing unease confirms this innocent chit-chat feels like exchanging not-so-pleasantries to him. *Where [...] going? Marguerite [...]. None of his [...] business.*

Kurt leans back. "I heard many companies are diversifying into less high-quality natural stone. To cater to a bigger clientele."

Juan shrugs. "I know little about it. You might be right." *Marguerite [...]. Not many people [...] difference.*

"What's her biggest contract right now?"

Juan's lips attempt to smile, but the wrinkles around his eyes don't bother. He holds his hand up in apology. "I don't know, I'm not that involved." *Why [...]? Not saying [...].*

Kurt's eyes flash. "Of course." He lets the ensuing silence hang heavily in the air.

Juan wipes his hands on his pants.

Kurt clears his throat. "How are the new government buildings coming along?"

Juan holds his breath and presses his back into the chair. *What [...]?*

Kurt swirls his finger over the rim of his glass, in a tantalizing slow movement. "Your daughter must've been so happy to get the exclusive government contract. Her company is the sole supplier for the marble floors and walls, right?"

Juan crosses his arms. "I...don't know." *Took [...] convincing*

Carlos to give [...] contract to Marguerite. [...] replacing for cheaper material.

The usual intense concentration of Kurt's mind mixes with what seems to be satisfaction. Fixing his eyes on Juan, he says, "Just out of curiosity, what quality of marble did the government choose for its buildings?"

Juan's I-don't-know-and-I-don't-care shrug is in complete contrast to the crimson shade creeping up on his neck. *He knows. Marguerite [...] no one can tell they use [...]. No proof. Money [...] fund to pay [...].*

"Ah well, good quality controllers will ensure the buildings are built to specification." Kurt sits up, indicating the end of the conversation.

Juan looks away and dabs his forehead with a paper napkin. *Need to warn Marguerite and Carlos. [...] pay quality controllers. [...] not find out.*

Kurt places his elbows on the table and leans forward. "Are you okay, Juan? Let's take a break. We'll continue in ten minutes." Kurt gets up and looks at me while jerking his head towards the door. I clench my fists. Would it hurt him to ask nicely, instead of making me feel like a dog following the master?

Kurt walks into the hallway and checks the meeting room next to us. It's empty. He grabs my elbow and pulls me inside. Has no one ever told him men can get sued for physically pulling female co-workers into empty rooms?

"What did you get?"

Just as no one apparently told him asking nicely might work better than barking orders. "Uhm, what do you mean?"

"Of his thoughts, of course!"

"Ah. It might've helped if you'd been clearer up front. You told me to just listen."

His eyes harden.

I shrug. "The conversation seemed odd to me." I massage my temples. Did Bernard mean this when he said I'd help 'smooth the process'? I don't want Kurt to use me as an unlimited view into other people's business.

Kurt squeezes my arm. For the second time within twenty-four hours, I jerk my arm away. He narrows his eyes. "Listen, Kathy, Juan is the Spanish delegate on the committee preparing the agreement for the new set-up of the EU. We can't have dirty politicians working on this new organisation. I need to know whether I have a disaster on my hands." He brings his face closer to mine and his breath brushes my cheek. "Is his daughter's company replacing high-quality marble with cheaper material?"

Besides the moral aspect of using my skills to tell on people, I can't be sure what I heard. I swallow. "His accent was hard to follow."

"But?" Kurt looks like he's about to stamp his foot like a child.

But who am I to question the morals of listening in on people committing crimes? I used to call the anonymous tip-line on people who committed crimes. Dirty politicians are not only a risk, but should be punished if they do something wrong. I cough. "I didn't hear everything. He did seem nervous when you mentioned the quality of the marble."

Kurt looks away. "Did he mention who's involved from the government?"

I stare at the floor. "I can't be sure." But Juan's thoughts were clear enough. Reluctant, I add, "He thought of a Carlos."

"Ah, interesting." Kurt strikes his hand over his chin. "And what about the money?" He grabs my shoulder. "Kathy, if he and his daughter swindle their own government and people find out, we'll have months of delay because his credibility is gone. Everything will be looked into, to ensure he didn't favour anyone in this particular process."

Right. Politicians shouldn't abuse their power and steal money. This is Juan's own fault. "From what I understand, there is some sort of fund." I frown. "But I didn't get what kind of fund."

"Probably a slush fund. Through such a fund, money is distributed outside of the books. That's illegal." Kurt rubs his hands. "You can stay here, I'll wrap up with Juan."

He barges out of the room. I take a seat, resting my head in my hands. Bernard hired me to help smooth wrinkles in the process, not to expose people like this. But if this Juan has a scheme making money from a government contract, he's a weak link. Kurt has a point in wanting to expose him.

I focus on the room next door.

Kathy's useful. Bernard wouldn't have used her to her full potential. Thank you, old man, you gave me the key to success.

I feel my mouth hanging open and close it. Wow, Kurt has relaxed his intense concentration. I can even see the room through his eyes and feel how he's seating himself. His self-congratulatory thoughts are interrupted when Juan enters the room. Juan's mind is as tense as Kurt's is relaxed. Through Juan's eyes I see Kurt, saying lightly, "Feeling better, Juan?".

[...] go. Kurt [...] dangerous.

"Juan, dear friend, I hear you're the Spanish delegate in the committee preparing the nomination for the new combined role of EU President."

Oh, no. "That's supposed to be confidential." Juan loosens his tie.

"The Syndicate is supposed to know these things. It's what we're here for."

Juan concentrates on sipping his coffee and swallows, as if to derive strength from the black liquid. *[...] careful. What does he want? [...] wait for him to say [...].*

"In fact, the Syndicate has been working on the exact same goal the EU strives to achieve. Advancing the European Union and its processes to act like one entity. Strengthening the EU, to make it more agile, more effective."

Juan's mind contracts, his focus on his coffee cup.

Kurt's determination intensifies. "Given my experience, everybody knows I'm the perfect candidate for the new President role."

Juan finally looks up at Kurt. *His eyes [...] insane shine.*

"Juan, you and I both know your daughter's company is saving money by using cheap materials but invoicing the good, expensive stuff. I know the difference feeds into a slush fund to pay you and your buddy Carlos off."

Juan's feelings sink into a heavy stomach. *Shit... What [...] do?*
"If I can find out this information, others can too."

Juan's despair washes over him, drowning him in fear he can't reach the surface in time.

Kurt adds, "But I can make it go away."

Juan freezes, his thoughts narrowing, hanging onto Kurt's next words like a safety buoy.

Kurt adds slowly, "I just need to know, do I have your loyalty?"

After a second of stillness, Juan nods, awash with the intense relief of filling his bursting lungs now that he's reached the surface just in time. His residual fear brings up one stubborn thought, *That's why [...] The Eraser.* But he lets it go and embraces his way out.

I pull back, my mind retracting into my body, pounding. I'd expected Kurt to ask Juan to step down. Or promise to clean up his act. Not to use it for his own benefit. He's worse than Juan. And I helped him.

I rub my temples to tame the hammering inside my skull.

CHAPTER THIRTY

The waiting area for takeout has a new soft leather couch. Well, 'gently used,' considering the creases in the seats and the lighter colour patches on the armrest. Maybe the owners bought a new couch for their living room and moved the old one here. For years, I sat on one of the uncomfortable chairs, lined up in a row of four, worrying whether the cane seat would hold. I sink back into the dark grey cushions of the upgraded waiting area and pat a cushion. *Nice.*

My favourite blue-black fish swims around the big fish tank, separating the waiting area from the rest of this Chinese-Indonesian restaurant. It has recently been fed, given its contented mood. Fish have soothing minds. They're happy swimming. Maybe I should get a fish bowl at home, the way people use a lavender candle to relax.

The door to the kitchen is propped open as usual. I try to avoid inhaling too deeply. A generous amount of a thick undistinguishable smell erupts through that door, combining odours of many individual dishes. The rich mix vaporises my appetite, but experience has taught me it'll fully return after the seven-minute walk home.

Through the sounds of pans clattering and oil spattering, two female voices audibly discuss something in a language I don't understand.

Stubborn. Seafood supplier unreliable. Doesn't want the one I negotiated.

Wait. That staccato, rational, and pressing manner of thinking feels uncomfortably familiar.

Suddenly, Cecilia emerges from the kitchen. For a mortifying second, we stare at each other.

"What are you doing here?" Cecilia asks, frowning.

"Uhm, waiting for my order. And you?"

Right. Of course. Just didn't expect to see her here. "My parents own this restaurant," Cecilia says, less terse. She picks up a notebook from under the cash register and opens it.

I slide my hands under my legs to stop them from wriggling. How ironic. The restaurant that instantly made it to the top of my takeout favourites once I'd tried it, is of course owned by Cecilia's parents. "They do a great job. I've come here for the last two years."

Cecilia looks up from the notebook, nods, and returns to study the book. *Last three deliveries all incomplete. Better get them to shape up if Mother doesn't want to change.* Cecilia sighs.

The woman who usually handles the cash register emerges from the kitchen without bags. She smiles at me. "So sorry, Kathy. No good. Start over. Ready in ten minutes." She smiles, bows slightly, and instructs Cecilia in another language.

Hmm. Okay, then. Might as well make the best of it. "I'm sorry, Kathy. Something went wrong, it will take another ten minutes. Do you like prawn crackers?"

Before I can decline politely as per a good rational response, my head nods enthusiastically. I love prawn crackers. Saliva squirts into my mouth. I swallow and pretend I don't feel betrayed by my taste buds. "Sure."

Cecilia reaches behind her, where several bowls of prawn crackers await customers. She walks around the cash register and towards the bar just behind the fish tank. She places the bowl on the bar and pours a glass of water from a bottle. "What would you like to drink?"

"Water for me as well, thanks." I get up and move to a bar stool. Less comfortable but for prawn crackers, I'll sit anywhere.

"Tough week?" Cecilia asks. When she notices my surprise, she adds, "You look tired. Don't worry, I won't ask any police questions here." *Too tired myself.*

"Well, yeah. This new job is…nothing like I've ever done. As you concluded yourself." Hoping Cecilia won't perceive it as an attack, which it wasn't, I smile and shrug.

Cecilia raises her glass in a toasting gesture. "Cheers. I know the feeling of not wanting to cook on a Saturday evening."

"You help your parents out in the restaurant?" I eye the basket. By my own standards, I've waited long enough to not seem greedy. I grab a prawn cracker.

"Sometimes, on business matters. Not with the cooking. Never had a flair for it. As a kid, I helped with the cleaning. Setting tables. Later with the business side." She sinks back in thought. *Disappointed them with my cooking skills. They disappointed me by never mastering Dutch properly. But they admired my business skills. Not every ten-year-old negotiates successfully with a new supplier. Or arranges a new permit with the city at twelve.*

"It's nice to be so close to your parents." I sigh.

With her mouth stuffed, Cecilia asks, "Take it you aren't?"

Cecilia isn't exactly the person I'd expected to share personal stuff with, but it's nice to have a normal conversation for once. And a person who loves prawn crackers as much as I do deserves a proper answer. "Not this type of close. My dad and stepmother live in Leiden. Don't see them too often, but we get along fine."

This time, Cecilia swallows before she asks, "And your mother?"

"Died when I was almost four."

Cecilia draws a pained face. "Ow, that's awful. Sorry to hear that. How?"

"Hit and run. Driver was never found." I take a sip of water.

"I'm so sorry." *Poor girl.* Cecilia swipes a drop of water from the side of her glass. "Do you still remember her?" *My parents weren't easy, made me work hard, but they were there.*

"I have a few memories." Instead of my mother's bloody face, the Hekate statue worms its way into my mind. Must be because of Cecilia's fierce and fearless stature. I shake it off. "You know, she used to work for the Syndicate, too." I stuff another prawn cracker in my talkative mouth and start chewing, to avoid other revelations that are none of Cecilia's business.

"She did? At the time she died?" Cecilia gazes at me thoughtfully. *Maybe her reason to take the job? Full circle kind of thing?*

I nod, chomping down on the next prawn cracker. Where is my food? Any time now, please.

"I did find it a bit of an odd job change" Cecilia admits. *Could explain why she hangs out with types like Kurt.*

Better divert her attention. "Any brothers and sisters helping out here, too?"

Cecilia shakes her head. "Only child."

"If you're not interested in taking over the restaurant, who will?" I give myself a virtual kick in the butt. She never told me she wasn't interested in taking over. "Well, I assume you're not taking over," I add hastily. "Given your completely different career choice."

"You're right. They'll have to sell at some point."

"No grandchildren to hand it over to?"

Cecilia grimaces. "No." Her thoughts go to her comfortable singles' apartment. Kudos to her male colleague, for guessing it's not unlike mine. Cecilia sighs. *No one to feel responsible for. Except the cat. Better that way.*

The tough, independent image she keeps up has a fray of loneliness.

"Kathy, here's your order, so sorry!" Cecilia's mother places a white plastic bag, knot on top, on the counter in front of me.

"Thank you." I get up and nod at Cecilia. "You too."

Outside, I take a deep breath of cold air. What did I thank Cecilia for, exactly? The prawn crackers? Or the first normal conversation I've had in a long while?

CHAPTER THIRTY-ONE

Yup, just as I thought, got takeout at that restaurant again. As if she ever goes anywhere in the evening. Don't understand why I still have to follow her.

That must come from the car slowly driving past me. I keep my eyes on the pavement and focus on the driver's mind. Took me a couple of years to act normal, while seeing myself through other peoples' eyes. Like when you catch your own image in a shop window and suddenly become aware of what you actually look like when you're not holding in your stomach.

Through the driver's eyes, I see myself opening the door to the staircase up to my apartment. His focus returns to the road. *That's it, I'm out of here for tonight.*

Police? Probably. Cecilia must've gotten permission from her boss to investigate me further. Maybe our run-in this evening at her parents' restaurant wasn't purely accidental?

Moody, I enter my apartment and bang the food on the table where Cecilia interrogated me. I hang my coat. My appetite seems to have gone. The table I usually sit at reminds me of being interviewed by the cops. I pick up the bag and move to the couch. Reluctantly, I tug at the knot of the plastic bag. It slides open and the delicious smells of Cecilia's parents' excellent cooking find their way to my nose. My stomach rumbles with delight and within a mere ten minutes, I devour the contents.

CHAPTER THIRTY-TWO

"Today, I would like to show you the research department." Kurt takes a sip of his latte. "You know, this past weekend I was thinking, maybe we could get you tested."

"Tested? For what?" I ask. And who is 'we,' anyway?

"We have an EEG facility here, on the second floor, among other things. We could get EEG readings on your brain." He studies me.

"Why would 'we' want that?"

"We could see whether your brain responds differently. Just curiosity, I suppose."

Curiosity. Right... "Who would perform the test?"

"Our scientists. They don't know about your skills. They'd see it as just another regular test. Most other employees have done EEG tests, including me. It's quite interesting seeing your brain flaring up. We have the equipment, why not use it?" He appears nonchalant, as if he doesn't care what I'll decide.

"Why would an organisation mediating in international matters have brain scanning equipment?" And where? Ah. The peek through the elevator doors on my first day. The young woman in the lab coat. And the care taken to ward everyone off the second floor.

Kurt leans back. "Brain research is the topic of the future. Imagine being able to heal the brain the same way we can heal the rest of the body. We know so little about behaviour, about intelligence. Governments, and certainly the EU, should have an extensive brain research facility. We're small here, but once I..." He stops himself and clears his throat. "We started brain research here to bring it under the wings of the EU when they are ready. In this facility, we help people understand how their brain works. To become more successful." Kurt sits up. "We might even find out how your brain works and teach others. Or help you understand your skill."

"You mean, I'm an oddity, interesting to study."

"Wouldn't it be nice if we could train people to be like you? Imagine, if everybody would have the same skill as you. Nobody would have to hide anymore."

I lean back. That would be great, to have other people like me around. But would it work like that? "I wonder if it's that easy. Someone who isn't born into mind-reading might find it quite a challenge." Would they have to learn, or would they be as 'fluent' as me in reading other people's minds right away? If so, they would have to instantly handle the continuous stream of someone else's thoughts. Might drive them crazy. I grew up with it and even I find it hard to keep my sanity. They'd have to go through a steep learning curve. And would the average person even want to be able to read minds?

"You might be able to share your knowledge and experiences with others. To teach them. Be their mentor." The corners of Kurt's mouth almost soften.

Teach them. That's an interesting thought. Helping people navigate this skill. Finally have others, to be with on my side of the river. To communicate with in my unique way. I shake my head. Impossible. But what if it isn't? Instead of searching for people like me, I might teach them.

"Listen," Kurt adds patiently. "You can just go through the tests and see for yourself. It's entirely up to you."

I slowly nod. It's not the era of involuntary human experimenting anymore. With all the privacy laws in place these days, they can't use the data if I don't want them to. It's tempting to learn more about how my brain works. Might answer a few questions I've had for a long time. I nod again. "It's worth a try."

We take the elevator to the second floor. "Are there no stairs?" Why would we take the elevator for just going down one floor?

"Only for emergencies," Kurt says, while exiting the elevator.

I shiver. Bright artificial light hardens the grey, untreated concrete walls. There's a complete absence of plants, posters or anything ornamental. The anonymity is extreme, even for an organisation like the Syndicate.

Kurt holds his pass for the turnstile, then hands it to me to go
through as well. The hallway has three doors on the right side and
four on the left. All simple white doors with no indication of what
lies behind them. No 'Dr. Whatsoever' name plates, no signs such
as 'lab' or 'staff only.' All doors are closed. The security to prevent
employees from coming here seems overkill. As if this uninviting
look would attract droves of visitors.

Kurt tenses up, places himself in between me and the rest of the
hallway. His thoughts are impenetrable, but it's as if his will shields
the rest of the corridor. His left hand shoots out and holds the pass
in front of the little black square next to the first door on the right.
He pushes the door open, stepping close to me. To avoid his body
brushing mine, I quickly move into what appears to be an office.

Along the wall to the right is a large cabinet, filled for about
two-thirds with hanging file folders. On the wall to the left is a desk
with two computer monitors on top of each other and a smaller
monitor to the side. The opposite wall has two large windows with
a door in the middle. Through the windows, I see a medical-look-
ing area with impressive machines, as well as the young woman in
the lab coat who shared the elevator with me on my first day. Kurt
knocks on the window to attract her attention. When she looks up,
he waves.

She hesitates, but then walks over. *That creep Kurt. He always
just talks to Aaron. Why does he come when Aaron isn't here?* She
takes a breath, opens the door and steps into the office.

"Nicole, meet Kathy. She started working here about two weeks
ago. We would like you to do an EEG scan on Kathy."

She nods, frowning. "Okay. Anything in particular we're looking
for?"

"No, just a scan to show her how her brain works."

Nicole raises her eyebrows. "Which circumstances would you

want me to test her in?"

"Aaron told me he uses a combination of showing subjects a video, letting them perform certain tests, and asking them a standardised list of questions."

"Right. Our standard test battery. Should I make a report?"

"Nothing special. Just explain the results to Kathy afterwards."

Nicole nods. *What a waste of research capacity. But let's get on with it. Hopefully, I'll still have time to search Aaron's files this afternoon.*

Kurt leaves, and Nicole invites me to sit down next to her behind the computer. She explains briefly how the EEG test works.

"The EEG measures electric activity of the brain, predominantly of the cerebral cortex. The neurons in your brain generate tiny electric impulses. We can't measure a single one, but many neurons together generate enough electric activity to be measurable on the outer side of the skull. When you see, do or think something, cognitive processes activate many neurons. By measuring their activity, we can see which parts of your brain are active, the intensity of their activity, and how the parts of the brain interact with each other. Does that make sense?"

I nod.

Nicole points through the window. "See the chair over there?"

"The dentist's chair?"

Nicole smiles. "Yes. You'll take a seat, and I'll first measure your head. I'll make a few marks on your skull to make sure I position the electrodes correctly. Don't worry, no one will notice afterwards. Then I'll place a cap on your head that has a lot of electrodes connected to it. Apart from the cap, you won't feel a thing. Let's get started, shall we?"

She holds the door for me. The chair does not look particularly inviting, even though it's flexible in three areas to position the parts for the legs, upper body and head separately. All three parts have nooks. Like for attaching straps, to restrain someone. *Come on, Kath, don't overreact... It's just your fantasy.* Must be the clinical atmosphere. I take a seat and ignore the goosebumps on my arms.

"Feel free to adjust it to a comfortable position," Nicole says. She gives me a remote control attached to the chair. "The buttons speak for themselves. Both the back and the leg part can be adjusted to any slope you like. I'll take the headrest off for now, because it would get in the way of the testing equipment." She drapes a measuring tape from one ear to another, then from the bridge of my nose to the back of my skull. I resist the urge to scratch the spots where Nicole marks my skull. She picks up a white, stiff cap with strange knobs sticking out. "Could you hold your head up and sit still while I affix the cap to your head?"

Dutifully, I sit up. The cap feels softer than expected. Nicole fiddles around for a minute to adjust the straps and make sure the cap fits tightly without being too tight.

"Close your eyes. I'll clean the sockets and the alcohol vapour might sting your eyes a little."

Nicole applies a light, quick pressure at all the knobs while the scent of alcohol dominates the air. She waits a few seconds, then plugs in the electrodes. Fascinated, I follow the process through her eyes.

She fixes the last one and steps back. "How does that feel?"

"Like wearing one of those old-fashioned swim caps, and the pool guard has her hand firmly on my head."

Nicole chuckles. She pulls out several privacy screens on wheels and arranges them at three sides around me, obscuring the office next door and the rest of the room. "This way, you can focus on the monitor without being distracted." She presses several buttons and switches on a monitor in front of me. "First, I'll show you a short video to see if everything works. Then, we'll get on with the tests. Try to sit relaxed, so you can keep your head still."

Nicole steps out of sight. After watching the short video, she comes back and shows me a thumbs up. "Everything works well. We'll start the tests." She hands me a wireless keyboard. "Just follow the instructions on the screen. I'll step out of the room so I won't distract you and affect your responses."

Right. But then the test won't come up with interesting data, at least not for me. Only if I can read her mind, the data might show something I'm interested in.

Nicole exits the room, and just when the test on the computer monitor starts, she exits the room next door as well. I lose track of her mind. Nothing else left for me to do, other than to complete the tests. I yawn.

After half an hour, I feel Nicole entering the office again, checking the progress on her computer. When the test is complete, she enters the test room. "I'll take the keyboard back now. Next, you'll just watch a couple of videos." She places the keyboard at the monitor, types in a few things and then sits down behind the desk in the next room. Good. Now I can read her mind and watch the videos at the same time. A real-life situation.

She opens a file on her computer and starts filling out details for my test-name, age and gender, and is prompted to fill out the field 'Purpose.' She hesitates, then types 'New employee generic testing.' *Have to ask Aaron how to classify this.* She continues to enter the types of tests and the time she started them. The phone on her desk rings. The wall between the test room and the office is thick enough to block the ringing sound from my ears, but I can hear it through Nicole's mind.

"Hi Kurt. Yes, we're in the middle of the testing. Sure, I've put up the screens so she won't see you. Okay." *Wow, the second time today Kurt talks to me. He never does. He even wants to come see for himself. Must be because of Kathy. That's why Jason is so negative about her. He doesn't like sharing Kurt's attention with anyone. But he's negative about everyone, anyway.*

Nicole startles, and her feelings turn uneasy. *Jeez, Kurt gives me the creeps! Coming in without a sound. Not even saying hello. Don't get why he comes in. Not much to see. And why would he ask to have the test results straight away?*

Indeed, why? So far, his interests only concern himself.

Kurt's thoughts are clear, the wall of concentration is gone. *Need to get these results to Aaron asap. Want to know how it works, to learn how to mind-read. Imagine the possibilities! Would've been useful twenty-five years ago. To know Jacques was using me, sacrificing me to get ahead himself. If I'd known, I'd have outsmarted him. I would've been President, not Jacques... Have waited decades for this second chance. Shame Mother isn't alive anymore. She'd be so proud... 'Kurt, you see what your father has achieved with only half your brain. You can achieve whatever you want.' When Jacques single-handedly ended my career, Mother was devastated... She was never the same. Fell ill. That* weasel! *Effectively murdered her.*

His mind is accessible, but only when he's in another room... Maybe, like Bernard, he thinks I can't mind-read through walls?

A voice close by makes me almost jump out of my skin. "Next test is coming."

Jeez... Nicole keys in commands on the computer. I'd been so focused on Kurt's mind, I didn't even notice her coming in. She smiles and leaves.

At least I made his son pay. The media fall-out was even bigger than I'd hoped. The damage a few well-planted pieces of evidence can do... Never got into politics anywhere ever again. Need to check in with Kathy about that Cecilia. Ben considers her a good detective. Smart. Relentless. Could be a threat. But Ben promised he can curb her if necessary.

"Getting useful results?" he asks Nicole. *Need to have good quality readings.*

Through Kurt's eyes, I see Nicole nodding.

Great. Let's see what Aaron can get from it. Then decide further steps. Looking forward to getting the tests done we prepared for this weekend. Amused, he pictures Sara, eyes flooded with utter terror, strapped in a chair. A dentist's chair. I jerk up, lift my arms in the air. Still unrestrained. No straps in sight. I take a deep breath to calm down the drum roll of my heart. What was that? For an actual memory, it seemed too vague. Maybe Kurt was fantasizing or planning.

I wipe my forehead.

CHAPTER THIRTY-THREE

By the time we finish the tests, it's almost noon.

"Did you bring your lunch?" Nicole asks.

"Yes. No canteen here, right?"

"No. Although this office would be big enough for a small canteen." Nicole ruffles through a large handbag and takes out a package in aluminium foil. *According to Aaron, Kurt doesn't want any caterers in the building. No outsiders past reception. Only cleaning services, who are handpicked by Jason. Screened too, apparently.* "We can have lunch now and go over the results." *Then I have the afternoon still to search Aaron's files.*

I point to the ceiling. "I've got my lunch upstairs. Mind if I get it?"

"Sure. I'll come with you, you probably don't have the clearance to get back to this floor."

In the elevator, I ask, "Why the secrecy?"

Nicole shrugs. "Aaron doesn't want busybodies to show up. Especially when we're testing, people stopping by could affect the results." *Paranoid Aaron. Doesn't want me to use the main elevator. Like we're pariahs, to be kept away from the rest of the organisation. Strange how Kurt seems as keen on building an excellent research facility as on keeping it a secret. Tough on Aaron, not being able to boast about it to former university colleagues...*

"What's behind the other doors?"

"I'm only allowed into the office and lab you were in. And a storage room for equipment." Nicole looks at her feet. "Aaron says the rest is empty for expansion in the future." *Don't understand why he's lying. When I get a chance to pinch Aaron's key card again, I'll exam-*

ine the rooms with beds again. Weirdest assignment so far.

The elevator door opens and Nicole shakes off her thoughts, happy to step into a bright sunlit hallway. Why would she work here if she's so freaked out by Aaron and the lab? She seems not to like anyone around here. Everyone seems wary or even suspicious of each other. All with their own motives to work in this unhealthy, sick organisational culture.

But look who's talking. The things I do... As soon as I've gotten all the info Kurt has on my mother, I'm out of here. Even if that means I quit a job at record speed again.

Back at the lab, Nicole explains the graphs and the results of the different tests. "Brain activity can vary between individuals, but we do see common patterns, of course. The first tests all are within the normal range." She moves on to another graph. "During the videos, there is a deviation outside of the normal range. Something we'd see when people are distracted, thinking about other things. Like we would normally see when people multitask, interacting with someone while at the same time having to focus on a task." She looks at me and smiles. "Your mind probably wandered off during the videos?"

"Uhm, yeah, I guess so." My mind wandered off all right. Into Kurt's thoughts. Reading someone's mind apparently triggers the same brain activity as when people are interacting or doing two things at the same time. Still doesn't explain *why* I'm able to read minds.

After another fifteen minutes of looking at data from my brain, I stifle a yawn.

Nicole winks. "I know, graphs aren't the most interesting subject. I'll email you the results. Just let me know if you have any more questions."

I go up to the third floor and enter the empty office Jason likes to stow me away in. I inhale and attempt to release the tension in my shoulders.

Suddenly, my shoulders tense up again, and I feel a cold wall of determination. I turn around. Kurt stands behind me and closes the door.

"How did the tests go?"

"Fine. Apparently, the results are not unusual."

"When Aaron, our head scientist, gets back, I'll ask him to go over the results as well. Nicole is his junior assistant, she started only a few weeks ago."

"Thanks." In my opinion, Nicole did just fine, but as the results seem harmless, Kurt and Aaron can have their fun studying them.

Kurt still leans against the door, not in a hurry to leave. He seems to feel a sense of apprehension, like athletes concentrating just before their performance.

"Uhm, is there anything else I can help you with?"

"Let's see what you can tell me." To my surprise, he switches to thoughts again. Slow and deliberate, like someone who has to make an effort to talk. Different from when he was in the lab, thinking of his disastrous political career. *I'd like to try more of that mind-talking Bernard did. See if you can hear exactly what I think. Let's see. What I got back from you so far, you don't seem to understand everything people are thinking. Hence the experiment.*

I suppress a smile. Not telling him exactly what everybody thinks might lead to that conclusion.

"Let's do a test." *Uhm, let me think. Something we discussed last week. Yes. Just repeat my thoughts.* His brows draw together in the effort. *Sara has another job.*

"Sara has another job."

Working for the BND.

"Working for the BND."

Kurt glances at the ceiling, relaxes, and says, "Thank you. That was more specific than I thought." He turns around and leaves me staring after him.

This doesn't feel right. If Sara is indeed betraying Kurt, she might be in trouble. He's ruthless, like with the son of Jacques, whomever that may be, where Kurt apparently even planted evidence to drown him in controversy.

I've got to warn Sara. The company directory shows office 311 is hers. I walk over, balling my fists to keep myself from running.

When I enter her office, she looks up from the report she's reading and raises her eyebrows. I close the door, running a hand through my hair. "Listen, I…"

Sara gets up abruptly. "Sorry, I need to go to the bathroom. Why don't you join me?"

I stare at her, baffled, but she's already halfway down the corridor, leaving me no other option than to follow her.

In the bathroom, Sara stands in one of the stalls with the door open. What an awful place to want to chat. Every sound echoes off the dull white tiles, demonstrated by the ricocheting noise when Sara flushes the toilet. Rushed, she steps up to me and whispers, "They placed cameras everywhere. Bathrooms are the only place with just microphones instead of cameras. Flush the toilet, and then tell me quickly what you want to say."

Ah, hence 'the building with ears'…

The rumble of the toilet she just flushed stops.

I flush the toilet in the other stall, rush to Sara and whisper, "Kurt knows you're working for the BND."

Sara's face turns white, and she steadies herself with a hand on the sink. She nods and rushes away. Again, I find myself staring after her, while she's already halfway down the corridor.

I trudge to my office. Sara passes me with a stuffy handbag hanging from her shoulder and a couple of files in her left hand. She presses the button of the elevator with her right, and steps aside to let me pass, giving me the slightest nod of acknowledgement.

This place gets weirder by the minute. The rest of the afternoon I find it hard to concentrate.

CHAPTER THIRTY-FOUR

On my way home, I get out early at Rotterdam Central station under a grey sky and a persistent drizzle. Station Blaak is closer to my apartment, but hopefully an extra twenty-minute walk will flush the grey sky from my head.

The sky seems to darken, as the buildings on both sides of the Karel Doormanstraat block the remaining dreary daylight. A few big plant troughs, with one tree each, scatter the sidewalks, supposedly to cheer up this three-dimensional concrete jungle. The insinuation that trees can only survive in a plant-trough-controlled habitat only emphasises the man-made nature of the city.

A scruffy man leans against one of the troughs, his mind hazy. The euro I drop in the cup next to him tinkles when it joins several other coins.

I walk towards the Schouwburgplein and inhale as the light brightens on the square. Of the four huge hydraulic lampposts bordering the square, two bend forward. As always, I marvel at the red crane-like masts, at home so close to the biggest port of Europe.

The clouds in my head thin out and I hurry home. On the stairs to my loft, I check my phone. Dad's 'we need to talk voice' strengthens the importance of his short voicemail, "Call me back." I bounce up the rest of the stairs two steps at a time.

Once inside on the doormat in my apartment, I return Dad's call.

"Thanks for calling back, Kath." His tone is serious.

"What's up? Alida okay?" I wedge the phone between my right shoulder and ear and struggle my left arm out of my coat.

"Alida is fine. I'm calling about the farmhouse. The tenants moved their furniture out yesterday, and when they came back this afternoon to do a final check, they found..." He clears his throat. "The house was broken into. There's a lot of damage. They found walls broken through, floorboards pulled up. They informed the police, who made a report. I called the insurance, they'll send someone to assess the damage the day after tomorrow. I think we both should be there. Would Wednesday afternoon suit you?"

"Of course. I'll make it work. What did the police say?" I hang the dripping coat on a hook on the wall and place a dirty towel I keep in the hallway for that purpose underneath the coat.

"They're not sure. Thieves might have noticed the tenants packing and hoped everything was wrapped up like gifts for them to take."

"But why damage the place?" I kick off my shoes and place them on the bottom shelf of the shoe rack.

"Possibly out of frustration for coming up empty-handed. Police don't think it's vandalism, they've got little of that on the island." He sighs. "We need to see the damage. Whether you want to sell or rent out again, you can't do it in its current state."

"I guess not." That farmhouse keeps being a pain in the ass. Getting rid of it isn't easy.

"The insurance surveyor comes at 3.30 P.M. I would like you and me to go through the house before that and assess the damage ourselves. Where will you be Wednesday?"

"In the office in The Hague."

Dad groans. "You know how I hate driving into The Hague. I teach at Delft University in the morning. Could you come to the Delft Campus station around 1 P.M.?"

"Sure. I'll be there."

We hang up. I walk to the fridge. I don't feel like cooking, nor like venturing out in the rain again for takeout. Not even to get my favourite Chinese comfort food. I cook bigger portions about twice a week and leave containers in the freezer for days like this. From one of the freezer drawers, I grab a container of boerenkool. My favourite Dutch winter dish of kale with mashed potatoes is exactly what I need right now. It'll heat me up and at least leave my body content.

Between dinner and tucking into bed early, I read for two hours in a chair near the window, although I catch myself staring at the river most of the time.

At 2 A.M. I wake up, sweating. Did I eat too much boerenkool? But it's not my stomach that woke me up. Something stirs in my mind. Something urgent.

I slip into a restless sleep. The Hekate statue in the garden of the farmhouse whirls into view. The three women, bonded as Siamese twins with their bodies and legs, run into the house and attack the intruders with their knife and torches. One of the torches grows and grows, the flame lighting the face of the woman holding it. Cecilia? No, it's my mother. She stares at me, opens her mouth. At first, I can't hear anything above the intruders hammering into the walls. But then my mother's voice comes through. "…at her feet, sweetheart. Turn the knife and you'll find answers at her feet."

CHAPTER THIRTY-FIVE

The next morning, Kurt enters the office I start to consider as mine, just when I end the call with Cecilia.

"Bad news?" he asks.

My face must show my displeasure. I'd hoped to shake Cecilia off. "That was Cecilia Yong, the detective. She wants me to report to the police station this afternoon."

"Don't worry. Remember, I can protect you. Try to pump her for information, what she knows about the Syndicate. When she stops being useful to us, I'll make her go away."

Hard to imagine this man was his mother's delight. 'When people stop being useful, I make them go away' would make for an excellent motivational motto on his office wall.

At the police station that afternoon, a constable shows me into an interview room. He leaves when Cecilia enters with two bottles of water. She doesn't sit down. A bad sign?

"Figured you might like some water." In her mind, she pictures me at the bar in her parents' restaurant last Saturday. *Simple taste. Like me.*

"Thanks."

Cecilia studies me. *Thinner and more baggy-eyed every time I see her.* "I'd like to know more about your four anonymous calls."

"Just one, remember?"

Cecilia walks a few paces back and forth. "Stop lying. You've had that sim card for years." *Doesn't know I'm bluffing.*

Thanks, now I do. "I haven't. Just bought it that day."

"All these calls, your work phone shows you were at the scene of the crime when you called in the tips. Too much of a coincidence.

Why don't you just tell me how you knew about these crimes? It doesn't seem like you were involved personally. Maybe I can help you. But only if you're honest with me." *Might be afraid of consequences from her criminal friends.*

"I really don't know what you're talking about." I suppress the inclination to roll my tensed shoulders.

Cecilia sighs. *Try different approach.* "I'd also like to ask you a few more questions about the Syndicate. Could you tell me what you do for them?"

"My job title is Personal Assistant."

"Assist with what, exactly?"

"Meetings the Syndicate's boss has."

Cecilia crosses her arms, and her eyes narrow. "Meaning? Be more specific." *Being evasive. Always acts like she's got something to hide. Can't put my finger on it, but something's not right.*

"I join him during meetings. We, uhm, prepare together, talk through the strategy on how to reach the deal, or finalise the policy, or whatever the topic for that meeting is. We discuss the people involved, what their background is and what the best approach is to convince them." Pleased, I sit straight. I made it sound like quite the respectable job.

Cecilia seats herself on a corner of the table and leans towards me, focusing her expressionless cat-like eyes on me. A little too close for comfort. I lean back.

Her next question comes out friendly. "Isn't that hard? You don't have prior experience with the European Union, or with any kind of politicians." *Completely unconvincing, her getting that job.*

"People are people. Behaviour is the same anywhere. Whether they work in profit, non-profit or political organisations."

"Why did Bernard hire you? He worked in Brussels and already had a PA."

I shrug. "I don't know."

"And then he died."

I wring my hands. "I didn't hear until I reported to the The Hague office on my first day." Only two weeks ago, on this day, Bernard and Kurt interviewed me. So much has happened…

"We suspect Bernard might have been murdered."

My jaw drops. "Murdered? How?"

Surprise seems genuine. "We think he was hit on the head and pushed into the water unconscious. Conveniently, the two cameras in the area stopped working during the afternoon."

Something clicks in my mind, and I blurt out, "You know, his PA in Brussels said Bernard never got drunk. She didn't believe it was an accident."

Cecilia shakes her head.

I frown. "Why would anyone murder Bernard? He seemed nice. His job didn't seem dangerous." Although he did fear being followed. And he was working on something secret.

Cecilia sighs, gets off the table and starts pacing the room again. "We don't know. Could've been a robbery. His wallet was in the water, empty." *Bet that's what the murderer would like us to believe.*

I steady my hands by folding them in my lap. Bernard murdered… "I hardly knew him, but I was looking forward to working with him."

Odd. "Why?"

I swallow. "He used to work with my mother."

Cecilia stops mid-pace and looks at me. "Right. You told me she used to work for the Syndicate. I didn't realise she worked with Bernard back then." *Strange coincidence.*

The addictive images Bernard showed me enter my mind. My mother laughing, talking. The asshole who killed Bernard killed his memories of my mother, too. I screw the cap off the bottle and try to get rid of the lump in my throat by drinking half the bottle.

She's emotional. Because of Bernard? She hardly knew him. Too many things don't add up.

I glance at Cecilia while listening to her thoughts. She's tough, but not hardened throughout. In other circumstances, we might even get along. Although two people keeping everyone at arm's length might not form the best ingredients for a warm friendship.

CHAPTER THIRTY-SIX

The train emerges above ground north of Delft city centre, in the middle of an industrial area. Buildings close to the tracks block most of the view eastwards, but between them, numerous pipelines weave from tanks to vessels and into the buildings. Several vents and chimneys emit puffs of steam. From here, the old, iconic industrial buildings don't show their best, but I've admired their grandeur from the front a few years ago.

The trains on this stretch are almost always busy, and downright packed during rush hour. People still walk past to find a seat. A woman my age enters the cabin, her face white apart from the circles under her eyes and her hand on her curved belly.

A man three rows ahead notices her. *Should give up my seat.* He prepares to get up. *Or... would she be insulted? She looks pregnant, but what if she's not? Instead of a gallant guy, I'll be the inconsiderate jerk.* He places his bag back at his feet. *Better not risk it.*

Poor guy. At least I know for sure a woman is pregnant instead of having a naturally protruding belly. Once a woman is aware of her pregnancy, it's on her mind most of the time, even if just as a background process. Often, when the woman is into her last trimester, I feel the baby's presence. This woman's pregnancy seems not that far advanced yet.

Full again today. It's not too bad now, but can I still do this in two months? She stumbles her way towards me. I get up and wave to my seat.

She looks back, confused. *No one behind me. She gets up for me? That's a first.* She hesitates, then sits down. "Thanks." Her lips curve into the serene smile pregnant women seem to have patented. She folds both hands on her belly, to be close to the new being made by her and the one she loves most.

I push my way to the vestibule, past standing passengers, tripping over bags and feet that go unnoticed by my blurry eyes.

At Rijswijk station, I jump out and stride towards the exit. Outside, I adjust my pace to the other people trudging to their workplaces, like ducks in a row. Their dull stream of morning thoughts is like background noise. Until one line of thought spikes up.

EEG results disappointing. Stronger theta waves and lower alpha waves, but that's more a result of mind-reading than an explanation of how she does it. Glad Kurt gave me someone for base level testing. Can't wait till Saturday!

What? This guy must be thinking about my tests. How does he know I can read minds? And what will happen on Saturday?

The guy, his height disguised by his stooping, enters the Syndicate building. I linger outside the door and concentrate on the receptionist. She says *Morning Aaron* and watches him go through one of the side doors.

Right, Aaron, the head scientist. Kurt must have told him.

I barge into the building and nod at the receptionist, who steps back. *What is the matter with her? Face like thunder.*

I soldier on to the elevator. I'll make it up to her another day.

That's the snitch who got Sara fired.

I turn around. A woman glares at me.

Suck-up. Kurt probably felt obligated to keep her because Bernard hired her. And madam makes sure she gets rid of the competition. She steps in after me, moves to the opposite corner and stares at the ceiling. *Hate those career bitches. We women should stand up for each other. Jason was right to warn us all we can't trust her.*

Great. This is turning out to be another marvelous day.

On the elevator's arrival, I march straight to Kurt's office. Jason stands in front of Kurt's desk.

I square myself in the door opening and look at Kurt. "We need to talk. Now."

Jason frowns. *Bitch. Thinks she's running the show here.*

Kurt nods to Jason. "It's okay. I need to talk to Kathy."

I should push you hard against the wall and smack you. Jason stomps past me without looking me in the eye, not restraining his elbow from 'accidentally' ramming into my ribs. I shove the door shut with a bang after him.

Kurt looks at me with raised eyebrows.

I ball my fists. "What's this shit about Sara?"

"Why don't you take a seat?"

"No."

An amused flicker interrupts his concentration on me. "Suit yourself. What did you hear?"

"That Sara got fired, and people blame me."

Kurt unplugs a cable from under his desk. That's the second time. Why? He leans back. "I had to fire Sara. I don't tolerate my people working for law enforcement or intelligence agencies. She was spying on me. But we do need to discuss the consequences of this." He gestures towards the chair opposite of his desk. "Better take a seat. It takes a bit of explaining."

Sighing as if it takes a tremendous effort, I sit down. I'm aware I come across as a grumpy, stubborn child, but that happens to be exactly how I feel.

"Jason is my security officer. We handle very sensitive matters here. We can't have any leaks. You've seen the extensive secrecy agreement every employee has to sign. To ensure compliance, Jason had cameras installed. He does weekly random checks to hear and see what's going on. Whether people do their jobs properly."

"Doesn't that invade employees' privacy?"

"Everyone signed for it. It's in the secrecy agreement."

"You mean it's hidden somewhere in those fourteen pages? No one reads an agreement like that in detail. What's the point. If you don't sign, you won't get the job."

"That's their problem. They signed. You signed. Jason stumbled on the footage of us talking about Sara. Where you tell me she works for the BND. Even if I had no intention of firing her, now that Jason knew, I had no choice."

"So now everyone here knows I can read minds?"

Kurt shakes his head. "No, not at all. I reviewed the video as well. We never mention you read her mind. Your secret is still safe."

"You *asked* me to spy on Sara. I didn't snitch on her by myself."

"That's not how it sounds on the video."

"What if Jason reviews the footage of our conversations in here?"

"I can switch off the cameras here."

The cable under his desk... I close my eyes. Kurt is so smart. That's why he came to my office. And why he suddenly talked to me in thoughts. And wanted me to repeat his thoughts to 'test my ability.'

In a patient voice, Kurt says, "Kathy, I tried to do you a favour."

My eyes jerk open. "A *favour*? How do you consider this a favour?"

"I never asked you out loud about Sara. On camera, it's as if you told me yourself. If we explain you answered questions I was thinking, people like Jason realise you can read minds." He leans forward, his fingertips against each other in front of his chin. "There are two options. Either you let people think you got Sara fired, or you tell them you can read minds. In the first option, people will come around. They'll understand Sara caused this herself and forget over time. I can help to ensure everything goes back to normal." He pauses, drops his voice half an octave and continues, "In the second option, nothing will ever go back to normal."

Another 'assurance' that's just a threat. I'm on a sinking ship in icy waters, the options being to jump into the freezing water to a sure death, or in a lifeboat where a hungry polar bear holds his paw over a hole leaking water. Because we hang on to any tiny speck of hope, we place our lives in the hands of the polar bear.

But this time, I won't dance to this polar bear's tune straight away. I cross my arms. "If you're so concerned about keeping my secret, then why does Aaron know?"

Finally, he's taken by surprise. A flash of intense irritation surges through him. He needs a few seconds to recover and concentrate on me again.

"Aaron studied your test results. He's much more experienced than Nicole and knew something was up. He asked me about it. I gave it to him as a hypothesis. A possibility. Nothing else."

He's lying. I can tell from his smug face. He's probably satisfied how he made this up on the spot.

He clears his throat. "By the way, how did it go with Cecilia? Anything I need to know?"

Sure, change the topic. I spit out, "Nothing much. Repeat of the previous conversation."

"She questioned you about the Syndicate again?"

I shrug. He has lost the privilege of receiving information from me.

Kurt makes a note. "I'll make the call this afternoon to get her off your back. At least that's one worry off your mind. You see, I'm looking out for you." He pauses, before adding with emphasis, "Remember that."

Isn't that hilarious. Both Cecilia and Kurt attack me, with the promise they can help me. Both are intent on digging their claws into me. In whose claws will I be better off?

I place my hands on the armrests and push myself up. I'm done talking.

Kurt waves me down. "Stay. I've found more information on your mother."

After hanging in midair for a moment, I lower myself into the chair again.

CHAPTER THIRTY-SEVEN

Kurt leans back, and his eyes focus on the ceiling. "What do you know about your mother's biological parents?"

His casual question, his studied relaxed pose, and his stare elsewhere remind me of the cat we had when I was little who'd sit bored next to the mouse she just caught. The mouse grows hopeful to get away, waits, and when it attempts to move, the cat jumps on top, relishing the renewed opportunity to see the mouse squirm.

And I squirm. "I only know what you told me. That they left her somewhere."

"That's what your mother had told child services when they found her. Bernard investigated further. Police found the bodies of a man and a woman in a burnt-out car, three days before and about fifteen kilometres away from where your mother was found."

My nails sink into the arms of the chair. "What happened?"

"Tire tracks indicated they were run off the road. Whether the car caught fire because of that, or whether it was set on fire, they couldn't tell."

"Run off the road? You mean someone else was involved?"

"Looks like it. The report is inconclusive to whether the couple died because of the fire, or were dead before the fire started."

"Didn't the police identify the couple?"

"The official investigation didn't try very hard. A woman passed the car before it caught on fire. According to her, the couples' car had a German license plate. She saw another car parked a bit further, thought they already helped out, and drove on. She called in when the bodies were found. The Dutch police handed over the details to the German missing persons unit and stopped investigating."

"So, we can't be sure they were my mother's parents." I drop my eyes down and study the lines on the carpet I previously thought of as rivers. They now remind me of smoke curling up. Or slivers of mist, hiding the truth. For decades, nothing was known about my mother's parents, and now I'm supposed to believe this random couple found dead are my grandparents?

"Bernard became convinced they were. He managed to obtain a copy of the police report and started a search. Took him more than a year. Eventually, he found a group of Roma who'd travelled for a while with a couple that left around the time of the car fire." Kurt opens a file folder in front of him. "They remembered your grandparents."

"How can you be sure they're my grandparents, without DNA or anything like that?" Sometimes, the mouse would be equally non-chalant as the cat, pretending all was fine.

"Not one hundred percent, no. But they showed Bernard some pictures. Here's one." The cat regains control. Kurt hands me an old photograph, curled at the corners. Two women and a teenage boy sit on one side of a large picnic table, a woman with a girl on her lap on the other side. A man standing next to the table carries a big pan. Everyone looks at the camera, smiling.

"The Roma gave Bernard this photo. On one side is their family. The girl on this side is your mother. She sits on her mother's lap. Her father is standing next to them."

I peer at the picture. The girl, about three or four years old, does remind me of the earliest photos I have of my mother. But all young kids have chubby, angelic faces at that age. I shrug. "Could be. But it could just as well be someone else."

Kurt picks up another photo. "Here's one of the family just before they left the group. About two weeks before your mother was found." He hands me the picture and watches me.

On the family portrait, a woman and girl sit upright on a couch. The man stands next to the couch, his hand on the woman's shoulder. The girl is about six years old and has a close resemblance to my mother's early photos. She holds something in her lap, like a doll. Or could it be…

Kurt's voice reveals excitement. "In this picture, your mother holds her little brother. When this family left the Roma, they had a seven-year-old girl and baby-boy."

I stare at Kurt.

"Kathy, do you realise what that means? You could have an uncle somewhere."

I swallow. "My mother never mentioned a little brother. She would've remembered that."

Kurt's mood turns dark and impenetrable again. "Or she hid that fact from everyone. To protect her little brother."

Blood rushes to my head, flooding it with images. Of my mother mourning the little baby boy… Of a young girl walking around with a baby… I stare at the floor, hand on my forehead, trying to pretend I'm thinking. Which I am, but most of all, I hope to shield the shock plastered all over my face.

"Well?" Kurt says.

I swallow and force myself to look at him. "I…don't know what to say. It's hard to believe my mother would never have told anyone."

Somewhere out there, I could have an uncle. Would he be able to mind-read? Would it be possible to find someone like me, after all those years of searching? A family member, no less? I inhale and manage a casual tone. "Where's that little boy now?"

"I don't know." Kurt checks his file. "Bernard's notes suggest he didn't find anything."

My body responds before my mind, by tensing up. Kurt is evasive. And eager. He hides it behind his mask of concentration. Why is he excited? He has never shown a genuine concern for my well-being. How could he benefit from finding my lost family?

CHAPTER THIRTY-EIGHT

The train crawls forward, as if hesitating which way to go.

How long will I let Kurt manipulate me? I dig my nails into my palms. As long as he gives me more information about my mother, I suppose.

The train enters the tunnel, slowing even further on the approach of Delft. I stare out at the cheerful, attractive underground station, probably designed to distract passengers from noticing they're trapped in a dark place.

Which is what Kurt does to me every time. Distracting me from his dark mind, dark motives. What would my mother think about what I have become? Her daughter a junkie, craving information, willing to sell her soul.

I press my fingers against my eyes. I don't want them to become puffy before meeting Dad.

Station Delft-Campus couldn't be more different from Delft, even though they're just two minutes apart. The station is partly tucked away under a viaduct. Further down the tracks, square grey office buildings stand on both sides. Weeds grow abundantly, emphasizing the emptiness of the area.

A car approaches and stops in front of the gap in the gates, serving as an exit. I slide into the passenger seat and hug Dad hard.

He raises his eyebrows. "Everything alright, sweetheart?"

I swallow. "The new job has been intense."

He sighs. "To be honest, I wasn't too happy you took that job." He focuses on the road.

Once we're on the highway, I ask him to explain.

He sighs. "Your mother was about to leave the job when she

died. I should've told you. But it was long ago. The organisation surely has changed, and I…" *was glad you found a different job, maybe to last for a while this time.*

"I would've taken the job, anyway. The person who hired me had worked with Mom. I hoped he'd tell me about her. He promised."

The car shoots forward. "Was it Bernard?"

"Yes."

"And did you get to know more?"

"He died the day before I started. He just shared a few memories." If only Dad knew how… "His deputy took over. He found Bernard's notes. He claims Mom's parents died in a car crash."

Dad's knuckles turn white from gripping the steering wheel hard. Pain floods him, like always, when we talk about my mother. *Oh Ysolde… Another thing you told him without telling me. Why wasn't I enough? That car crash…if that coward had helped you instead of fleeing…*

Before, I always backed off at this point. But before, I just had questions. Now, I might have a few answers. We could work together. I touch his arm. "Why did she want to quit?"

"Your mother first liked Bernard. But after a while, she felt used. She assured me he didn't mistreat her, but she questioned the organisation's morals."

"Did you know Bernard investigated what happened to her parents?"

"She told me he was looking into it. A few days before…" My mother's face, when he was asked to identify her, pulses into his mind. He swallows. "She wasn't pleased. It scared her. She said it was none of Bernard's business."

My mother didn't want Bernard to find out what happened to her parents? Why not? Didn't she trust Bernard? I rub my temples. It makes no sense…

Dad exhales when his car kit announces a phone call. His emotions ebb away, while he discusses the results of an experiment with one of his PhD students.

Maybe it's wrong to bother Dad with this. It happened so long ago. He's happily remarried. It's not fair to remind him he didn't really know his first wife, nor to taint his memories of her.

While Dad and his student talk about scientific details far beyond my comprehension, I stare out of the car window. We enter the Hoeksche Waard, where the farmhouse is located. Technically, the Hoeksche Waard is an inland island. Its outstretched agricultural landscape couldn't be more different from the bustling city of Rotterdam, only minutes away. Many creeks traverse the reclaimed land, serving as irrigation or drainage, depending on the weather. A highway runs from the north, accessing the island through a tunnel, to the south, where it crosses the 1200-metre long Haringvliet Bridge. On the east, another tunnel provides access to the mainland, and on the northwest, a busy ferry service connects the island.

Dad leaves the highway, but the view stays the same—wide agricultural fields, interspersed with farmhouses. The rows of typical knotted willows along the creeks stand strong—their collective angle hints at the direction of the winds they brave every day. And although I still don't understand why my mother was so happy here, I must admit the landscape, though by no means beautiful, has a roguish appeal.

By the time we pull into the driveway of the farmhouse, Dad and his PhD student discuss how to revisit the hypotheses to get back on track.

I glance at the house I haven't seen for twenty-three years. Dad took care of the repairs, arranged the lease agreements through an agent, paid the bills. I never had to face my inheritance. Did he protect me from painful memories, as much as I protect him from his?

I exit the car and close the door softly, the animated voices in the car now muffled. I square my shoulders and walk towards the house.

The white plastered front has taken on a grey hue. Ivy curls up around two paned windows in the front. In a few weeks they will bear leaves again, but for now, the barren brown roots add to the deserted atmosphere.

The pebbles in the driveway lost their fight against weeds and grass. I follow the cobbled path to the right of the house, which curves around the corner to the front door. Although the front door is now black instead of the dark green I remember, it still is the traditional two-part door, of which the upper half can open separately.

To get inside, I'll have to wait for Dad with the key. I first walk along the outstretched side wall. When my mother grew up here, the farmhouse consisted of a small house in the front and a big barn at the back, attached through a small hallway in between. After my mother's adoptive parents sold the land, they started to convert the barn. When they died, my mother finished the first half, and left the back half as shed and storage. You can tell from the outside, the first half of the barn has big floor-to-ceiling windows, followed by traditional small, half-circle windows in the second part.

Through the windows, a terrace is visible through the French doors on the opposite outer wall. The high ceiling, with rustic wooden beams, gives the room a cozy but sturdy feel. My pained memories might have not done the house justice. No wonder we never had a problem getting tenants. Although right now, the rubble on the floor will turn everybody off.

Footsteps approach. "Kath?" Dad waves a key in the air, then opens the front door. I follow him in. The hallway still has the checkerboard black-and-white tiles on the floor. Several are broken, and a few differently shaded tiles suggest repairs.

Dad ignores the kitchen to the left and walks through the door on the right, into the hallway. I suck in air. Several gaping holes in the internal walls allow a view into the study as well as the living room. The wall of the utilities room is almost gone. Pieces of plasterboard, plaster and wood are everywhere, and chunks of yellow fluffy insulation material cover what is left of the floor.

Dad sighs. "I'd hoped it wasn't as bad as the cops said. I talked to them again yesterday. Most internal walls, installed when your mother and her parents restructured, are at least partly destroyed. As if they were searching for something inside the walls. They left the original brick walls alone, just removed part of the plaster in some places."

We walk through the door to the living room and stumble upon a similar scene. The wooden floor has fared little better than the internal walls. Several planks have been broken away, the floorboard below removed, resulting in gaps big enough to stick your head through.

I touch the brick outer wall. At least that seems sturdy and intact. "What a mess."

Dad swallows. "I see why the police think the burglars were looking for something."

We finish the tour of the house. All converted rooms are in the same chaos. And although the original walls in the house are mostly intact, cupboards, floors and ceilings have been broken open everywhere.

We return to the living room. There's no place to sit, rubble covers the entire floor. I ask, "Do you think they've found whatever they were looking for?" A stupid question, he knows as much as I do, but it suddenly matters.

He shrugs. "The police said they might not have found what they were after, otherwise they would've stopped their destruction at some point. But I'm afraid we'll never know." He sighs. "Let's walk around the house and see how they got in."

The French doors are locked and undamaged. Dad opens them and we step onto the uneven cobbled terrace. The grey-blue square cobbles are destined for the same fate as the pebbles in front. The weeds haven't progressed as much but are about to take over. On the other side of the terrace, one tenant installed a kids' sandbox. The black tarp affixed as cover has come loose on the far-right corner, and flaps in synchrony with the wind.

Along the wall of the barn, a lawn stretches towards the small creek that separates this land from the farmland behind. A small path, made of the same cobbles as the terrace, meanders through the lawn. Hesitantly, I follow the path to the end of the barn, bracing myself for the view at the end. There, the path splits, one part leading to the other side of the house, the other leading to the creek at the back. And tucked in the corner of that junction should be the statue. Unless they smashed that as well. I don't even know what I'm hoping for.

I pass the end of the barn, looking ahead.

It's not there. The bastards took it.

I step forward, and the statue suddenly catches my eye. The last time, this threatening statue towered above me, the larger-than-life knife and torches in my face, the snake curling up above my head. Now, the three females don't even reach my ribcage. The details of their faces and robes are beautiful, their arms hold their weapons alert but not aggressive. Why did I fear these protective creatures, this goddess of conveying messages between worlds?

I kneel in front of the statue and remember my mother's voice from the dream. 'Turn the knife and you'll find answers at her feet.'

Dad's footsteps behind me jolt me out of the mesmerizing memory. I stand up and turn.

"Your mother loved that statue." From his right eye, a tear runs down his cheek.

I walk up to him and give him a big hug. "I feared that statue. It was so…threatening. I didn't get why she loved it. Why she named me after this goddess. But it's beautiful."

Dad squeezes me, then grabs his handkerchief and blows his nose. "She bought it after your birth. She wanted this house to be yours one day. I never understood why, but she was convinced this house would suit you."

I shake my head. I don't understand either.

A buzzing sound comes from Dad's pocket. He takes his phone out. "It's the surveyor. I better pick up." He taps the screen. "Hi." He listens, then responds, "We're already at the house. Ten minutes? Sure. See you then." He pockets his phone. "His previous appointment was quicker than he thought. He'll be here in ten minutes."

I point to the back of the barn. "That's probably where they got in." The back has a set of two traditional big barn doors that, when opened, allow a tractor to drive through. At the far-left end, a normal door stands open a crack.

"The lock is broken." Dad opens the door and we stick our heads through. Along the wall to the left, a variety of garden equipment hangs or has fallen to the ground. Old, mismatched cupboards stand along the right wall. The door in the back wall, leading to the living room, is smashed.

The crunching sound of a car driving onto the pebbled driveway brings us out again. Dad walks around to greet the surveyor. I turn back to the statue.

CHAPTER THIRTY-NINE

'Turn the knife and you'll find answers at her feet.'

I reach out and touch one of the faces.

It wasn't just a dream. It was a memory. A message from one mind-reader to another. My mother thought of the statue and tried to imprint it on my mind. Maybe that's why the statue seemed larger than life.

I study the knife and trace it with my finger. Just below the blade is a crack, running around in a circle. The crack is straight, an intentional one, not a fracture. I grab the blade. Should the knife come off? Or does something happen when the knife turns?

I wriggle, pull, and push. It's not as solid as stone should be. My hand trembles and my heart races. Breathe, Kath. Think.

'Turn the knife.' With both hands, I grab it again. In my memory, my mother showed how to turn it. Clockwise. I increase the pressure on the blade. Something seems to give way. I throw in my body weight as a lever.

Suddenly, I crash to the left of the statue, stone blade in hand. I stare from the blade in my hand to the handle still held by the stone female figure. I peer into the handle. In the hollow lies a small key. I fish it out and place the stone blade back.

'You'll find answers at her feet.' Yeah, well, she has six of them. On my knees, I crawl around the statue. The concrete base seems big compared to the statue itself. No keyhole. What did I expect? A visible keyhole would've been too obvious. But she wouldn't hide a key if there was no point. With eyes closed, I focus on my mother's memory. What was the next visual she tried to imprint? The foggy memory comes into focus. My mother turns the key at the base of the statue. But how did she get to the keyhole? No matter how hard I try, the middle part remains hidden. Frustrated, I open my eyes. There's still no keyhole at the base. What's the missing part of that memory?

I crawl around the statue, inspecting the areas between the feet. I spit on my fingers and rub a bit of dirt and green moss away. Along two rows of toes, moss grows in a straight pattern. Frantically, I scratch it away, the moss building up under my nails. There's a crack! The same straight-lined unnatural crack as on the handle of the knife. I scratch and rub along other cracks that angle downward along the base. The cracks form a rectangle. I try to wriggle the key into the crack. The key bends, the unyielding stone oblivious. I need something sturdier.

I hurry into the barn, grab a garden hoe, and run back to the statue. Hopefully, the blade of the hoe is thin enough to fit into the slit. I place the blade along one of the vertical cracks and kick the hoe three times. A few millimetres of the blade disappears into the concrete. I lean into the handle of the hoe, increasing the pressure bit by bit. The wooden handle of the hoe bends and groans. Then the hoe shoots away and propels me to the ground again. Damn, the hoe probably broke. I sit up. A slab of concrete came loose and lies at the base of the statue. I crawl forward, heart racing. In the base's cavity sits a metal plate with a keyhole.

My fingers tremble. The key meets resistance from the lock and won't turn. I pick up the garden hoe, hang it back in the barn, and search for anything suitable to grease a lock. Next to four old paint buckets, a bottle of frying oil sits on the shelf. I pour some over the key and walk back to the statue. The dripping key slides into the lock, and after wriggling and applying some force, it turns. The metal plate comes off, revealing a dark opening, about five centimetres high, the back end not visible. I swallow and reach in. My fingers meet with paper. I retrieve a green file folder. I reach in again and come up with an envelope. The third time I come up empty.

From the barn, Dad's voice and that of another man come closer. I thrust the metal plate back in place, lock it, place the slab back, and shove the folder and envelope under my jacket. I stuff the key in my jeans pocket.

"Kathy?"

I walk over to the barn door.

"This is my daughter Kathy. This is…"

"Steve. Nice meeting you. I was just telling your father I'll need to come back with a contractor for quotes on the cost of repairs. There doesn't appear to be structural damage. Our insurance gives you two options. One, we take care of the repairs to return it to the state it was before. Two, after we have the full quote, we pay you the money and you take care of the repairs yourself. You don't have to decide now. When we have the quote, I will get in touch."

Dad looks at me. *A shame she never had a good feeling about this house. Option one is what Kathy wants.* He opens his mouth.

I hold up my hand, flushed with shame for having left him to deal with these decisions until now. "Dad, you've always taken care of this house for me. It's time I take the responsibility." I turn to Steve. "I'll give you my number. When you get back to me, we'll decide."

In the car, Dad asks in a gruff voice, "Are you sure you want to deal with this, honey?"

"Mom left the house to me for a reason. I…need to think about what I want to do."

Dad blinks a few times. *Ysolde wanted Kath to have it. I never understood why she thought the house would be good for Kathy. But they're so much alike… One moment they're symbiotically close to me, the next, they could as well be in another galaxy.*

I pat my dad's arm. Under my jacket, the file folder presses into my ribs.

CHAPTER FORTY

I lean against the kitchen counter and lower the tea bag one more time, even though the colour of the steaming liquid is already darker than I usually prefer. The envelope and file folder wait on the table where Cecilia interviewed me four weeks ago. On the way home, I couldn't wait to see what's inside. But now… What if it contains nothing special?

I lift the bag and drop it in the sink. With the steaming mug, I sit down at the table. The thin envelope can't contain more than two or three pages, tops. I wriggle my pinky nail into a small gap in the corner of the envelope and freeze. This envelope is about twenty-five years old, before the time of glue strips. My mother probably sealed the envelope by licking it the old-fashioned way. This envelope deserves special treatment.

I stand up and choose a sharp cutting knife from a kitchen drawer. The knife fits in the small slit in the corner. I wiggle it until the slit is larger and carefully slice it across, leaving a nice, even tear to make sure I don't cut whatever is in there too. The envelope contains two pieces of lined paper. I take a deep breath, unfold the pages and smooth them on the table. They're filled with precise, small writing in blue.

It's dated 26 March 1997. About five weeks before my mother died. She must have been the last person to touch this letter, this envelope. And now I'm the first person to open it, to read the contents. I caress the paper with my fingers and start reading.

'My sweet little Kathy,
With all my heart, I hope to help you grow up into an amazing

adult. I hope that one day, we will talk about this letter and laugh about why I ever thought I needed to write it. But if anything happens to me, I want you to know about your family.

Soon after you were born, I knew you could mind-read as well. You're the only person who shares my ability. I want to help you navigate that gift, a gift the world is hostile to.

Your grandfather, my father, was a mind-reader as well. He trained as a psychologist and helped numerous people with his gift. But some grew afraid of his knowledge, or they believed dark powers were at work. He had to flee the south of Germany just after I was born. He planned to disappear alone, so my mother and I could live a normal life somewhere else. However, my mother couldn't bear to be without him, nor to deny him his own daughter. They joined a group of Roma, who embraced his, and later my, ability.

After several years, some people somehow turned up at the Roma camp, looking for my father. My parents grabbed me and my little brother Dieter and drove for hours. It was dark when my mother woke me up. A car blocked the road in front of us. My mother thrust Dieter and his diaper bag in my arms, pushed us out of the car and told me to hide. I crawled into the bushes my father had almost parked into. The men in the other car came over. My mother screamed. I held Dieter tight and ducked into a ditch. A flashlight swept over the bushes. There was more yelling and screaming, and then an awful silence. Smoke stung my eyes and throat. I peeked out, and our car was engulfed by flames. I'll never forget that horrible smell.

We stayed in the ditch until the flames were gone. In the moonlight, I peered into what was left of the car, and of my parents.

I don't remember much else from that first night in the woods. When daylight came, I looked at Dieter's peaceful, chubby face, sleeping in my lap. I promised him a normal life. No running from other people. A new start. I believed that if he would grow up without another mind-reader around, he would not be cursed, like me.

After walking one day and one more night, the milk in Dieter's diaper bag was finished. Early morning, I placed him at the door of a church in a little village, hoping it would give him the highest chance of survival. I walked two more days, increasing the distance between me and Dieter, and where our parents were killed, hoping we would never be chased by the same people.

Then I was caught stealing bananas from a supermarket. Child services came, and I pretended I didn't remember much. The first two foster families where they placed me found it hard to care for a girl who didn't want to talk or interact in any way. Then I was placed with Jan and Aaltje de Jong, on their farm. I loved their animals. The cows and sheep didn't judge me for knowing their feelings. I knew when they became sick, or were expecting. Jan and Aaltje believed 'only good, loving people can bond with animals that well' and officially adopted me.

In my last year of high school, Jan became ill. Once they knew he wouldn't recover, they sold the land and the animals. Aaltje died six months after him, assured they left me enough money to sort out what I wanted to do with my life.

Soon after, I met your dad. I found his mind so comforting rational and single-minded. As a scientist, he only believes in explanations by equations. And he's the kindest man I ever met. I was offered a job and my life was perfectly normal. I wanted a family I could call my own.

I was so happy to be pregnant. I named you after Hekate, the Greek goddess with three identities I'd admired as a child. With her torches, she brings wisdom to the world. With her key, she opens the gates between worlds and can access the hidden knowledge beyond. With her knife, she severs the umbilical cord at birth.

When I was pregnant, the questions I had as a teenager about destiny and responsibility bothered me again. I thought, maybe the world has changed, maybe there are people who can be trusted. I told my boss, who'd often wondered about my insight into people, about mind-reading and what had happened to my parents. But I still didn't dare tell your dad the truth about me. About you. It's sad how we fear trusting the people closest to us. Our fear of rejection prohibits us from being ourselves with the ones we love most.

Then my boss betrayed my trust and told Evan, a colleague, who loves power. Evan's fascinated by the possibilities of having unique knowledge.

Luckily, I never told Bernard details about my baby brother. I wanted to find Dieter first and warn him. He wasn't difficult to find, but his mind was troubled and confused. He's not ready for the truth yet. I will try again soon, but as Evan has someone following me, I need to be careful.

With this letter, I'll hide my files containing information about Dieter, the work I do, and mind-reading. I'll update the information every year. If for some reason I can't give you this myself when you're ready, I hope you'll find it through the thoughts I conveyed to you, and that you'll hopefully understand when you're older.

I love you more than anything in the world, and if there's one thing I could ask for, it's to see you grow up and be there for you every step of the way. But, like my father, I have brought danger to you, and for that I am so, so sorry, my dear little Kath… You are such a beautiful, wonderful girl and I love you more than anything in the world.

Love you forever,
Mom'

The floodgates burst open.

I cry for the little girl, walking around clutching her baby brother, desperately figuring out how to keep him safe.

I cry for the orphaned child, rejected by two foster families.

I cry for the shy teenager, feeling safer with farm animals than with humans.

I cry for the young mother, full of love for her little girl, determined to be the mother she had to miss herself.

And finally, I cry for myself. For growing up without a mother who could've taught me so much, the one person who loved me unconditionally despite knowing everything about me.

CHAPTER FORTY-ONE

After fifteen minutes, the flow of tears stops and my head throbs. I fetch a fresh hot tea and swallow two painkillers. I sit down and study the rest of the materials my mother left me.

The file folder contains information about Dieter, or Rick, as his adoptive parents named him. There is an address, a business card from the director of a rehab clinic, and pictures. I stare at the pictures again. They show a teenage boy, tall but hunching, as if to hide his length. He has a glazed look in his eyes. Eyes framed by the same straight shaped eyebrows as my mother's.

I open my laptop and type the address into the search bar. The house was for sale six years ago, and the people living there now have a different last name than Rick's adoptive parents.

The search on his name, Rick Veenstra, on LinkedIn leads to fifty-six hits. I scroll the list. Maybe I'll recognise him from his profile picture straight away. The fourth profile looks promising, but when I click it open, his listed education shows he can't be older than thirty-five. I need to search methodically. I rub my eyes and go back to the first one.

Out of the forty-two profiles listing enough details, I can figure out their approximate age. After half an hour, I've brought my list down to ten men. I cross off the ones whose high school stood further than thirty kilometres from where Rick grew up. Then I cross-link with information from other social media and internet searches. After another hour I stare at a list with three possible candidates for my 'uncle vacancy.'

I say it out loud. "My uncle." Is there really someone else out there who is related to my mother? Who might even have the same ability? I need to know. I have to find him.

Two of the three on the shortlist work at places within an hour's drive. For one, I could even find a home address. The third works further away, in the east. I paste their information and pictures into a word file. I grab the picture of the dopey teenager and hold it up to the screen. None of the three men resemble the picture in the file.

Maybe he's not on LinkedIn. Or he is, but as one of the 'ghost' profiles I skipped. Or maybe I crossed the right profile off, misinterpreting the information. I groan and glance at the clock. 11 P.M. I better get some sleep. Tomorrow, my head will feel clearer.

After six hours of restless sleep, I get out of bed. It's Thursday, but today I have more important things to do than work. I text Kurt, 'I'd like to take two days off, until things cool down at the office around Sara.' He responds within five minutes, 'Ok.'

I have a busy day ahead. Under a hot shower, I absorb the warmth, the energy. With a coffee and yoghurt, I study my list of uncle possibilities.

I could wait at their workplaces and try to read their minds when they come outside. And then talk to them. Yeah, sure. What will I say? 'Hi, I'm the daughter of the older sister you don't know you had.' Might be better to call them.

Before I talk myself out of that plan as well, I call the company where the first one works.

"Mr. Veenstra is on leave right now. I could put you through to one of his colleagues?"

"No, thanks, it's okay. I will call back later." Damn. I don't have his home address, so I'll have to wait until he's back.

The second one has been thrifty with personal information on social media. I'll have to confirm where he spent his teenage years. I call the bank where he works. To my surprise, the receptionist connects me straight away. Maybe she thinks I'm a customer.

"Veenstra."

"Hello, Mr. Veenstra. I am organising a high school reunion and was wondering if you're interested in attending."

"Just had a reunion last year."

Shit. "Oh, really? That must not have been, uhm, the Stedelijk Lyceum then?"

"No. There is no such school in The Hague."

"Oh, my apologies, sir, I must have gotten the wrong information. Sorry to bother you." I strike his name through. The Hague is too far from where my uncle grew up.

With the third one, I have no luck either.

"Mr. Veenstra doesn't work here anymore," a man answering the phone says curtly.

"Would you know where he went?"

"Sorry, we're not allowed to give any information." He hangs up on me.

In what now seems a previous life, but in reality was just over a month ago, I did many reference checks on applicants. Such a curt response, from a company still listed as employer on the man's professional LinkedIn profile, usually means they 'parted ways' not very amicably.

The bright side: my list of three is down to two. But for the first guy, I'll have to wait until he's back at work again, and for the second, I might have to wait until he's got a new job.

Time to check the other information my mother left me. I open the file folder. Her neat print covers several pages. A few are about Evan, his research department, and his employees. She marked one of them as 'dangerous.' Next to a picture of him, she wrote, 'Kurt is intelligent but even more ruthless than Evan. Had dreams of becoming President of his country one day, but party expelled him after a couple of incidents. Kurt often follows me, observes me from a car. He and Evan probably know their thoughts are safe at a distance.'

Then I turn to her notes on mind-reading. She listed the situations in which she can and can't mind-read ('up to a distance of about one hundred metres without obstacles,' 'sometimes through a window,' 'never through a brick or concrete wall').

On another sheet, she wrote, 'To build good relationships, better learn to switch off mind-reading.' She tabled her attempts, with whom, and the extent to which they were successful. I swallow and go through the column 'how to block thoughts.' My cheeks burn. 'Focusing on self' seems to come out as the most promising method when she didn't want to read her husband's thoughts. She rated the success of each category—'focusing on physical senses and sensations' and 'focusing on own emotions' were rated higher than 'focusing on other people or animals around' or 'focusing on sounds.'

The next page is titled 'Do's and don't's when someone knows you're a mind-reader.' It must be based on her relationship with Bernard, as he was the only one who knew. The list of don't's is longer, and more detailed. The first don't—*Don't confront people with their thoughts. Pretend you don't hear them, leave them their dignity by pretending you don't hear everything.*

The first do—*Be as honest as you can about your own thoughts, so the other person perceives a balance.*

I lean back. My mother was so much better at this than I am. She was about my age when she died, and she had put in a lot more work into dealing with mind-reading than I have. I just try to survive. And when it puts me in an awkward situation, I run. At my age, my mother had managed to build a steady relationship with my father, and was a mother to a little girl. She had devised a statue with a lockbox in it, to hide secret information. What have I done in comparison? Nothing, really.

I push my chair back. It is time I follow in my mother's footsteps and do something.

CHAPTER FORTY-TWO

The stiff wind finds its way through my jeans and shawl, chilling me to the bone. The first half hour of waiting, I pretended not to feel it. Now, I'm past caring what other people think of that young woman walking in small circles mumbling to herself.

I'll add to my mother's files, starting with Aaron. He travels by public transport, so I'll follow him when he leaves work.

The throng of people increases. I check my watch. 5.15 P.M., time for people to go home. I adjust the shawl wrapped around my head. Even though most people complete their daily short walk to the station by staring at the sidewalk or their phone, the shawl will minimise the risk of being recognised.

Five minutes later, Aaron strides out of the Syndicate's building. I follow him towards the train station. His thoughts are easy to pick up.

This research will definitely earn me my PhD! They won't be able to dismiss me now. 'Hypotheses not concise enough. Research not accurate.' Pfff. Professor would be drooling if he knew about the equipment I get to work with. Kurt finally approved buying the new electrodes. I'm so brilliant, to claim he might be able to learn how to mind-read himself. His obsession is a little creepy. I guess that's what happens after twenty years of practising daily how to avoid thoughts coming into your head.

I bump into a woman, not a cursory brush, but full body contact.

The woman's piercing blue eyes stare into mine, irritated.

"Sorry. Was absorbed in thoughts." I hurry into the station.

So Kurt practised for *twenty years?* Then my mother was right, he knew she could mind-read. And he prepared himself. For twenty years. That guy is sick.

I spot Aaron entering a train. I run to the next door and enter the carriage in the direction where Aaron boarded. He enters the other side of the carriage and makes his way towards me. I better sit down. I gesture to a grumpy-looking man, not very well groomed, to remove his duffel bag from the seat next to the window. In normal circumstances, I wouldn't even have considered squeezing myself past him, only to be stuck between the window and his body odour. I sit down, ignoring the irritated grunts of the man. Aaron takes a seat five rows in front of me.

I was so certain mind-reading originates in the cerebral cortex. But if that were the case, the EEGs would have told us more. I need to measure her limbic system. Open her brain. Kurt won't give me permission until he's done with her. Hope he's done soon.

He projects in his mind exactly what he'd like to do to my brain. I swallow. His joyful anticipation is sickening.

At the next stop, the old man in the spot opposite of Aaron leaves and a young girl takes his place, distracting Aaron.

Lovely shaped skull. EEG equipment wouldn't take a lot of adjustment on that one. A bit like Kurt. He has quite a symmetrical skull as well. His monthly test is tomorrow, isn't it? Boring. He has mastered the skill of focusing quite well. Don't see the need to keep testing it. Shame he doesn't want Nicole to know. Would rather have her do these stupid repetitive tests. If Kurt does become the new European CEO, as he calls it, I'll need more assistants, anyway. Now that Kurt is close to finding another mind-reader.

The girl with the symmetrical skull takes off her coat. For a few seconds, Aaron appreciates her other lovely shapes. Then he resumes his thoughts. *Glad Kurt's giving me a live brain to test. Didn't think he had the guts. Bernard's death unleashed him. Dreaming of building a legion of mind-readers, becoming the most powerful man on earth. Promising me unlimited funds.*

He envisions a huge lab, with all sorts of brain scanners, and even a surgery room. Although my body has warmed up by now, I can't stop shivering.

CHAPTER FORTY-THREE

I compare my scribbles with my mother's notes. I like the idea of keeping our notes together in my mother's file folder. Computers are too easy to hack into, anyway.

Although my print is also small, it isn't as neat as my mother's. Probably the difference between growing up writing or growing up typing.

I glance around the apartment. There's no safe place to hide the documents. For the moment, a cereal box will have to do.

I stroke my mother's letter. We both made the same naïve mistake, thinking we could put our mind-reading to good use. It's obvious we can't trust anyone. Our ability is too unique, too powerful for others to handle.

My mother was traumatised into a distrusting child, bonded mainly with animals as a teenager, but then started to reach out and built relationships in her twenties. I stare at her table with techniques to curb her mind-reading. Why did she keep her ability from Dad, but trusted her boss? For me, keeping an important part of myself from a friend or lover felt like basing a relationship on an inequality. Keeping people at arm's length means no moral dilemmas or problems with opening up. A great solution, or so I thought, to prevent feeling guilty about keeping an essential part of myself from others. Although I miss out on important parts of life, with that kind of self-punishment.

I glance at my mother's envelope on the table. If I'd kept up the self-punishment, if I wouldn't have let Bernard break through my defense and would've declined working with him, my secret might still be safe. History repeats itself. My grandfather, my mother, and now me. All in trouble, or worse, because we let others know about our mind-reading.

But to be honest, Bernard approaching me like that was a welcome adventure. Apart from knowing more about my mother, the idea of someone accepting me for who I am, to be myself completely, had been very appealing. As well as putting my ability to good use.

I snort. The only ones who got to put my ability to use are Kurt and Aaron. One wants to become the next top dog of a world power, the other wants to redeem himself by ground-breaking research.

Sighing, I stow the file folder and letter in a cereal box and go to bed. Sleep doesn't come. Sentences of my mother's letter swirl in my head. 'I want to help you navigate your gift, a gift the world is hostile to.' 'I wonder why so many people fear to trust the people closest to us.'

My mother thought she figured out the right approach by suppressing her ability. But not before she felt threatened and had to go to great lengths to hide information about her background. I thought I figured out the right approach by keeping to myself, pulling away more and more. Not functioning properly in the real world.

The three-faced goddess Hekate was supposed to bring wisdom to the world by opening the gates between worlds and accessing the hidden knowledge beyond. But how?

I glance at my phone. 2 A.M.

Maybe my mother and I were both wrong. Maybe I should try the one thing both my mother and I avoided.

Maybe I should try trusting the right people.

I grab my phone and type in a brief message. Despite the late hour, Cecilia responds within three minutes. 'Ok. Meet me there at noon.'

I inhale deeply. Tomorrow, in the spirit of my mother's experiments, I'll try something new.

CHAPTER FORTY-FOUR

Cecilia's mother beams. "Come in, come in!" She leads me towards a table in a corner, on one side fenced off by a high plant trough, on the other side by a privacy screen. A big basket of prawn crackers sits ready at the table. "You're early," she says, beaming with approval. Most of her thoughts are in an unfamiliar language, but emotions speak to everyone. She seems to be happy Cecilia is meeting someone.

Cecilia's staccato thinking wafts towards me from behind—*Don't like police business meeting here.* Her mom greeting her interrupts her grumpy thoughts.

I cringe. At 2 A.M., this spot had seemed a logical choice. After a few hours of sleep later, not so much. Since then, I'd practised several openings.

'Why do you think I know so much about crimes and criminals?'

Or, 'Have you ever wondered about mind-reading?'

Or, 'Let me tell you what you're thinking.'

I discarded them all. Cecilia's a rational thinker, who values honesty. At the same time, I have to give her time to process what I'm saying.

She nods to me, unsmiling, and sits down. *Don't feed me bullshit stories.*

My throat burns. Cops are suspicious by nature. She's never going to believe me. But there's no way back now.

I take a deep breath. "I did have the sim card for a longer time."

Cecilia's eyes narrow. *I knew it.*

"The thing is, I can read minds. I hear other people's thoughts."

Cecilia's eyes widen, and her eyebrows rise to her hairline. *Oh, come on. Texting me 'Ready for the truth?' and then giving me this crap?*

"I understand that sounds unbelievable. Impossible. But think about it. How would I otherwise know about all these crimes? Like the guy kidnapping Lily. I stood behind him at the cashier and saw the girl in his mind."

Cecilia stares at me. *And the hint about the trapdoor to the girl's hiding place. No…absolutely impossible. She would know what I'm thinking right now.*

"I do know what you're thinking right now."

Cecilia jerks back.

The words now tumble out of my mouth. "Think about the other tips. The truck with refugees inside, smuggled into the country. I drove past them on the highway and felt their despair. Then the body in the back of the car that got stuck in traffic during the Marathon of Rotterdam. I was cheering on a fellow student and passed the car on my bike. I heard the thoughts of the impatient driver and passenger. Or the dealer with the contaminated meth. The one time I go to a festival, I walk past a drug trafficker thinking about the dirty pills he's selling."

Cecilia's jaw drops. *Fits the details of the calls. But hearing thoughts? Impossible. She has to have a source. Well, multiple sources, as the cases don't seem related. Hearing thoughts would explain… No, it can't be. Never heard of people hearing thoughts.*

"No criminal sources. I really do hear thoughts." I fiddle with my hands in my lap.

"Right." She closes her mouth and swallows. *Oh, my. So…is she hearing every thought? Everything I think?*

I clear my throat. "If I concentrate, I can hear everything someone is thinking indeed."

Her eyes widen and then narrow. *What did I think about when I was with her? She knows everything?*

"I don't know everything. But if people are close, I can hear their thoughts."

Cecilia's stomach clenches. "*All* of it?"

"Not necessarily. In a crowd, only certain thoughts stand out. Or if I'm preoccupied, then I don't hear everything."

"But if you listen in to people, if I could call it like that, do you know everything?" Her stomach knots again.

"I wouldn't say that. I hear thoughts and feel people's emotions. But emotions are often triggered by an external stimulus, not by a thought. So, if people feel scared, or angry, as a result of a trigger, I only know they're scared, or angry. I don't know why." I swallow. "Like now, I can feel you're scared, but I don't know exactly why."

Cecilia's brows furrow. A flash of irritation and anger surges through her.

I open my mouth but think better of it. She might not appreciate being confronted with all her emotions.

She looks at me, eyes angry slits again.

I want her to understand so badly. So much depends on it. I wring my hands and check into her mind. Maybe I shouldn't but I can't resist.

She studies me, her gaze going over my slumped shoulders, my head hanging. Her feeling towards me softens. "You do understand this is very hard to believe, right. I—can't imagine what it's like. To read other people's minds. Would be convenient in my job. Bad in relationships, I guess. To know everything… Not sure I would want to. How does it work? When did you develop this ability?" *So many questions. And possibilities. Mostly for the wrong people.*

"As to how it works—I don't know. They tested my brain at the Syndicate, but nothing much came out of it. Since when, well, I've always been able to hear thoughts, but learned early on to keep that to myself." I meet her inquisitive eyes. "I once read research by Shaunti Feldhahn on how men blame a beautiful woman for being distracted by her. By wearing those tight clothes, their mind is on that sexy ass or her cleavage instead of the topic, so they feel their preoccupation is clearly her fault. I figured fear of mind-reading works the same. People would blame me for knowing thoughts they are ashamed of, even though their thoughts are not my fault."

Cecilia leans back and crosses her arms. "Well, our thoughts are one of the few things that are still our own. And now you're telling me they aren't. When we don't tell anyone about our ugly thoughts, nobody knows. Except, you see us at our worst, before we can correct ourselves."

I smile. "But you see, *everyone* has bad and ugly thoughts. That doesn't bother me at all. Bad thoughts don't make bad *people*. What matters is what they do with those thoughts." I clear my throat. I never had to explain before. But I want, no I *need*, Cecilia to understand. "After a life-time of mind-reading, I've learned not to judge people on a few bad thoughts."

Cecilia rubs her temples. "I can't even begin to imagine what your world looks like."

I shrug. "It's never easy to be different."

Cecilia flinches. *You don't say.* A surge of loneliness floods her, and then she concentrates back on me. "Why did you call in tips to the police?"

"At university, studying psychology, the morality of my unique ability bothered me. Or, more specifically, the responsibility I felt came with it. I couldn't let crimes happen, or leave criminals unpunished, once I knew about them. To call in tips, I bought a simple phone and that sim-card, and called from outside locations and switched that phone off before getting home, so you guys wouldn't find out my location." I look down. "Made me feel smart and righteous for a while, reporting frauds, murders, abusing husbands. But more often than not, culprits got away with their crimes. A year ago, I got into serious trouble. In a previous job, the finance manager was committing fraud. I informed the CEO. They didn't understand how I knew, and kept interrogating me, thinking I must be an accomplice. They couldn't prove anything, but fired me anyway. I'd sworn to stop interfering and stuck to it. Until Lily's Amber Alert."

More questions tumble through Cecilia's mind, fighting for her attention. She settles on one she feels most strongly about. "Why tell me?" *Must want something from me.* "What do you expect from me?" *Need to know your motive.*

"I know I can trust you. You're honest. Fighting crime for the right reasons. I—" I look into her eyes, pleading. "I wish you could read my mind. Trying to find the right words to describe your worst fears, your deepest desires, is impossible." I swallow. "I don't understand how people do it."

Cecilia chuckles. "That makes two of us. I just don't."

Cecilia's mother arrives with several dishes. She places the first dish close to me. "Your favourite."

My mouth waters, smelling the babi-pangang I always order for takeout. Which technically is an Indonesian dish, historically incorporated in the menus of many Chinese restaurants in the Netherlands. The spiced pork strips have a crunchy outside, are soft inside and are generously covered in a red sweet and spicy sauce.

She places three other plates on the table and points to one of them. "Try. It's our specialty. You'll like it!"

One dish I recognise as koe loe yuk, fried meat balls in a sweet-and-sour sauce. The other dishes I've never had before. I smile at Cecilia's mother. "Thank you so much! This feels like a big treat."

I feel Cecilia's embarrassment when her mother retreats.

"Don't be embarrassed. Your mom is so sweet. I wish my mother—" I swallow. "My mother could read minds, and her father as well. He was killed for it, together with his wife. When my mother was killed, it seemed a hit-and-run, but now I'm not so sure anymore. Bernard, the boss of the Syndicate at the time, knew about my mother's mind-reading. I felt my secret was safe with him. But then he died, and it turned out Kurt knew. He's been using me, lying to me. I don't know what to do anymore." I bite my trembling lip. Cecilia seems the type that hates it when people cry. As am I, usually.

Cecilia leans forward and asks, a little more friendly this time, "Why are you telling me now?" *Need to know. Don't use me.*

"I don't want to use you. But I do need you."

CHAPTER FORTY-FIVE

"I thought joining the Syndicate meant I'd be working for a good cause. Instead, I'm using my ability to spy on people so Kurt can blackmail them. I could just leave, but besides making my life difficult, he'll keep his blackmailing schemes up." I wring my hands. "I'd like to expose him somehow. But I'm not sure how."

Cecilia sighs. *Need to tell her. This could work out. Or she's lying, and I blow the whole operation.* She inhales. *Have to risk it.* "I was approached last Monday by a special unit. They're investigating Kurt and the Syndicate. When they realised I'd been talking to you, they involved me. To pump you for information. I'm sworn to secrecy but…" She coughs and continues dryly, "that might not work in this case." *Unfair.* Her eyes bore into mine. "I feel at a disadvantage. You know everything I'm thinking. But you can hide things from me."

"Ha! That's not how I felt when you interrogated me. You seem to sense very well when I'm not telling the whole truth."

"Comes with the job. Still, it's not the same to *think* you know, or to *actually* know."

I return her stern look. "I promise I'll tell you everything. My whole life I've been hiding this essential part of me from everyone. Even from my dad. When Bernard approached me, it felt wonderful to be fully accepted. Now, I just feel used. My natural response would be to run, to go back to hiding who I am from everybody. One part of me really, *really* craves that option. Or, I can try something different and trust the right people with my secret. I owe it to myself to try."

To my surprise, Cecilia's eyes flood, and she blinks several times. *I know all about hiding an important part of yourself.* Irritated, she swats at an escaping tear, slapping herself in the process.

She rolls her eyes and looks at me. We both snicker.

I lean forward, a little more hopeful. "I need help. From the right person."

Cecilia thinks for a moment and then smiles. "Loners like us don't usually ask for help. I'm honoured you trust me." She clears her throat. "The Syndicate, under Bernard's leadership, has been very instrumental in starting the EU, and since then, in managing difficult situations. However, Bernard gave Kurt too much leeway in building a network his way. Evidence of an affair, a mistake, an addiction—he would make it go away. A big circle of politicians owes him. They don't necessarily like him, but they like what he did for them."

I nod. "I met politicians who think of Kurt as 'The Eraser,' someone who can make problems go away. I've witnessed Kurt blackmailing a Spanish politician. And apparently, Kurt sometimes even planted evidence to incriminate someone he didn't like."

Cecilia's eyes cloud over and she frowns. "Wait—you can just read Kurt's mind. Why don't you use that against him?"

I shake my head. "Kurt's the only person I ever met whose mind I can't read. Apparently, he has trained for years to be able to block his thoughts."

Cecilia's shoulders drop. *Really? Strange.*

"Yes, very strange. I can only read his mind if he wants me to. And then, of course, I can't trust what he's thinking. He chooses what thoughts he admits through." I recount how Aaron thought about Kurt training for years to avoid his mind being read. "It's so frustrating… I can't read the mind of the one dangerous person I really need to."

Cecilia slams the table. "Damn. I'd hoped you'd be able to give us more information from reading his mind."

I lean forward. "I noticed he keeps a second phone. Uses it to store information. He might keep all his blackmailing info on there. If we get to that, would that help?"

Her eyes widen. "Definitely! The task force has accessed his personal and Syndicate networks and checked all his linked devices. They found nothing. That makes sense if he uses a separate device that he never connects to any network." *Need to get to that phone. Inform the task force.*

Cecilia's mother hovers around the entrance, glancing at our table with uneaten dishes. To comfort her, I spoon bits of all the dishes on my plate. Cecilia does the same, and we both eat.

After clearing half her plate, Cecilia says, "The task force is specifically worried about Kurt's meddling in the talks the EU started on reshaping the way they work. With the recent changing political world arena, the EU wants to strengthen cooperation between countries and establish a stronger global presence. But for that, they need to work more efficiently, have a better operating apparatus." *Shall I tell her everything? This is all so strictly confidential. Paul Schipper—I could get fired for this.*

"I'll tell you what I know first. Kurt asked me to look into Paul Schipper. To read his mind. I don't understand why. He got me dressed up as a waitress in the same room as Paul Schipper and Greta Beck. Is Schipper the envisioned leader of the EU?"

Cecilia gasps. "I don't think so. But they plan to streamline several EU organisations, and want Schipper to lead that effort. Kurt apparently wants that position himself, so he can 'reform' the EU to his taste and then step up to the role of the new European Prime Minister. His main opposers are Paul Schipper and Greta Beck, who influence some of the others as they're two of the longest serving political leaders in Europe. He apparently dug a lot in their past for dark secrets, but has found nothing yet."

I slap my forehead. "That's why Kurt wanted me to follow Paul on his way to work. He hopes to find something to disgrace him."

We both sink into our thoughts while chewing. When I order takeout, I often consider trying something else but go for babi pangang every time. To be able to try a variety of dishes, instead of just one delicious dish, is a big treat.

Cecilia pushes her empty plate aside. "I'm curious. You said you never told your father?"

"No. I tried, but I seemed to only scare him. Apparently not even my mother told him." I give her a brief description of what I've found at the farmhouse.

Her eyes widen. "Wait, is the farmhouse located in the Hoeksche Waard?"

I nod.

"Kurt uses two employees at the Syndicate for dirty jobs. The task force has put a watch on them since Bernard died. Last weekend, they broke into a farmhouse that sounds like yours."

My jaw drops.

"Their phones are tapped. One of them texted Kurt 'didn't find it.'"

"Kurt's responsible for all that damage?" Heat rises in my face. I spear a piece of koe loe yuk on my fork and pulverise the fried meatball between my molars.

Cecilia places her elbow on the table and rests her head in her hand. She stares for a long time into a space to the left of my head, thinking. After a while, she sits up. "Listen, I'll discuss a plan with the task force. With you, we have a terrific source on the inside. I'll get back to you."

I nod. "Uhm, I would like to ask you another favour." Haltingly, I tell Cecilia about the brother of my mother, recounting my clumsy attempts to narrow the possibilities.

She writes his name down, and the names of the church and the village where my mother left him. "I'll do a search. Should know tonight."

CHAPTER FORTY-SIX

Just when I walk up to Rick's house, the door opens. My jaw drops. Trembling, I sit down on the nearest bench. Cecilia didn't prepare me when she called me back last night and gave me his details. She must have known. Or maybe I didn't give her a chance. I was so excited when she gave me Rick's address, I didn't leave room for her to say anything else.

During the fifteen-minute walk from the train station to his house, I imagined how I would ring the bell and introduce myself. That plan is literally out of the door, that he just came through to stroll to the park close by.

How stupid of me to not even contemplate this possibility. He's in his forties, after all. I steal another glance. The little girl lets go of his hand and climbs on a swing. "Push me, Daddy!"

He smiles and starts pushing.

She squeals with delight. "Higher, Daddy! Higher!"

I do not only have an uncle. I have a sweet little cousin, too...

Rick tells the girl it's enough and stops pushing. The girl mopes for a few seconds, and then asks, "Daddy, are you the uncle of that woman?" She points at me.

Startled, I sit up.

Rick stares at me. *Uncle? Who's that woman?*

I stand up and take a few steps towards them, looking at Rick. *You are the little brother of my mother. You were adopted, right? My name is Kathy.*

Rick frowns, shakes his head like a wet dog. In his mind I read he has heard fragments, but he hasn't understood.

The girl smiles. "Hi, Kathy."

Her father grabs her hand and starts to walk away. He hesitates, stops, and turns around.

I focus on the girl. *Can you hear what others think, too?*

She nods happily, her long dark blond curls joining in the movement.

I'd imagined talking to my uncle, having a reasonable, grown-up conversation, pretending we're not the weirdest related people on earth. Now I just stand here, unable to move.

There really is another person in this world who can read minds. For so long, I thought I was alone, a freak of nature, destined to keep an important part of myself hidden forever. And now... now a cute girl knows what I'm thinking.

The girl pulls away from her father, runs towards me, and hugs my legs. "Don't cry. Please?"

Only then do I feel the moisture on my cheeks.

Rick approaches us. He extends his hand to his daughter, and she places her chubby hand in his, in that automatic, intimate move, common for parents and children everywhere in the world.

Rick studies me. "Why don't we go to our house? We obviously need to talk."

The girl gives me her other hand, and like a family, we walk back to their house.

"Would you like something to drink?" Rick asks, once I've settled on their couch. "I have either strong coffee or tea."

"Strong coffee is perfect."

He disappears into the kitchen. The girl busies herself with two stuffies. I don't even know her name.

She smiles at me. "I'm Isabella."

Right, she reads my mind. "What a beautiful name."

"Thanks." She bounces towards a bookcase and grabs a picture frame, then plants herself next to me on the couch. "This is my mom. She died when I was two. She was very sick."

"Wow, you've got your mom's long curly hair, I see."

"Yes." She stands up and places the frame back.

Rick enters and hands me a cup of coffee. He raises his eyebrows when he lowers himself in a chair opposite of me. "Go ahead."

I glance at Isabella.

Rick shrugs. "I could send her to her room, but she would hear everything anyway."

Isabella nods. "I know what other people think, even if I'm upstairs."

I laugh. "Me too. My mother also knew what people think, but couldn't when there was a wall in between." I look at Isabella and blink. "My mom also died, just before I turned four." I place both my hands around the coffee cup, deriving the courage to go on from the heat. "I just found information about my mother. She was adopted. I never knew anything about her life before. Apparently, her parents were…" I glance at Isabella and clear my throat. "They died."

"In a car fire," Isabella explains to her dad.

I grimace. "Yes. Sorry. You saw that in my mind."

"Of course." Her big, knowing eyes are too old for her age. Eyes like mine.

I look up at Rick. "She had a baby brother and left him outside a church. I believe that boy was you."

"I was indeed found at a church." *Could be just a coincidence. But…* The image of a young woman appears in his mind. She resembles my mother in the picture on my nightstand.

"But?" I plead.

He bows his head. "I was approached by a woman when I was nineteen. She said she was my sister. I…wasn't in a good place at the time." *Had moved on to heroin by then.* "My parents didn't understand my mind-reading. They thought I had ADHD. From when I was six, I was given medication that must have suppressed the mind-reading, because when I turned sixteen and refused to take the meds any longer, the mind-reading came back full force." Rick rubs his neck, as if the memory still gives him a headache. "I thought I was going crazy. By the time your mother approached me, I was…angry with the whole world. For being different. I didn't want anything to do with mind-reading." He looks up, his eyes glistening. "And then this woman approached me. Told me she was my sister. That our father could read minds. I think I yelled at her. Told her to go away…"

Isabella crawls onto her father's lap. She wraps her arms around his neck. Rick plants a kiss on her hair. He continues, "A few weeks later, my parents kicked me out of the house. Couldn't handle my addiction. I don't blame them. I stole money from them, wouldn't show up for days, then come home in a mess." He closes his eyes and leans his head against Isabella's. I feel his embarrassment when he thinks about the pain he caused his adoptive parents. "I lived on the streets for a couple of months. One day, the same woman approached me. She took me to a clinic. I did a program for three months. Later, I found out she paid for my treatment. But the clinic said they didn't have a name. I went back to my parents, finished an education. I hoped the woman would come back."

My words come out in a whisper. "She was dead by then."

He sighs. "I screwed up. In that period of my life, I screwed up a lot."

"What about your mind-reading?"

"At that point, it was completely gone. After a few years, I sensed people's emotions again. But it never fully returned. If I concentrate, I can feel bits and pieces. Nothing like Isabella." He gives her a warm smile, his face lighting up. "Now I wish I still had the ability. For my daughter's sake. I don't want her to feel different from everyone else in the world."

"And now I'm not," Isabella states, beaming at me.

Rick and I talk for hours. Rick in his armchair, me on the couch, and Isabella playing on the floor with figurines from a popular kids show. Isabella's presence in my mind is warm and symbiotic, and it brings back memories of my mother. At three, I didn't understand that special closeness, that full understanding two mind-readers develop together. It's like a tight hug and I don't want to let go.

I show Rick the file my mother put together. He tells me about his childhood, how he struggled, and his concern for Isabella.

Isabella drops a figurine in a toy bed and looks up. "Daddy worries about me. Especially after that time that I told him our neighbour hung up a rope and thought of killing herself. He went over to her and later called someone. She's feeling a little better now."

Rick's jaw tenses. "Isabella shouldn't have to deal with such things. How do you do it?"

"As a kid, I also tried to talk to adults about it. You did well, talking to your dad, honey." I smile at Isabella and feel her satisfaction and pride.

Freely, Isabella talks about other situations she struggles with. For Rick's benefit we talk out loud, but Isabella and I also feel each other's emotions, see the visuals of the other's thoughts, and our interaction accelerates until Rick throws his hands in the air and complains he can't follow us. But he smiles and hugs his daughter.

Isabella asks, "Can aunt Kathy come to judo?"

"Sure." Rick looks at me. "Although I can imagine you have things to do on a Saturday."

I smile. "Nothing better than spending time with the both of you."

Rick makes grilled cheese sandwiches for lunch, which we gobble up at the kitchen table. Then Rick drives us to the gym. In the car, Isabella brags about her accomplishments. "I'm the best in my class. Even with older kids."

I turn and wink at her. "Well, you do have a bit of an advantage, knowing what move they're about to use."

She laughs deviously. "I forgot you know."

In the gym, Rick and I sit down at a quiet spot, away from other parents. Two mothers glance at me, and whisper to each other.

"They think you managed to get a young girlfriend," I inform Rick.

He shrugs. "Doesn't bother me." He glances at me. "Does it bother you? Knowing everything people think about you?"

"Not really. Sometimes it hurts, of course, but I've gotten used to it. It's always been like this."

He sighs. "That's what went wrong for me, I guess. For years, the meds suppressed the mind-reading, so I didn't learn how to deal with it when I was young. When the mind-reading came back at sixteen, I couldn't stand it. Just couldn't deal with the bombardment of all those thoughts." He holds his thumb up to Isabella when she looks up. "She probably felt my misery." His eyes cloud over. "When Mary was pregnant with Isabella, I pleaded with the universe to not curse the baby with my ability." He bows his head. "When Mary got sick, she didn't tell Isabella. Isabella became very caring, would lie down with her, hug her. Her perceptiveness touched Mary. But then I knew."

Isabella throws a concerned look at her father.

I wave at her and think, 'Don't worry about him. We're talking.'

She waves back and joins her group again.

Rick sighs. "I worry a lot about Isabella."

"She seems a happy child."

"For now. But she knows way too much about what adults are thinking. She continuously listens in on the neighbours on both sides. I've been thinking of moving, but it's hard to find a place with hardly any neighbours."

"I think she handles it remarkably well." I touch his arm. "And she has you."

"But what if she grows as confused as I was as a teenager? Is it humanly possible to have this—this weird capability and become a normal person?" He glances at me and smiles sheepishly. "Sorry."

I grin. "I still wonder myself."

Rick grabs my hand. "Will you help us? It would make a huge difference for Isabella, to have an aunt who knows how she feels."

I place my other hand over his. "Of course. I'd love to."

See, they're holding hands.

I roll my eyes at the gossipers.

CHAPTER FORTY-SEVEN

Cecilia jumps in straight away when I pick up the phone. "Hope you don't mind me calling about work issues on a Sunday."

She already struck me as the type with very little private life. Like me.

"No worries. To me, this isn't about work anyway. It's personal."

"Had a long talk with the leader of the task force working on the Syndicate. I got permission to tell you most details. Didn't want to wait until tomorrow. You met Nicole, Aaron's assistant. She works undercover for the Dutch intelligence agency. I think you should know who you can trust." Cecilia inhales. "She's one of us."

She sounds tense. This is the reason why, with anyone other than my dad, I prefer face-to-face conversations. Her tone indicates something's off, and without mind-reading, I won't know what the tension in her voice means. "Are you sure I can trust Nicole?"

Without pausing, Cecilia answers, "Absolutely. She used to work for the police. Moved to the intelligence agency two years ago. Smart. Strong-headed though. Not always easy to work with." Her voice trembles.

"You and I aren't exactly pushover kittens either."

Her laugh sounds strained. "You're right. I'll bet you two get along famously."

Jealousy. That's what I hear in her voice.

"Be careful, Kathy. To the task force's dismay, the German intelligence agency had infiltrated the Syndicate as well, but their informant is missing. They asked for our help, since they haven't been able to contact her the past few days."

My stomach clenches. "You mean Sara? Kurt knows she works for the BND. I warned Sara about that last Monday." The phone almost slips from my trembling hand.

"Around what time Monday?"

"It must've been around 3 P.M. She left immediately. Maybe she went into hiding from everybody? Just to lie low?"

"She would've let the BND know. They can keep her safe. She isn't in her apartment and her phone is offline since Monday afternoon."

I shiver. "This could be my fault. I was the one who told Kurt she worked for the BND. I didn't know then what the BND was."

Cecilia curses. "*Please*, don't tell him anything, even if it seems innocent. Certainly, don't let him know about Nicole!"

"Of course not." But Cecilia is right to be pissed off. My cheeks burn. Sara might be in danger because of me. "I'm sorry. I won't tell Kurt the tiniest detail anymore."

Cecilia sighs. "Although I'd normally agree with that, you might have to go along with him to find out what he's up to."

"But how? I rarely know what he's thinking. I've only been able to read his mind if he wants me to. Or if he didn't know I was close."

"Is he really that good at hiding his thoughts?"

"Yes. His thoughts flare up only occasionally. Like when something unexpected happens, or when he's angry."

"It's harder to repress emotions than thoughts. Try throwing him off balance. Draw him out one way or another. Make him angry. Give him unexpected information. Or sneak up on him."

"That'll be hard when his doormat Jason is around. I don't know if I'm able to get much." Then I think of Sara, and the urgency in her serious face last Monday. And now she's missing. I clear my throat. "I'll try everything I can."

"Thanks." Cecilia pauses, and her tone changes. "Have you contacted your mother's brother?"

"I went to see him yesterday." I smile at the memory of Isabella, and the connection we had on all possible levels.

"And?"

"And it was great. Did you know he has a *daughter*? I have an uncle *and* a cousin."

Cecilia's voice grows softer. "I did see there was a girl registered at his address, with the same last name. I'm glad you got to meet them. Are they mind-readers like you?"

I hesitate. I came out to Cecilia, but whether they want to some day, is up to them.

But before I can say no, Cecilia apologises. "Sorry, none of my business. I'm glad you found them. Did you tell your dad?"

"No. I'm not sure whether he wants to know. We generally don't talk about my mother. It's too painful for him."

"Hmm. I bet he wants to know. Regardless of his pain." For a moment I think Cecilia hung up, until she continues, "You doubted whether it really was an accident?"

I sigh. "Someone hit her, left her to die at the roadside. Probably just a hit-and-run. But since I learned how her parents died, I don't know."

"I can see why you're suspicious. Terrible thing to go through as a child."

"It was. Although you didn't have the idyllic childhood either."

"Oh, it wasn't bad at all. By helping my parents at the restaurant, I got to play grown-up really young. Very useful training for a cop." Under the irony, her voice doesn't seem to have a trace of self-pity. Just matter-of-fact statements. "The eyes of the food safety inspectors almost popped when they visited and were forced to talk to a twelve-year-old. But they got over it. It had advantages too. My teachers complained little about me, as I attended parent-teacher conferences as a translator. Or if they did, I, uhm, modified the translations." She laughs.

"Your parents must be so proud to have a kick-ass detective as a daughter."

"They'd rather have me in the restaurant. And be married, with a husband taking care of me. I guess I'm a bit of a disappointment to them in these areas." Cecilia sounds curt.

I frown. In the restaurant, I'd felt the warmth of Cecilia's mother, as well as her concern for her daughter, but no trace of disappointment. "I don't think you disappoint them. Your mother clearly loves you."

Cecilia sighs. "I guess. Anyway, gotta go. Talk later."

We hang up and I focus again on the drawings I was studying when Cecilia called. Dad still had the blueprints of the farmhouse, and the renovations my mother had done. Some details are not clear, lost in translation by my dad scanning the originals and me printing the scans on a low-resolution printer. But those details don't matter for what I'm trying to do. My mother would be pleased.

CHAPTER FORTY-EIGHT

I stride past Jason's office and halt in Kurt's doorway, without him noticing me. He leans back in his desk chair, sips his precious latte and stares at his screen.

Need to get that Schipper out of the way. I'll manage the Germans. Greta Beck can't keep up the resistance forever once she's alone. There MUST be a scandal in Schipper's past. He can't be squeaky clean as he pretends to be. And otherwise I'll invent one. Who's—? KATHY!

A fierce flash of anger disappears behind the solid wall of focus Kurt pulls up. He slams his cup down.

"Kathy." Through his rigid lips and clenched teeth, my name sounds like a weird sneeze rather than a greeting.

In a chipper voice, I say, "Morning Kurt. Checking in to see if you've got any assignments for me to work on."

"Haven't had time to think about that. Most of my employees are independent enough to know what to do themselves."

"Most of your employees haven't been hired to read other people's minds." I add a cheerful wink.

He narrows his eyes while raising his left eyebrow, deepening the wrinkle above it, illustrating the flash of irritation escaping the defense wall in his mind.

"Listen, Kurt. Why don't you tell me what you want? I've got the feeling you're giving me small assignments without disclosing the ultimate goal. You're really just using my mind-reading, while you could use the rest of my experience as well."

He waves at the door to signal I should close it and only continues when I've done so. "What do you suggest?"

I seat myself in the chair opposite his desk. "Bernard told me the EU is changing the organisation in an attempt to become more effective. I'd like to know what role the Syndicate envisions to play. With my HR experience, I could help."

Kurt studies me, his mouth still a grim line.

I need to up my game. Flattery is the most effective tool for getting people to open up, if applied properly. "The thing is, I don't see you in the same passive role as Bernard, the proverbial backseat. He helped people mask their incompetence, smoothed over the mistakes they made, and then melted back into the shadows. He knew he'd never be able to be in the limelight, make the hard decisions and face the music. Although he had the brains, he didn't have the personality for a big political impact. You do. You can do a better job than most of those politicians you are protecting from the messes they made themselves."

I rub my sweaty hands on my pants. The scary thing is, what I just said is not even untrue. He just completely lacks the ethics and empathy to be a good politician. Or a good human, for that matter.

Kurt relaxes his jaws and shoulders. "Bernard indeed preferred the veiled approach." His focus on me has lost his usual aggressive tinge, but he doesn't reveal any thoughts.

Beads of sweat trickle along my back. "How much use is there for an organisation like the Syndicate, anyway? Let's face it, if politicians could solve their own issues or know how to prevent causing a mess in the first place, they wouldn't need someone to patch things up." I tilt my head and force a trace of admiration into my voice. "As a politician, you wouldn't need outsiders to take care of your problems. You would solve them yourself."

He nods. "Thanks for your confidence."

I search his face for sarcasm. He's not a fool. Maybe he saw through me right away.

I stand up, walk over to the door, then turn to face him. "Apologies for my frankness. I didn't intend to overstep. It's just…the EU has been slow in making progress over the past decades. It would be nice to see them take the lead in global politics."

Although defrosted, Kurt seems to remain sceptical. "I thought you weren't interested in politics, let alone have a passion for it."

I smile. "I didn't. Working here has affected me, I guess. I want Europe to succeed, and with the right leaders, we will." I open the door.

"Close the door and sit down."

Luckily, me and my hopeful expression face the door. I force my face to neutral and walk back to the chair.

Kurt waits until I sit and leans forward, locking eyes. "I couldn't agree more. For years, I've been watching Bernard help fools clean up their messes, close negotiations they didn't have the balls to fight themselves. Most of them are too concerned with pleasing their constituency. Too focused on keeping everyone on board. Sometimes you just have to make hard decisions. Kick some asses about."

He might be right, but politicians who do so gather more enemies than the ones who don't. And although voters say they want the establishment to be shaken up, they are just as quick to turn against someone actually doing that.

Kurt's eyes fire up and dart around the room. "Sometimes people don't know what's good for them. As a politician, you have to make the *best* decisions, not just the ones that please the people. The average Joe just has no clue. You can't listen to them."

I stifle a snort. I'm sure such a speech would go down well with voters.

"The continuous delay because of all the compromising is *sickening* me. The way I drive decisions fast, I'll bring much more wealth and power to the EU." *I'm perfect for this. Have been preparing all my life.*

I clench my fists, nails pinching into my palms. Finally. His feverish passion and thoughts surface in his mind. I keep nodding, afraid to interrupt his flow, his personal crusade glowing and growing.

"Several southern countries support me, you know." *They owe me.* "I just need to convince Germany and the Netherlands, and the remaining countries will go along." *Paul Schipper in the way.* Suddenly, he searches for my eyes with a maniacal blaze in his.

My body jerks back, wanting to run for shelter. I grasp the arm-rests to keep myself seated.

He bangs his fist on the desk, the cup rattles on its saucer. "Help me, Kathy. If you help me get rid of Schipper, I'll make it worth your while. I can make sure your mind-reading is kept a secret. Even better, I'll search the world for other mind-readers so you won't be alone. But I need all the shit on this Schipper guy there is. You are the best person to find out. We just need to get you close to him."

Not trusting my voice, I nod.

CHAPTER FORTY-NINE

The organiser of the legal conference I'm about to attend must've been in an obstinate mood when choosing the venue. The bright colours of the striped circus tent stand out against a grey sky above and a trodden, muddy field below. Two flaps are held to the side and people wearing their standard lawyer attire stream into the colourful tent, which almost seems to fight a bland world by swallowing masses of dark grey and blue suits. For a moment, I envision a wild crowd exiting the tent on the other side in colourful festive clothing, cheerful and dancing.

I shake my head back to reality and enter, my own blue suit blending in. To my surprise, there's no evidence of security at all, despite the prime minister attending in about an hour.

At a table where registration takes place, a man asks, "Your name, please?"

"Kathy van der Laan."

He picks up the list with 'L-O' handwritten on the top. His finger moves down the list and he frowns.

"I might not be on the printed list. I was only added as a participant yesterday afternoon." After my enlightening talk with Kurt in the morning, he bounced into my office in the afternoon to tell me about the great opportunity to get me close to Schipper.

The man's face lights up. "Ah, let me check." He fishes another list from the table with handwritten entries. "Yes, you're on this list." He highlights my name in orange, grabs a blank name tag from a box and hands it over. "My apologies, given the short notice we weren't able to print a name tag for you. Could you please write your name and organisation on this one?" He points to a box with pens, hands me a linen bag with contents, and turns to the next in line.

I scribble 'Kathy' on the tag and pin it on my jacket while I continue deeper into the tent. On the right, the staff pours coffee and tea behind two long tables. I grab a coffee and gulp it down. Filter coffee simply isn't made for savouring each sip.

I dump the cup on an empty table and follow several people through another opening into the inner part of the circus tent. In the middle, they have set a circular wooden stage. On the stage are several tables, chairs and a lectern.

The seats closest to the stage have a dark blue cover, embroidered with 'VIP' in white. The rows behind them are filling up, interspersed with several single seats where people decided not to sit too close together. I pick such a single seat in the first row behind the VIP area, between people chatting with the person on their other side, minimizing the risk of being drawn into a conversation and having to pretend I'm a lawyer.

Several posters on the poles announce the start of the circus performances this weekend, detailing the dates of the shows for the next two weeks. Such smart marketing, to rent out this temporary venue for conferences and meetings. Extra income for the days the tent isn't used while the performers are settling in, and the potential of many parents coming back here next week, boasting to their children about their work conference here.

I browse the contents of the linen bag. A bottle of water, a notebook with a fancy black and gold cover, two pens, a program, and several brochures. According to the program, Paul Schipper will be interviewed at 10 A.M.

During the first half hour, the organiser introduces the program, several speakers and gushes about the esteemed board members having made this possible. He revels about recent developments in European law he's sure we're all excited about.

I study the entrances and exits, and the people in the VIP rows. Kurt said someone in the audience will ask Schipper about the circumstances of some former lover who died, and wants me to read Schipper's first thoughts to that and 'get something useful.'

No one in the crowd stands out. Given Kurt's broad influence, the person asking the question could be a legitimate conference attendee, who owes Kurt a favour.

Just before ten, the organiser raises his voice and his face beams. "Ladies and gentlemen, our first guest is someone from our own community. After finishing law school, he worked as a company lawyer for almost ten years, before becoming a full-time politician. Please give our guest a great welcoming applause. Here is—Paul Schipper!"

The audience claps, and Schipper enters the stage from the right.

The two men shake hands and smile at the audience, posing for a photographer coming out of nowhere and the many cellphones in the air. Social media feeds will soon be flooded with people showing off seeing the PM live, possibly tagging the circus location.

Hopefully, the circus pays their marketing person well, he or she deserves it.

"Thanks for coming, Paul, it's a pleasure to have you here."

Schipper smiles again at the audience. "It's great to be here, amidst like-minded people."

They reminisce about their university days together and their first years as young lawyers. The organiser asks Schipper several innocent questions about the similarities between being a lawyer and prime minister, and the importance of lawyers and laws in general. The glowing contentment and pride of most attendees, hearing someone important praising their profession, fills the tent. After thirty minutes of feel-good chatting, the organiser announces the PM will graciously answer a few questions.

I scan the crowd. Among the many people eager for a brief interaction with the prime minister, boosting their own importance, there is a sharp alertness somewhere to my left. I scan the rows, but nobody stands out.

The first few people ask the usual long, elaborate questions which aren't really questions, trying to maximise their moment in the limelight, showing off their own knowledge and brilliance, rather than genuinely posing a question.

The organiser points to the next person, and the sharp alertness flares up. A young man with dark hair and glasses rises. I'm pretty sure I never saw him at the Syndicate. He clears his throat. "Prime Minister, can you tell us more about the legal implications of being prime minister while police investigated the death of a woman who was rumoured to be your lover? Especially given the fight you supposedly had with her the night she died?"

The tent grows as silent as if it was empty. Everyone holds their breath.

I focus on Schipper, whose smile lies frozen on his face. His shoulders sag.

I should never have... The thought is cut off by a wave of emotions—mostly grief, but it seems laced with guilt. He shivers.

The organiser shakes off his shock. "My apologies, ladies and gentlemen. Although the intricacies of the legalities around a prime minister are interesting, the major topics of this conference are European versus Dutch law. I propose we move on to the next question about this topic." He scans the crowd, desperate for a familiar face. *Need to find the right person for an innocent question.* I follow his search in his mind. His gaze rests on someone behind me. *Erik! Yes, he's perfectly harmless.* He points over my head. "Yes, sir, go ahead."

During the next few minutes, the organiser answers the question by digressing and distracting, until Schipper chimes in. A few other questions and answers follow, and then the organiser cordially thanks Schipper for coming. Schipper leaves at the back of the stage instead of past the seats to the right where he came in.

Despite the attempt by the organiser to move on to the next item on the agenda, the tent buzzes. Even though amplified through the microphone, the organiser's voice drowns in the excited chatter. I check the thoughts and talk around me.

"That was a bold question..."

"I'd say stupid. Career limiting move."

"I'm sure Schipper had no part in her accident. Must've been hard on the fellow to have all those rumours circulating."

"Always thought that Schipper looked guilty. Truth will never come out, though. He's got ways to hide the truth."

The organiser's jaw sets. He yells into the microphone for silence. In the three minutes it takes for the noise to die down, I sneak out and leave the tent. Just in time to see a car leave. Schipper's presence in the car stands out, rather from his depressed mind than his silhouette. *I should never have... It wasn't worth it...*

The car, and Schipper's mind, are swallowed by busy traffic. Well, at least I'll be honest when I tell Kurt I got nothing. But I must admit I'm curious.

CHAPTER FIFTY

I close the front door behind me and groan. I trudge down the stairs, scolding myself. Look who's calling herself an early riser, but barely manages to leave at 5.45 A.M. for a meeting.

In the street, the city mocks me. Rotterdam buzzes with masses of hardworking people in all sorts of jobs at all sorts of hours. Though the streets are empty compared with their state two hours later, plenty of people are out. Some people seem to return home from a night shift, others hasten to a bus stop to start their workday. Many apartments have lights on, and the shadows on the curtains are eating breakfast, or getting dressed.

I stifle a yawn and step aside for a black labradoodle, tongue hanging out, stuffing his wet nose against my other hand. No matter at what time I'm out, there always seem to be people walking their dog. The owner is in a tired, almost thoughtless state, but the curly dog's cheerfulness lifts my mood. A little.

By the time I reach the police station, my blood circulation is up and running and has cleared the fog in my brain. I scan the area. Cecilia might already be waiting for me.

The window of a white compact car whirrs down. I peer through the opening and Cecilia reaches over to open the passenger door. I slide into the seat next to her.

She pulls out and concentrates on navigating the narrow streets. When we've reached the highway, she asks, "Are you up for meeting Paul Schipper in person?" She adds dryly, "Legitimately this time?"

"*Meeting* him?" I look at Cecilia. The streetlights flash over her face, on and off, on and off. She's one with the steering wheel, exuding confidence. Hopefully, some of it wears off on me by the time we arrive.

"We first meet with the task force leader, Tony."

"What did you tell him about me?"

"He doesn't know about your mind-reading. He just knows Kurt is digging into Schipper's past to slander him and that you're partially aware of Kurt's plans. We believe Schipper himself needs to be involved."

I massage the knots between my shoulders and neck. Not everyone is as morally sound and trustworthy as Cecilia. If I don't tell them I can read minds, how do I explain why Kurt uses me to find incriminating info on Schipper? If I do tell them, how do I ensure not ending up burning in a car like my grandparents?

CHAPTER FIFTY-ONE

"We need evidence to prove Kurt is holding several politicians on a leash." Tony widens his stance, folds his arms, and stares at a whiteboard with the names of the politicians believed to be under Kurt's influence. *Depressingly long list. Two presidents, one prime minister and numerous high-ranking politicians. This guy has spent decades preparing.* He swivels his head towards me. "Cecilia said you've seen Kurt using a second phone but he's secretive about it?"

I nod and open my mouth to respond, but Tony cuts me off. He's the type who needs to share his own train of thought before he's able to take in someone else's. "We haven't been able to find any registration for a second phone for him. It's likely he stores information on there. My guess it's about his blackmailing schemes."

Cecilia leans against the opposite wall of Tony. "You don't think he has that information stored elsewhere, besides that second phone?"

Tony runs his hand through his hair. "At least not on the servers of the Syndicate, nor on his personal computer at home. We've hacked into everything we could access, but I would expect that, besides that phone, he has several copies. It's his way of controlling people within the EU, and it's his insurance policy if things go wrong. We need to get our hands on it."

In a friendlier tone, Cecilia asks me, "Do you think you can find out where he stores it all?" *By getting him to think about it?*

I smile at her, to let her know I've heard her thought. "I'll try, but it won't be easy." So far, Kurt dropped the guard on his mind only once.

Tony's eyes are on me. *Don't understand why Kurt works with someone who's clueless about politics. She could be spying for Kurt. She was the one telling him about Sara... We can use her to get at Kurt, but prepare to cut her loose if needed.*

I try the terrible machine coffee we picked up before we started the meeting and wince. Tony sees me as a pawn in his investigation. A pawn to sacrifice if necessary. I can't blame him. Sara weighs on my mind too.

Cecilia says, "What if we frame Kurt for trying to blackmail Schipper in a situation we control? Kathy could feed Kurt information about Schipper, and if Kurt bites, we expose him."

Tony frowns. "Then we still don't know what power he holds over others."

Cecilia shrugs. "Once he's the new EU President, it will be a lot harder to get at him. We're running out of options."

I stare at the floor. Whether we focus on finding the compromising data without leaking it, or on framing him by feeding him false information, I'll be a major part of their plan. If Kurt finds out I'm working against him, I'll be in deep shit. On the other hand, the way Kurt uses me now, I'm in deep shit already.

All three of us jerk up when there's a knock on the door. A police officer comes in, followed by Paul Schipper. Even at this early hour, he looks crisp and well-groomed, with the trademark kindness already in his eyes. He's holding a decent take-away cup of coffee. I wipe my mouth to make sure there's no drool leaking out. See, that's why he became Prime Minister, as he's smart enough to buy a decent brew before entering a building with criminal tasting machine coffee.

Tony flushes. "Hello. Mr. Schipper. I'm Tony Dekker, the leader of this task force."

Schipper smiles. "Please, call me Paul."

"Right, right." Tony smiles nervously. *Nicer in person than I'd expected.* "This is Cecilia, my colleague, from the Rotterdam force."

Schipper nods to Cecilia, and she nods back, smiling but with her arms crossed. From her thoughts, it's clear she's not as easily impressed as Tony. *Turns the charm on, but let's see how useful he really is.*

"And this is Kathy, an, er, informant, working for the Syndicate."

Schipper blinks twice. *Hey, don't I know her? Those eyes. That lonely, hunted look.*

I raise my hand, not trusting my voice, and gaze at his coffee. Talking about Kurt, being scrutinised by Tony, Schipper reading my eyes too well—it's too much to handle before I've had my proper caffeine shot.

Tony places his feet wide and clears his throat. *Need to show Paul we're useful. Get him and his own EU investigation unit to cooperate with us. Better yet, give me the lead over them.* "We were discussing Kurt's ambition to become the new leader of the EU and his tactics to get there."

Schipper takes a seat on the other side of the table, eyes still on me. "Right. We've had two complaints about those 'tactics.' But no hard evidence, and no one's willing to testify." He leans forward. "Kathy, I understand you work for him." *Can we trust her? I'm sure I've seen her before. She could be spying for him. Need to be sure.*

I force myself to look at him. "Yes. Bernard, his boss, hired me, but he died before I started working at the Syndicate."

Schipper raises his eyebrows. "So you've only worked for Kurt, what, two weeks now?"

"Three."

"That's short." *She can't have found out much in three weeks. Experienced detectives have worked on Kurt for years and failed.*

I clear my throat. "It's short, but Kurt's showing his true colours now that he took over from Bernard. He's eager to implement changes."

Schipper nods. *He seems to have gotten bolder indeed. Maybe he's sending her to spy on us.* "Right."

"Kurt seems to think you're in his way, with you leading some EU committee. Maybe even as a candidate for the new EU job, which he wants himself."

"For years he has wanted to re-enter the political arena. But he lacks the skills. I don't see why he would think he qualifies."

"As I understand it, he sees the EU as the next world leader, now that the US has lost that position. The new EU President would be the most important person in the world. He wants that role, no matter what."

Schipper rolls his eyes. "That sounds like Kurt. But it's not the intention of the EU to play 'follow the leader.' We need the world to cooperate and use each other's strengths, not to have a strong dependence on one country. Take the 2008 financial crisis. You could say it started as the Wall Street flu, but it caused a worldwide financial pandemic. We shouldn't create a new situation where one country, or region, can be the single domino tile that topples over the rest." He winks. "Not even if it's our own European Union."

"That's a noble viewpoint."

"It's the sensible viewpoint. Long term, we all benefit from collaborative cohesion instead of domination. History has proven again and again that individuals or groups who want to dominate the world, or even just their own geographical area, don't get to enjoy long-term success." Schipper drums his fingers on the table. "We aim to simplify and strengthen the EU by combining the European Commission and Council. But first, we need a major clean-up. We're setting up an anti-corruption EU committee. Kurt doesn't want that to succeed, because he digs up dirt on politicians himself, to use against them. I've spoken to several politicians who've been approached by Kurt, two of them received blackmail threats. We need to take Kurt down." He rubs his forehead.

Tony still stands with his feet wide and his arms crossed. "With Kathy on the inside, we could think of a way to frame Kurt."

Schipper sips his coffee. "It would help to get evidence of his blackmailing games." *But how can we know she won't double-cross us?*

I need to win his trust, but how? A whiff of his coffee creeps across the table. I close my eyes and sniff, light-headed. "We need to draw Kurt out, in a bold way." I glance up at Cecilia. "I'd prefer to talk it over with Paul Schipper alone, though."

Tony snorts. "No way. I'm heading this task force, *I'm* the one making the decisions here."

Schipper smiles at Tony, but his eyes harden. *Pompous fellow. Doesn't like me setting up a similar task force in the EU. Didn't get results in the last two years, needs to move over. Whether it dents his ego or not.*

I lean towards Schipper. "Kurt's out to frame you. I'd rather discuss that with you alone."

Schipper squints his eyes. *Shit, what does he have on me?* Then he relaxes and smiles again. *Better get to the bottom of this without unnecessary witnesses.* He nods to Tony. "Okay, I'll hear Kathy out. Will update you afterwards."

"But—" Tony protests. *No way! I'm working on this for years and when it gets exciting, I will not be left out!*

Cecilia steps towards Tony and touches his elbow. "Let them have their talk."

Tony shakes his head. "You can talk with us present. I need to be in the know."

Cecilia turns to Schipper. *Need to mitigate. Kathy won't talk with Tony in the room.* "I can imagine you two need to discuss details together, but the task force has to be involved in any plan to catch Kurt."

Schipper nods.

Cecilia presses Tony's elbow. "Let's step out for a short while."

Tony presses his lips into a line, but walks with Cecilia towards the door.

I glance around the room. Is this an interrogation room, with cameras or a one-way window, where they will listen in?

Cecilia seems to understand, as she looks at me and thinks loud and clear: *You and Schipper can talk without us listening in.*

CHAPTER FIFTY-TWO

The door closes behind them and instead of relieved, I feel nervous. After all, I'm alone with the political leader of the Netherlands, a guy who I respect but have spied on. I drink the rest of my coffee in one gulp. Maybe we could start with some small talk. "You were smart, getting a coffee outside. The machine coffee here is awful."

"Yeah." Schipper studies me. *Now where have I seen her before?*

"What kind of coffee do you prefer? I usually take a double espresso." I feel Schipper's irritation and cringe. Small talk never has been my strength.

"How did you get mixed up in this?"

I take a deep breath. Here we go. "I presume you know Bernard, the previous Syndicate leader."

He nods. *Useful, years ago. Syndicate long outlived its purpose.*

"Bernard approached me because my mother used to work for him years ago. He suspected I had the same unique ability as she had. I read minds." I spread my fingers on the table, and add, "I know what people think."

Schipper laughs, incredulous. "You mean, like a psychic?" *Jeez, had not expected her to be one of these vague people.*

"Not like a psychic. I hear thoughts word for word. And I'm not vague. It's real."

He sits up, taken aback. *Did she say vague? Like I was thinking?*

"Sorry about that, it must feel threatening. I always kept silent, but Bernard knew because my mother was a mind-reader as well. And then Kurt found out and tried to use me." I look down. "Kurt wants me to spy on you. Two weeks ago in Brussels, at the meeting between you and Greta Beck, I was the one serving coffee and tea." My cheeks flush. "I also followed you twice while you biked to work. And yesterday, I attended your session during the lawyer's conference."

"You *followed* me?" *The nerve! My God, what did she get on me?*

I glance at him. He's horrified. My eyes sink to his coffee cup on the table. "I'm really, really sorry. If it's any consolation, I hardly told Kurt anything. He told me it was to help the EU progress. And he promised me information about my mother, who died when I was three. Still, I should never have done it." It sounds lame, even to my own ears.

Schipper thunders, "Kurt is a rotten apple. If you truly can read minds, you should've known." *Bullshit story. Did Kurt really think I'd fall for that?*

I look Schipper in the eye. "Kurt is the first person I've met whose mind I can't read. He has found a way to not think when I'm around. Apparently, he trained for years."

Oh sure. Kurt the superhuman. He's so into himself that he thought I'd actually believe this.

My throat constricts. "Really, I'm not sent here by Kurt. I want to take him down as much as you do. He has threatened to tell other people about me. And as you can see for yourself, knowing about my ability won't go down well with most people. I've been hiding my mind-reading all my life. My family members have been hunted down for their skills. I don't want to end up like them."

There are more? Really? Imagine the possibilities... No, it's simply not possible.

"The possibilities aren't as great as you think."

Schipper jerks back. *Unnerving.*

"You see, thoughts are not evidence. And apparently, it's possible to block thoughts. At least that's what Kurt seems capable of."

Schipper narrows his eyes. *Impossible. She could have deduced that I'm worrying about what I thought. She's just very empathic.*

I roll my eyes. What a stubborn guy. But I guess being gullible doesn't make one prime minister. "Let me repeat your thoughts to prove it. 'Impossible. She could have deduced that I'm worrying about what I thought. She's just very empathic.'"

A deep red creeps up his neck. *Oh shit. This is embarrassing. What did I think of? The meeting with Greta was all business. But when I biked to work—wait, the interview yesterday—*

I raise my hands, palms towards Schipper. "I didn't get anything embarrassing. Really. I don't want to know. Besides, I'd never tell on you."

He springs to his feet, his chair falling over backwards. "You better not." He raises his finger and points at me. "I don't want to see you in my vicinity ever again." He strides out of the room and bangs the door behind him.

I bow forward and lean my head in my hands. See, that's why I shouldn't tell people. Cecilia was an exception to the rule. Schipper ran away, while I told him I wanted to help. I'd expected someone of his stature to remain calm. To face the situation. If Schipper reacts this way, other people's responses will be much worse.

The door opens and Tony storms in. *Should have stayed. My task force! Should never have allowed her to fuck things up.* For the second time in a minute, an angry man points a finger at me. "What did you say to Paul?"

I clench my teeth. "We discussed how much Kurt loves him."

Tony snorts. "He rushed out of the building. Didn't even want to talk." He stares me down.

I stare back. "He made that choice. I didn't tell him to run." And yes, I feel guilty. But not towards Tony the bulldog.

He raises his hands to the ceiling. "Oh sure. You just delayed an important investigation, I don't know how nor why, and you blame him?"

I get up and walk towards the door. "I really do want to help. With or without Schipper."

Tony steps aside to let me out. "Cecilia went after him. Let's hope she can calm him down. But I doubt it." *That'll teach her to bring in unqualified informants. Suits me. I'll bring Kurt down with the task force. Much better.*

I halt and look Tony in the eye. The next words hardly ever leave my mouth, but this time, I know they're true. "I can't stop Kurt on my own." I swallow. "Neither can the task force. We need each other. I'll get in touch with Cecilia to discuss the next steps."

On my way out, I check my phone. Three missed calls from Kurt.

CHAPTER FIFTY-THREE

Outside, rain falls steadily, and a faint rumble in the distance warns for worse. But finding shelter isn't a priority right now. At least the deserted streets offer privacy.

After eight rings, Cecilia's voicemail kicks in and I hang up. Maybe she's still talking to Schipper. Or she's mad at me. By now, we were supposed to have a plan. If I don't feed Kurt something on Schipper, he might try framing him another way and we've lost our chance to be in control.

I sit down on a bench with my head in my hands, and feel the water soak into the seat of my pants. Serves me right. Why did I want to tell Schipper everything? My whole life I've been able to get by with lying. One more lie wouldn't have hurt.

I take a deep breath. Moaning about it won't help. I heave my cold butt up and set off in the Syndicate's direction. At a coffee stand, I allow myself the first decent coffee of the day, to go. Sipping, I drag my feet towards the Syndicate.

When the phone rings, my heart lifts. Until I see Kurt's name on the display. I hover over the red button, but decide it's better to let it go to voicemail automatically.

There's just one person I want to talk to right now. I dial Cecilia again. This time, she picks up on the first ring.

"Hi, Kathy." My stomach sinks at the guardedness in her voice.

"I'm so sorry, Cecilia, for messing up. I told Schipper about my mind-reading. You responded so well to it. But Schipper, he…" My voice quivers and I swallow.

A click of a door is followed by her voice, much warmer now. "Had to get into an empty room. Tony was on my back as soon as

I returned. Listen Kathy, *you* didn't mess up. You've been honest, with perfectly good intentions. Schipper messed up. I told him not to be a pussy."

"You…what?"

"He ordered me to stay away from you, claimed you are dangerous. I told him how I got to know you. How you've used your skill to good use in the past, and how you've agreed to help bring Kurt down. How special he is for being the second person *ever* you told your secret to yourself. And how he's frustrating the process by not being able to overcome the shock of finding out something unusual."

I choke on the coffee. After coughing a few times, I croak, "Wow. How did he take it?"

"At first, not well. But he's the type to see reason."

"Will he, uhm, talk to others about my mind-reading, you think?"

"I asked him not to do that, to which he agreed. To be fair, I think he wouldn't because he's afraid of you, of what you may have read in his mind. He won't risk you disclosing his secrets by putting you on the spot. I'd say you're squared off for now."

I frown. "I don't know anything embarrassing about him."

Cecilia chuckles. "He doesn't know that. I told him Kurt expects you to come back with incriminating evidence."

"Definitely. Something on the death of a rumoured former lover."

"That's not gonna happen. Schipper was adamant we wouldn't use anything from his private life. But he offered another idea. In the past years, several companies needed government support. Schipper suggested you could tell Kurt he's meeting the CEO of one of those companies about additional government funding. And that Schipper seems to be getting something in exchange."

I frown. "Isn't that even riskier for him?"

"Might be, but that's his problem. You can tell Kurt, Schipper is meeting with the CEO of Van Rijn Offshore tomorrow at 8 P.M. in hotel Des Indes. Kurt will for sure try to get evidence. But, uhm, try not to let him talk you into listening in on them."

I snort. "As if I want to." Then Cecilia's careful choice of words sinks in. "It's probably Schipper who doesn't want me there. Right?"

"We better keep you out of his vicinity for the time being. Kath, I'm sorry, he's a bit of a pussy in that regard. But I guess he's got a lot to lose."

I snort. "He's not the only one."

"Yeah. Take care of yourself. You're a brave girl."

I smile. Cecilia ends the call before I can thank her.

A ping sounds. Kurt has not only tried to call but has texted as well. 'Got busy signal so you still seem to know how a phone works. Call me!'

Finally, we're getting somewhere. Without my usual hesitation, I enter the revolving door of the Syndicate building.

CHAPTER FIFTY-FOUR

White room. Where am I? What…why can't I feel my body? Why is he coming at me with a syringe??

My body freezes at the exact time the elevator stops on the third floor. I stumble out, gagging, sweating and feeling cold at the same time. Whose thoughts were those? What's happening? With my hand pressed on my chest, I attempt to steady the frantic boom-boom, boom-boom inside, as if the heart wants to jump out and rescue this person. My left hand seeks the wall. If only the wall could answer where this terrified mind can be found. I scan along all the minds I can sense. Among the usual stream of thoughts, mild emotions and feelings, nothing intense stands out.

The image of a rabbit with inflamed eyes swims into my head. As a sensitive teenager, I'd been a member of an organisation fighting animal cruelty. To wring out donations, they used to send horrible pictures, like the effect cosmetics testing had on animals. Based on the glossy images on rich paper, emphasizing the inhumane conditions the animals lived in, I'd imagined the animals' feelings. They were exactly like I just experienced.

In the bathroom, I run cold water over my wrists. Watching water flowing from the faucet, over my hands, into the sink and down the drain hole slows down my breathing. I turn the faucet off and grab a greyish rough paper towel. Funny. Such a shady, selfish place as the Syndicate making an environmental statement by using recycled paper towels.

I take another look in the mirror. *Come on Kathy, go get something from Kurt.*

In the hallway, I pass Jason, who for once is too absorbed by his thoughts to pay attention to me. *Schipper seems determined to take out Kurt. The meetings next week will be crucial. We'll have to get at least two out of the three over to our side. Have to dig deeper into the financial failure of that Italian's previous business. If we can get anything tangible, he'll have to see it our way.*

I grit my teeth. Not if I can help it. We need to remove this drunk driver from the road before he can cause additional damage. I inhale and step into Kurt's office.

Kurt looks at his watch and thunders, "Did you take half the day off?"

"Alarm didn't work, sorry." I glance at my watch. It's 10 A.M. Hardly half a day, but Kurt might not be in the mood to discuss semantics right now.

"Why didn't you call me back earlier?" In a flash of irritation, he can't stop himself thinking *Incompetent bitch!* Then his intent focus returns.

"I preferred to tell you in person. I could hardly tell you while being on a busy train."

His eyes narrow. "Tell me about Paul."

"Which of the questions was asked by your guy?"

Kurt crosses his arms. "What do you think? Do you mean to say the public asked several provoking questions?"

"Well, no. I guess you mean the question about the death of some woman."

"Not just 'some woman'! A lover, who died just after they'd been reported to have seen each other."

I shrug. "I didn't get anything. His mind closed down when he was asked the question."

Kurt raises one eyebrow. We hold a staring contest, both trying the cops' technique of silence.

Kurt asks, "And?"

I shrug. I should feed the information to him casually. "And nothing. There wasn't anything, I swear. He closed down and only had thoughts about work."

Kurt's stare intensifies. "You expect me to believe you?"

I study Kurt. Until now, I didn't see through it, but he has that wary distrust of people, a sign of what some of us in HR call 'being empathically challenged.' I first noticed it in a fellow student. The young woman only saw things from her own perspective. She didn't understand why others behaved differently than she would, and therefore was disappointed in them, over and over again. Over the years, misunderstandings piled up, and she soured into a cynic, believing people couldn't be trusted and rallied against her. Her acidic radiation of distrust affronted people, causing them to avoid her, increasing her conviction the world was hostile.

In my various jobs I've met more such people, ranging from early to advanced stages of steering towards a lonely life, blocking any attempt by other people who reach out. It's sad when people ruin their own lives and don't realise it.

Kurt slams down his fist. "Am I talking to a wall?"

He's definitely beyond an advanced stage. He can only be contained. I sit up. "I'm sorry. I actually might have heard something interesting. Paul seemed excited about a meeting tomorrow with the CEO of Van Rijn Offshore."

"A meeting? About what?"

"Something to do with government funding. At first, it sounded normal to me, but his excitement about the meeting stood out."

Kurt tries to regain his focus, but his eagerness to process the information wins. *Van Rijn Offshore? About to go bust.* "That company has received more than their normal share of government funding already. Paul should be careful if he proposes pumping more money into them, as the parliament won't be too forthcoming."

"Schipper seemed to think he would succeed if he could negotiate the right terms with Van Rijn. He seemed excited about what it could mean for him personally."

A hungry gleam appears in Kurt's eyes. *Bribe? Personal favour?* "What do you mean, personally?"

"I don't know. He was in a celebratory mood though, thinking about it, before the interview started."

"Where would he meet this CEO?"

"Apparently Hotel Des Indes. At 8 P.M. tomorrow."

Have to be in on the conversation. Then Kurt manages to control his thoughts again, by focusing on me with an intense satisfaction.

I shiver.

"Did you follow him after the interview?"

"No."

"Why not? I want as much on this guy as possible."

"You didn't say I should follow him again. I didn't want to run the risk of him starting to recognise me."

"Next time, do everything you can to get me information. You need to anticipate what I need from you."

"Like, reading your mind?" I bite my lip. Challenging Kurt is the stupidest thing I can do right now.

His eyes become slits. "You know what I mean."

I nod and leave.

On the way to my office, I listen for thoughts. There's the normal steady murmur of people working in several offices along the hallway, but nothing like the terror I felt exiting the elevator earlier.

CHAPTER FIFTY-FIVE

Early Friday morning, I walk to the restaurant of Cecilia's parents. They don't open until 11 A.M., but Cecilia asked me to meet for breakfast and an update.

Her mother's heart flutters when I enter, happy that Cecilia found someone. That seems a little over the top, even if Cecilia is a loner. Although I can never be sure what people think in a language I don't understand. Cultural differences complicate interpreting feelings in another language.

Cecilia sits at the same table as last time. She jumps in right away. "Last night, Paul Schipper met with the CEO of Van Rijn Offshore. Only cops and security people were around the meeting room at the time. We didn't see Kurt or any people we didn't know."

My shoulders tense. "He didn't take the bait?"

Cecilia shakes her head. "Not that we can tell." She taps her fingers on the table. "But just in case Kurt had a different way of listening in, Schipper and his friend the CEO put up a show, discussing a 'favour.'"

I sigh. "What if Kurt did record it, and he decides to bring it out in the open straight away? Instead of first trying to blackmail Paul Schipper?"

"Not his usual modus operandi. We took precautions. Paul Schipper and the CEO discussed the strategy at the police station yesterday early evening, with members of the task force and even a journalist we trust."

"But if Kurt doesn't respond at all, we have to start over."

Cecilia nods. "Check with Kurt this morning. Try to find out whether he did something with it." She shifts in her chair. "We tracked several of Kurt's confidantes to know who showed up in the hotel's vicinity. None of them did. But one, who was part of raiding your farmhouse, has been to the location of your uncle's house last night."

"Oh shit." I get out my phone, fumbling, and nearly drop it on my plate. I dial Rick's number twice, and both times get voicemail straight away. My voice trembles. "Most people wouldn't pick up at 6:30 A.M., I guess."

Cecilia watches me. "I didn't tell the task force. I didn't want them to ask questions about your family. But if you and Rick agree, I can have a team watching their house." *Especially now that we've found Sara...* A mixture of fear and anger flows through Cecilia.

I sit up. "What about Sara?"

Cecilia clears her throat. "The BND found her in her apartment yesterday afternoon. Alive, but..." She swallows. "They found a few strange holes in her skull. For the rest, she seems physically okay. But she can hardly talk, and seems to have no memory of what happened. Not even of who she is. She was transported to a hospital in Germany."

Eyes wide, I stare at Cecilia. This is my fault. "It must have been Kurt." I hardly recognise my own voice. "And now Rick doesn't answer my phone. Shit." I put my head in my hands. "What am I going to do?"

Cecilia places her hand over mine. "I know you've always relied on yourself. But you don't have to do this alone."

My eyes burn.

Cecilia stands up. "Let's drive over there."

CHAPTER FIFTY-SIX

I stare down at the stain I just made on the sidewalk. Mostly coffee, mixed with bile probably.

Rick's house is dark. Nobody answered the door. I don't feel any presence inside. They should've been awake by now.

In the car, Cecilia's on the phone with someone in the task force. I open the door and slide into the passenger side.

Cecilia's face is drawn. "No, he doesn't have to pick Veenstra up. He should just watch until someone gets home and contact us for further instructions. And have Veenstra's number tracked. I'll text the number right away." She hangs up and looks at me.

I send her the number, and she forwards it. I wring my hands. "Something's terribly wrong. They should be home, having breakfast, getting Isabella ready for school."

"Do you want to wait for them here? You could wait together with the cop they're sending."

"Somehow, I think they won't come. Could you bring me to the Syndicate?"

Cecilia starts the car. "Better come with me to the task force."

"No. I need to find out what Kurt's up to. Our best chance to get additional information is for me to get something out of Kurt." I slam my fist on my thigh. "We're getting nowhere. We need to break this open." The image of Isabella's smile blurs my vision.

"Right." Cecilia drives fast, weaving through the morning traffic. When she pulls into the street of the Syndicate, Cecilia receives a call on her car kit.

A male voice jumps right in. "The number you just sent is offline since yesterday evening. Maybe switched it off during the night.

We'll let you know when it comes online."

I grab the door handle.

Cecilia places a hand on my other arm. "Are you sure about this?"

I nod and exit the car, anxiety morphing into anger. This must all be Kurt's doing. But if I storm in and blame Kurt, he'll have the upper hand and will be able to disguise his thoughts. I need to stay calm for Rick's and Isabella's sake.

The building's emptiness is emphasised by the single sound of my echoing footsteps in the main hall, the solitary elevator ride, the vacant hallways on the third floor. Not even Jason peeking around his door to see who exits the elevator.

I check my watch. It's early, but not that early.

I walk to Kurt's office. Another empty space. I run along the full corridor. Every office is empty. In the last room, the one where Jason and Kurt like to stow me away, is a note. 'Kathy, meet Aaron on the second floor when you get here. I'll join you soon. K.'

What's this? I don't want Aaron around when I'm grilling Kurt. But do I have a choice?

I rub my forehead. Aaron and the second floor scare me. Part of my instinct says to run away. But I've run away so often. I can't run from Isabella and Rick.

"Kathy?" I jump at the sudden appearance of Jason in the doorway. "Kurt asked you to come to the second floor."

"I can't go there with the limited access you gave me, remember?"

"I'll get you there." He walks me to the elevator, holds his card against the black little square and gestures for me to push the button for the second floor. While the doors close, Jason's sarcastic little goodbye wave makes me nauseous again. Yeah, no lost love here as well, asshole.

My phone pings to announce another text message. Cecilia. 'Several syndicate employees told to stay home. Be careful.'

That explains the emptiness. Something's going on. My finger hovers over the ground floor button. But I have to stay. I need to know about Rick and Isabella.

I pull my hand back when the elevator stops. The doors open, and Aaron stands outside, his hands on his back. *There she is. Now act!*

I feel adrenaline surge through him, while he retrieves a taser from behind his back and pushes it against my arm. A sharp jolt spreads through my body and my breath falters. I try to back away, but Aaron keeps pushing. My legs buckle. I feel sweat and chills at the same time, the floor rushes towards me fast, then a blunt pain spreads from above my right ear through my skull. Focus, Kathy… take a few breaths. Where's Aaron? I can't find his mind…

Wheels whirr towards me. I turn my head and a desk chair rolls into view. Then Aaron's hands slide under my armpits, pulling me up. I should leave now. Why won't my legs work?

Aaron hoists me on the chair and pushes me into the hallway, past the office. I'll probably finally find out what lies behind the other doors. Another wish granted.

The first door on the left looms closer. Aaron bumps my knees into the door, opening it. The room has no windows but is far from dark, lit by a round harsh ceiling light, revealing a bare space apart from two metal framed single beds, one against the left wall and the other against the right. A motionless body occupies the one on the left.

First, Aaron's breath brushes past my right cheek, before he articulates, "Can you see him Kathy? Can you see Rick?"

I try moving my lips, to ask for Isabella, but I only hear a gurgle and feel a sliver of saliva escaping the corner of my mouth.

Aaron seems to understand, though. He pushes me into the hallway again, into the second door on the left, again opening the door with my knees. This one has a bunk bed, with Isabella lying on the lower one. Like her dad, she's strapped to the bed and is motionless. The worst fear leaves my stomach. Dead bodies don't need to be restrained. They're still alive.

Aaron's breath precedes him again, and he says with emphasis, "And now for your accommodation."

We enter the hallway again, this time going through the third door on the left. This door seems harder on my knees. I wish he would stop using me as a door opener.

The room is the same as Rick's. I feel Aaron's hands under my armpits. My lips try to tell him off, but they're still useless dry pieces of skin. He drags me onto the bed and I feel a pressure on my legs, arms, and chest. The clicks of clasps being shut make clear I won't be able to leave this bed on my own terms.

"Tucking me in?" My words slur, but given Aaron's rolling eyes, he heard me fine.

He reaches behind him and when he turns, a syringe glistens in his hand, a harsh shape against the single bulb hanging from the ceiling.

"Sleep. I want your brain nice and rested for later."

Aaron leaves the room, taking the chair with him. I give in to the darkness.

CHAPTER FIFTY-SEVEN

Where am I? What happened?

Still half asleep, it takes me a second to realise those thoughts aren't mine. But whose are they? And this bed, why is it so hard? Where's my comfy duvet?

Oh my. I hardly dare open my eyes. Did I end up in someone else's bed? Haven't done that since I was nineteen. What the—

Who's that? Female. Isn't it that mind-reader? Oh shit.

I turn my head and open my eyes. On a bench about a metre away lies the last man I'd expect to be in one room with. "You? What are you doing here?"

Schipper scowls. "Why don't you tell me." *No coincidence, being put in a room with her.*

My head hurts. A stupid bulb shines into my eyes. I wriggle to sit up, but my arms won't move. I look down at the unwilling bastards.

Right. Aaron strapped me in. I'm at the Syndicate. I close my eyes but the harsh light still shines through my eyelids, although now with a reddish tone.

"Why are you here?" Fear and anger grow in Schipper's mind until the fear deals with itself by fuelling the anger. A common strategy from the brain in an attempt to regain control.

"I don't know. Aaron, who's heading The Syndicate's research department, locked me up here." I turn my head as far as I can to scan the room. Looks like just me and Schipper here. "How did you get here?"

"I'm not sure. I was on my way to meet..." *should keep Milou out of this.* He jerks his head towards me. *Oh shit, she already heard that.* His hostile feelings towards me increase. "I was on my way to meet someone. Last thing I remember, I parked my car in a parking garage and walked to the elevator. Then I woke up here. What's happening?"

"I don't know."

Schipper snorts. *Sure. Go all innocent on me. After you spied on me several times.*

"I really don't know! Listen, I'm sorry I followed you. But I never told Kurt anything important."

Fear surges through Schipper's mind again, this time mingled with grief. A woman's face, a sweet smile softening her features, flashes before his eyes. He pushes it away by focusing on his anger towards Kurt. A speedy and knee-jerk response to a painful memory.

A strategy I know all too well.

Schipper snaps, "If you're so innocent, you shouldn't have spied on me at all." *What game are they playing?*

I roll my eyes. For an experienced politician, he's not very good at judging honest people. Or maybe, as a politician, you lose the belief there still are honest people. "I'm not playing a game. Please understand, I don't care who Milou is, or the woman with the sweet smile you just thought of."

A powerful emotion overcomes Schipper, and he turns away. He swallows twice, and his emotions flow away, until there's just the vast emptiness only a tidal wave of grief leaves behind. He fills the emptiness with angered determination. "Don't mention them again. Ever!"

"If you're so in favour of people being open, why are you so afraid of sharing your own secrets? That's why people don't trust politicians anymore."

Schipper snorts. "Oh yes, because if we always tell the truth, people will love us and not go on a witch hunt at all." He turns to me, eyes blazing. "Some people, who would never take a stand themselves, will happily hang anybody who does. As a politician, you have to develop a thick skin for that, and try to stay alive for as long as possible to achieve the positive things nobody will ever give you credit for."

My eyes blaze back at Schipper. "You're saying it's okay to deceive people, as long as you get them the right results? Isn't that a bomb of deception under the morality of our society? What if we all start acting like the destination is more important than the journey?"

"What if we don't? What if every year politicians step down because the public is all over them for a minor, irrelevant mistake? Do you think that instability helps a society?"

I shift on my bench. "Well, no, but I still think honesty weaves the fabric of a well-functioning society."

Schipper laughs. "Look who's talking. How many people know about your mind-reading?"

"Hey, I'm not heading a committee telling others to come clean."

"You don't have to. You just follow them for a while and you know everything they're thinking. Not quite a level playing field, is it?" He stares at the ceiling, at the harsh light, as if he likes the discomfort.

The light shoots through my head. I close my eyes, but the torturing light remains in Schipper's mind and that I can't shut out by closing my eyes.

Softer, he says, "I fight dirty politicians. I want politicians to conduct their business in a clean way, to not give out favours for personal gain. But I do think politicians have the right to a private life, which the public doesn't need to know everything about. We all need a private space. My thoughts are mine, and mine alone. One of the last places I can still be myself completely. Or so I thought."

What was it that my mother wrote in her notes? 'Don't confront people with their thoughts. Pretend you don't hear them. Leave them their dignity by pretending you don't hear everything.' She was right. I take a deep breath. "I'm sorry. I didn't mean to violate your thoughts."

He grunts. *Whatever.* He scans the room and wonders how to escape from this situation. Quick thinkers usually don't brood long. Schipper enters the problem-solving mode, another strategy to take back control. *Milou probably already reported me missing to the po-*

lice. Ben will for sure look into the Syndicate after our talk yesterday. Good thinking, to inform someone else than the task force.

Ben? I spat, "Don't tell me you talked to Ben, the police chief, yesterday?" And there goes my resolve to follow my mother's advice of pretending not to hear anything.

Irritation rises in Schipper, together with a feeling of triumph. "Yes. My insurance strategy against Kurt. I informed Ben of our plan in case the task force proved incompetent. Good thing I did."

"On the contrary! If you hadn't, we probably wouldn't have been in this mess. He's on Kurt's side."

"Sure, and although Kurt's your boss, you're not?"

"Ben is Kurt's informant within the police force. You informed Kurt's informant of our plans to frame Kurt. If you'd left it with the task force and me, Kurt might not have been on to us and we might have framed him today. Great job of relying on the wrong people." The words echo back to me through Schipper's mind and sink in. My cheeks burn. Often, we recognise the blind spots in ourselves all too well as faults in others. I avert my eyes and add, "And so did I. We might not have been here if *I* hadn't decided to play along with the wrong people."

Another one of my mother's notes comes to mind. 'Be as honest as you can about your own thoughts, so the other person perceives a balance.' Given my lecture to Schipper on honesty, I should've thought of it sooner. I sigh. "Let me tell you something about myself." I tell him about growing up with my secret, the death of my mother. About how Bernard shared his memories of my mother with me, and promised to share all the information he had. "Kurt kept feeding me bits and pieces of information. I was blind sighted, I craved to know about her so badly."

Through Schipper's eyes, I see tears escaping my eyes. He softens towards me, but his suspicion remains.

I keep talking. About how my mother's parents were killed. How my mother tried to protect her brother and was successful until I fucked up and now he's in another room on this floor. I even tell him about Isabella. Then I close my eyes. I feel naked. No, worse—I feel like the crab I once saw squirming in a seafood restaurant, pinned on a cutting board, pieces being sliced off by the server to provide dinner guests with the freshest sashimi imaginable. I've just presented myself on a cutting board to a stranger.

Schipper's mind is processing. *Sounds weird. So weird that it's credible.* He chuckles. "Basically, what you're saying is you're just like me. By hiding your ability, you try to stay alive for as long as possible to achieve the positive things nobody will ever give you credit for."

My cheeks burn and I don't know what to say.

Schipper's voice drops to a whisper and I'm not sure if he talks to me or himself. "That's what struck me that day in the elevator. Those eyes. They told me of loneliness, of the burden of a heavy responsibility. And loss. Losing a loved one, that's brutal."

I open my eyes and force myself to face him.

Schipper nods. "Thank you. I…know what it feels like to lose someone you love more than life itself." He clenches his fists and when he opens them again, the last resistance leaves his body. *With her, it's easier to give up resisting thinking about it. She'll know at some point.* His voice quivers. "I guess it won't hurt to tell you my story."

"If you prefer, think it. It'll be easier for you to express yourself. And nobody can listen in."

He nods again, then lays back and closes his eyes. *Right. Well… I fell in love about twelve years ago. She was married. It should never have happened. But it did.*

He works hard to keep his mind rational and suppress his feelings.

We tried to keep a distance but… A strong emotion bubbles up and Schipper gives in to it. He sees the woman walk, talk, laugh. *Elections were coming up and I led my party for the first time. I wanted to postpone any decisions until a few months after the elections, at least, but she couldn't go through with the deceit to her husband anymore. She asked him for a divorce. He threw her out, and she drove to my place. I told her she couldn't stay with me. Not the week leading up to the elections.* His stomach knots and he clenches his fists. A strong desire to change that moment overcomes him. He swallows. *I didn't want any scandal to break at that time. She left angry and sad. A drunk driver hit her and she died three days later in the hospital. Because I wanted to keep my reputation intact. I swore to never enter a relationship during my political career again. And to succeed as a politician. Because it felt like I would betray her, to give up being a politician after she died.* He inhales deeply. *The only one who knows the full story is my sister, Milou. She's a psychiatrist. I talk to her every few weeks.* He turns towards me, searching my eyes. The empty sadness returns to his mind. "I was such a fool." He blinks several times.

"That's terrible. I'm so sorry."

We both lie still for a while, busy with our own regrets.

Kathy? Dad?

I jerk up against the restraints and fall back.

"Isabella!"

Kathy! Can you hear me?

Yes! Yes, Isabella, I'm here. How are you?

I'm okay. What's happening? Dad and I have been here since yesterday evening. They kept us asleep most of the time. But I can't reach Dad. I know he's awake sometimes, but he doesn't hear me.

Schipper raises his eyebrows.

"I… I'm sharing thoughts with my cousin, Isabella. She's awake."

"Seems Kurt is arranging quite the party here. Any others?"

I close my eyes and concentrate. I can't feel Rick's presence. He could be asleep like Isabella says. "I'm not sure, but I think it's just you, me, Rick and Isabella."

Then, I sense someone walking through the corridor, and I tune into that person's mind.

Finally, I get to use the equipment!

CHAPTER FIFTY-EIGHT

Isabella barks, "You let go of my dad and aunt right now!"

Isabella, Rick, and I are in the lab, all three restrained. I'm closest to the door into the office. Isabella is in the middle and Rick at the far end of the lab. Privacy screens between us prevent us from seeing each other. Futile for Isabella and me, because we can see through everyone's eyes, even Kurt's. He must've let his guard down.

Kurt paces up and down.

"Well, well, three mind-readers in one room." Kurt's face has the same expectant expression as the lioness had in a zoo where I once attended a feeding. While the caretaker was explaining the eating habits of lions, carelessly dangling the bucket with meat scraps from his elbow, I wondered if he'd still feel so relaxed knowing the lioness was calculating how to not just get at the food, but the juicy-looking arm holding the bucket as well.

Kurt halts in front of Isabella.

Rick, still groggy, groans. "What the hell's going on here? Where's my daughter??"

Kurt raises his eyebrows. "You don't know? Really? You don't have the skill? Then you're wasting my time."

I shiver. If I hadn't searched for Rick, if I hadn't visited their house, they wouldn't be here. It's my job to protect them and so far, I failed horribly. The only thing left is damage control. "Kurt, he's still groggy from the sedative. It takes a while for the mind to become fully operational."

Kurt shrugs. He steps toward Isabella and stares at her, intensely concentrating.

Calmly, Isabella says, "It doesn't work like that."

Kurt steps back and I feel he's shocked.

Isabella continues, "Mind-reading, I mean."

She responds in her mind to my surprise.

He tried to read my thoughts. But his brain's fuzzy. Like our neighbour who sometimes smokes weird smelling cigarettes.

I see Kurt's face through her eyes, the wrinkles between his eyebrows deep in concentration. I focus on his mind.

Little brat. They're blocking me somehow. But I'll be their leader. Nobody can stop me.

Isabella is right. His thoughts jump from one floating cloud to another, making sense only to the brain that thinks about them. I had mind-watched enough students experimenting with drugs to recognise the weightless feeling, the larger-than-life thoughts, jumping from one place to another and then converging seamlessly into the most insightful vision they feel they've ever had. Like an unfolding weird dream—inevitably logical as long as you're asleep, but embarrassingly bizarre after you wake up.

With the others, I'll form a mind-reading army. Me, the first President of the European Union, and the visionary who expands it into the World Union.

Suddenly, I feel Aaron's presence in the office. Through the window into the lab, he watches Kurt with a scientific interest. *The drugs seem to have a stronger effect than the first time he took them. A shame he won't let me measure his brain to my new protocol. It would be easy to compare him with the three freak-shows.*

I snort. I've been afraid all my life to be called a freak-show, and now that someone does, it feels wrong, because Rick, Isabella and I aren't the biggest freak-shows in this room.

Aaron raps on the window with his knuckles, impatient. *Need to get on with my testing protocol. And Kurt will need another injection.*

Isabella shivers. *Testing protocol? Kathy, what is happening? What are we doing here?* She tries to feel brave, but her fear and anger keep winning.

I reply in my mind *I'm not sure, honey. Don't worry, we'll get out of here'* But my apprehension is probably as clear to Isabella as her fear is to me.

Aaron walks into the lab, towards Kurt, the syringe in his hand.

Kathy? Isabella? What's going on? Rick's mind seems to have woken up fully now. Maybe under stress, his mind-reading improves.

I concentrate on him. *Rick, calm down. Isabella is doing fine so far.*

Rick stops wriggling in his chair to focus. He seems to have picked up something.

I try again. *Rick. Can you hear me?*

Kathy?

Yes. Can you hear me?

I hear some of your thoughts. Where are we?

In the Syndicate's lab.

A…shit lab?

I laugh out loud. Quite the shit lab indeed.

The Syndicate's lab. An organisation I work for. Unfortunately.

You work here? Did I hear that correctly? No, no, it can't be. Damn, I wish I could mind-read as well as you both.

Yes, I work here. Used to work here. I never knew Kurt was such a dangerous guy.

Who's Kurt? The guy with the syringe?

No, that's Aaron. In my mind I recall their faces, and try to flash it like cards to Rick. *Aaron… Kurt… Aaron… Kurt…*

Right. Why are we here?

I'm not sure. But it's not good.

Isabella interferes. *That man Kurt wants to lead a group of mind-readers. But he's afraid of you, Kathy, and he thinks you are no use, Daddy.* She starts crying.

Rick's heart swells with the sobs of his daughter. "Honey, don't cry." He yanks at the straps restraining him. "Damn it. Aaron! Get over here. You let us go *right now!*"

Disinterested, Aaron listens while staring at a monitor to my right. The screen shows EEG recordings from our brains. He jumps, however, when Kurt swivels to face Aaron.

"I need that injection, NOW!"

Aaron nods, walks towards the office, gesturing Kurt to come with him.

What injection? What does Kurt need an injection for?

A few minutes later, Kurt darts into the lab, eyes a fanatic gleam, a combination of frustration and determination. *My new plan is so brilliant. I'll drag Paul's name through deep shit for wanting to frame me.*

At his wolfish smile, all three of us shudder simultaneously. I yank at the straps. But there's no way I can wriggle myself out of these.

He walks over to Rick and waves Aaron towards him. "We don't need him anymore. Put him back in his room." In his mind, he already discarded Rick.

Isabella reads it too. Her panic waves so strong, I feel my stomach turn.

Aaron rolls the bed, with Rick on it, out of the room. Kurt's thoughts still swerve from one grotesque idea to another, too fast and incongruous for me to understand. He shifts his focus to Isabella.

If he focuses on me, he might forget about her, leave her alone. I clear my throat and try to sound calm. "You think you can mind-read like us, but you're deluding yourself. Just like you're deluding yourself about your capability of being a leader. Let alone of the European Union. Your mother was wrong. You are not, and never will be, a better politician than your father was."

Kurt freezes. In his mind, I watch the flame I ignited develop into a blaze, and then into an engulfing fire, only leaving room for his hot-red rage towards me.

Impulsively, he carts Isabella out of the lab too.

Oh shit. Will he take it out on Isabella? I close my eyes to concentrate on Kurt while he pushes Isabella through the office, into the hallway, and then into her previous cell. I'm glad he's back straight away. But that relief evaporates when I feel his mind consumed by the desire to hurt me.

He walks up to me and slaps me hard across the face. Two, three times. Then he moves his face close to mine, his breath on my cheek. He sings, "I'm so glad I killed your mother."

CHAPTER FIFTY-NINE

Aaron's icy fingers attach a clip to my middle finger and then insert a needle into the back of my hand. From there, he attaches a tube to a drip-feed. I struggle against the restraints.

With a light smile, Aaron hovers over me. "Don't wear yourself out, Kathy. You're in the test chair, well restrained."

I focus on his mind, and through his eyes see a syringe being injected into a drip-feed.

"Close your eyes. You'll be here for a while. I'm going to prepare. You won't feel much pain, I promise."

Prepare? For what?

Aaron attaches a strap over my forehead and pulls it tight.

I try to find the minds of Rick and Isabella but come up with nothing. Their cells are on the opposite side of the hallway, with two doors and a couple of walls in between.

Aaron hums while he keeps busy behind me. He picks up an electric razor and shaves parts of my head. What the hell?

"What are you doing? Didn't like my hair?" The shaved spots feel cold.

Aaron chuckles. *Whatever.* He walks into the lab office. *Why did Kurt tell me to wait? I want to get started.* He looks at a notepad, and goes through a checklist.

I can't see Aaron, as the window to the office is blocked by the privacy screens, but I can see everything through his eyes. *Let's see. I shaved all the spots. Clean them before drilling. New drill at her bedside. Good thing I practiced on Sara, that drill was one size too big. Hope Kurt is done with the pictures soon.*

What was it that Cecilia said about Sara? She had a few strange holes in her skull, didn't remember who she was, had trouble talking. The fear I felt two days ago, about someone with a syringe coming. That must've been Sara, while Aaron practiced on her. A test-ride, before going all out on me.

A door bangs shut. Kurt, mind still in tunnel view mode, dances through the office. He pushes a bed past Aaron, without acknowledging he's there. He crashes the door of the lab into the wall with the bed. My heart thumps in my throat. Isabella? But no, the shape is larger, and has a balding head. It must be Schipper. Kurt places the bed in the middle section, next to me but behind the privacy screen. I can't reach Schipper's mind. He's probably sedated.

Suddenly, Kurt appears from behind the screen. "Oops. Did I scare you?" He giggles.

Oh boy. I might like him better in a sour mood after all.

He walks towards me, left finger pointing like an arrow. A tiny piece of white foam is forming in the right corner of his mouth.

"You tried to set me up. You and that police task force. AND Schipper." *Knew it would come in handy to keep Ben on my payroll. Good boy, for running straight to me after Schipper called him.*

I try to sound calm. "You can't keep running your blackmail schemes forever, you know. Some day it will catch up with you."

He grins. "No, it won't. I'm too smart for them all." His look at me seems to contain regret. "I wish you saw things my way. We could've been great together." *Too uptight, like her mother.* He pulls up a chair next to me and places his elbow on my arm. "Bernard's notes on your mother were so educational. She left you information on her little brother, the scheming bitch. Somewhere at the house. My people couldn't find it, but apparently you did. Where was it?"

I return his stare. This guy claims to have killed my mother, has hunted down my uncle and cousin, and thinks he can either own or kill us. I fight the urge to spit in his face. He's not even worth that energy.

Kurt leans into his elbow, into my arm. "Come on, indulge me."

Is he able to read my mind? I'm checking into his, but there's no echo, like when Isabella and I communicate through thoughts.

Kurt wiggles his elbow to roll the muscle over the bone in my arm, grinning when I wince. "Two of my people searched your mother's house. They might have caused a little damage." His face contracts in a frown. "But we didn't find anything. I wonder, what else did she leave you, other than the information about your uncle?"

"My mother left me information? If she hid it, as you say, how do you know about it?"

Kurt smirks. "Bernard was a fool. He tried to help your mother. He knew she felt responsible for her little brother. She told Bernard she found him, but the boy wasn't doing well. She didn't want Bernard to do anything about it and kept the details from him. Once she let it slip she would leave you the information. In a secret hiding place. Out of respect, Bernard left it at that." Kurt almost spits out those last words. *Soft idiot. He didn't realise the enormity of their potential.*

To Kurt, we're nothing more than a tool.

Kurt removes his elbow. "You probably feel superior, knowing everything about everybody, but I can't allow that if you don't want to work with me."

He stands up. *Don't need her anymore. Aaron can have his fun with her.* He waves to Aaron, then turns to me. "I hope your little cousin Isabella will be more useful." *Young enough to shape. She'll accept me. After a few years, she'll hardly remember her dad.* "Aaron, go ahead."

Aaron arranges his surgery tools on a metal platter on my right side. He ticks his finger against a syringe, and then I feel a small prick at four places on my skull.

"Don't worry, you won't feel much. That was a local anaesthetic, so you won't feel pain during the drilling. I'll place the electrodes in your brain, but as the brain doesn't feel pain, you don't need to worry about that." *At least not about that.*

I wriggle frantically, pull at my hands, but the restraints restrict even small movements.

"You'd better lay still, Kathy," Aaron says dryly. "You don't want me to drill too deep."

I hear him flicking a switch, causing a grinding sound, followed by a pressure on my skull. Kurt stands at the door, arms folded, watching with a sadistic smile. *Aaron gets his research, with a bonus. Guess he won't be mentioning damaging her brain in his thesis.*

My grandparents were hunted down and set on fire. My mother was left dying at the side of the road. My brain is being drilled into by a psychopath who holds Isabella and Rick as well. This might be the end of us. And that makes me feel reckless. I snort. "You can do whatever you want. You will never be the super politician you want to be. The police know about the extensive blackmailing files you have built up over the years. All those politicians that 'owe' you. All on that second phone of yours."

Kurt's eyes flicker. *She knows?* He shrugs. *Doesn't matter anymore.*

I try to smile confidently. Which isn't easy, while someone sticks probes into your brain. "And the back-ups, of course. We know where you keep them." Hopefully, my guess of Kurt taking the precaution of more than one back-up is correct.

Damn! They know about both back-ups?

In his mind I see a hard-drive, hidden in a clock on a dresser. Another hard-drive, taped to the back of a painting.

"Ready," Aaron says behind me.

A soft moan escapes from behind the screen. Schipper is waking up, but his mind is still fuzzy.

Kurt glances at Schipper, then shrugs. "Good. Let's start." He grins at me. "Why don't I show you my memories of the evening Bernard died." He recalls Bernard sitting in a bar, talking. "We had a few drinks. After the first one, he didn't notice they tasted strong." Kurt closes his eyes, remembering his hand pouring something in Bernard's glass while Bernard walks away to the washrooms. "He started to sweat after the second one." Kurt smiles at the memory. "We took a walk, as he wanted some fresh air."

"And you hit him on the head. Emptying his wallet, just in case they'd suspect the head wound was not caused by a fall." I aim for a conversational tone, as if there's no Aaron behind me fiddling with the equipment lodged into my brain.

Kurt frowns. *How does she know? Doesn't matter.* "They'll never find out what really happened." He glances up at Aaron. "Are you able to locate it?"

"I think so. Let me make one readjustment."

Through Aaron's eyes, I see my own brain exposed. He slowly drags out a needle, and with concentration sticks it into the grey matter again. Fascinating. And repulsive at the same time.

Kurt closes his eyes and thinks of carrying Bernard from the trunk of his car. In slow motion, he relives the moment of rolling him over the grass into the river. How he sank slowly. He opens his eyes and looks at me. "Could you follow that?"

I open my mouth, thinking Kurt must be addressing me. But then Aaron yells excitedly, "Got it!" *Perfect response. Finally figured out the part responsible for the mind-reading.*

"Kurt?" Schipper's voice is weak but demanding at the same time. "You let me go right now."

Kurt grins. "Ah, our beloved Prime Minister woke up. Let me show you the pictures that will hit the media tonight." He fishes a remote control out of his pants pocket, pushes the screen to the back so that Schipper and I can see each other. Schipper's body is covered by a sheet. Schipper glances around the lab. The fuzziness in his mind is enhanced by a massive headache.

Kurt points the remote at a screen on the wall and clicks a button. A picture appears. A picture of Isabella and Schipper. Both naked.

"What the hell?" I pull on the restraints as hard as I can, but they won't budge.

Panic clears the fog in Schipper's mind instantly.

Kurt covers his mouth with his hand. "Oops. That's quite the compromising picture, don't you think?"

I squint. They're lying next to each other, both with eyes closed. "You monster! You touched Isabella! If you hurt her in any way…" The empty threat sticks in my burning throat and hot tears scorch my eyes.

Kurt shows three other pictures, variations of the same, the naked bodies of Schipper and Isabella arranged together, touching.

My mouth is dry but I manage to yell, "It's clear both bodies are limp and arranged. You won't get away with this."

Kurt shakes his head. "Tut-tut. You're so naïve. It will take some time to enhance the pictures, but when they're released, they're the bomb I need to blast Schipper's credibility." He walks over to the bed and brings his face close to Schipper's. "It will be the scandal of the century."

Schipper tries to lift his arm.

Kurt grins. "Don't bother. You won't be able to fully move for the next hour or so. Just lie back and watch the show." He jerks his head towards me.

Kurt walks over to the monitor next to my chair.

Aaron points to a line in a chart. "Here you see a peak of activity when she read your mind. Let me adjust one probe, and we'll do a test again." He takes out a probe and inserts it again. Kurt's distorted, satisfied face looms above me. That's even more frightening than seeing my brain being poked at.

Your cousin Isabella is very trusting. She's now on her way to a safe place, and when she wakes up, you and her father will be dead. Through his mind, I see Rick lying unconscious on his bed in the white room.

Then I feel other people present in the next room, the office of the lab. I groan. Kurt's goons? The odds are bad enough as it is, without more people on Kurt's side.

But then I pick up staccato thinking. Cecilia! I exhale. The odds just improved nicely. I focus on the other mind but can't tell who it is. I focus on Cecilia again. *Feels good to do this with Nicole. Like old times.* Through her eyes, I see Nicole peeking through the window into the lab. She hunches down again, and mouths to Cecilia 'Kathy, Paul, Aaron, Kurt.' Then Nicole shakes her head.

Cecilia curses in her mind.

They need to know who else is here. I yell, "You'll never get away with holding me, Schipper, Rick and Isabella hostage here!" Hopefully Kurt thinks I'm just angry.

"Of course I will," snaps Kurt. "I had to improvise, but I came up with a brilliant plan, if I may say so myself."

I concentrate on Cecilia and see Nicole nodding at her.

Dripping with sarcasm, I mock Kurt. "You call it brilliant to keep them sedated in the room on the other side of the corridor?"

Through Cecilia's eyes, I see Nicole crawling out of the office into the corridor, punching away on her phone at the same time.

Kurt's right eyebrow twitches. "Isabella is on her way to a safer place. I need her, but—" He waves at the screen behind him, "once those pictures go viral, the police will be looking for her. And I want her for myself."

Bile rises into my mouth. I swallow it down. Gross, but safer than vomiting while your head is fixated and you've got needles in your brain.

Even Aaron is disturbed. *He's really getting worse. Scary.* But he checks himself. *He's enabling all this unprecedented research, though. Couldn't do it without Kurt.* His attention focuses on the monitor again.

Satisfied, Kurt continues, "They'll find a nice suicide in Rick's house tonight, with Rick dangling in the shed. He'll confess selling his daughter to Paul." He drops his head and looks sorrowful. Who would've guessed Kurt was capable of all these facial expressions? "But the poor fellow felt remorse, decided to kill his daughter, and hang himself out of shame. No one will be able to find Isabella, and they'll just assume he hid her body well." He perks up. "Meanwhile, she'll become the first to train in my mind-reading school. If she chooses wisely, more wisely than you, she'll rise to fame together with me." He smiles and places his fingertips together. He asks Aaron, "Ready now?"

Through Cecilia's eyes, I see Nicole crawling back into the office. Nicole whispers to Cecilia. I try to listen in through Cecilia's mind, but Aaron's intense, strange excitement stands out.

Aaron tries to keep his voice procedural. "Yes. The heat will go up automatically when the readings rise above this threshold, which I established through the tests we just did."

Loud, I ask, "What are you going to heat up my brain for?"

Cecilia beckons to Nicole, who now crawls through the door into the lab, slowly inching behind the screens towards Aaron and Kurt. Cecilia feels worried about Nicole. *Would prefer she carried a weapon instead of a syringe.* I also feel admiration. No...something stronger.

"And the heat will destroy that part of the brain?" Kurt asks.

I feel Cecilia waiting, tensed. And funnily enough, that eases my tension a little. She and Nicole are here to help. Now I need to do my part and protect Rick and Isabella. And Schipper.

Aaron answers, "Yes. We then test if she still responds to your thinking and repeat until we don't get a reading anymore."

"Great work, Aaron. Let's get started." Kurt walks back to the spot where he stands in full view. He seeks my gaze. "If you're not with me, you're against me. I will make sure you, and every unwilling mind-reader after you, will never read anyone's mind again."

He reaches behind his back and retrieves a gun. He strokes it and then points it at me. The gleam in his eyes evolves to a manic sadism. "Do you want to know how I killed your mother?" Kurt closes his eyes. He sees my mother walking along a road. He drives up to her.

"No!" I scream at her, to warn her, to will her to jump aside. More bile rises in my throat. I'm going to watch my mother die.

A burning scent diffuses into the air. I sniff at it. What could it be?

And then it makes sense. Kurt asking, 'The heat will destroy that part of the brain?' Kurt letting me read his mind voluntarily. All so Aaron can fry away the part of my brain responsible for the mind-reading.

CHAPTER SIXTY

A wheel of one of the screens to the left squeals. Kurt opens his eyes, his arm shoots forward, gun aimed at me. Or maybe behind me. "Aaron, was that you?"

Nicole bumped into a screen. Have to protect her. She's almost there. Cecilia cocks her gun and readies herself to jump out and shoot Kurt.

I feel Aaron's panic, his attention not even on my brain. "Uhm, Kurt? Could you please not point that gun at me?"

"Keep going. I'm an excellent shot." He grins, and adds, "I only hit the target I want to hit. Just do your job."

Shaken, Aaron looks down. *He's definitely losing it. As soon as I've got the data I need, I'm leaving the Syndicate.* "Turning up the heat, Kurt. I get something, but we're not there yet."

"Right, then let's continue the show." Kurt focuses on my mother, walking, and his hands turning the wheel.

The burning smell strengthens.

Can't wait for Nicole. Don't want Kathy to end up like Sara. Cecilia jumps out and aims at Kurt. "Kurt, put the gun down. You just confessed to killing Kathy's mother. It's over." *Please Nicole, hurry…*

Kurt swivels his gun towards Cecilia, frowns, and then laughs. "Come on, Cecilia, it's far from over. Your friend in the chair here is having her brain fried away. In the bed next to her lies the Prime Minister of the Netherlands, whom I can shoot at any moment. What makes you think you have the upper hand?"

"Kathy, listen to me." Cecilia sounds desperate. "Remember your mother's notes. Focus on yourself. Focus on something in the room. Anything. But not on anyone's thoughts!" *Hurry, Nicole!*

Kurt teases, "Oh Kathy, you don't want to miss the last moments of your mother's life, do you?"

I close my eyes and focus. The feeling of the head clamps. The bands around my wrists. Air breezes over my body, blowing calm determination through the open spots of my scalp.

Isabella. I need to save Isabella. So what if I'm the next one in the family line to become hunted down? I need to figure out where Kurt keeps her. Even if that means having my brain cells slowly scorching away.

I open my eyes, looking straight into Kurt's. While I force the corners of my mouth to curve into a smile, his angry frown simultaneously seems to deepen.

Kurt yells. "What are you so happy about?"

"You think you've got it all figured out. You think you can use and manipulate whoever is around. But you can't." I need to guide him to the right thought. I only might have one shot at this before Aaron bakes my brain into a useless blubber.

He snorts. "What makes you think I can't? I seem to be doing pretty well so far."

"Oh, come on. You had to improvise. You kidnapped the Dutch Prime Minister. No one will let you get away with that."

Kurt narrows his eyes. "Once I release the disgusting pictures of Schipper and Isabella, no one will listen to him."

I swallow. I check in with Cecilia thoughts.

Shoot now? No, Kathy in danger. Shoot when he's distracted by Aaron collapsing.

The smell of burning increases.

Excited, Aaron yells, "It's working, Kurt. I've got the intensity right."

Shit. I wish I could focus on Cecilia's steady thoughts, to ground me and give me strength to go on. But I can't. I have to focus solely on Kurt now. "Did you know Isabella and I can mind-read at a distance? Because we're both mind-readers, the reception between us two is much stronger."

Aaron yelps. "Ouch. What was that?"

I feel Nicole's relief. *Syringe fully emptied. Won't take long.*

Kurt narrows his eyes and looks up. "Keep your focus, Aaron." Then he looks back at me. *Mind-reading at a distance Really? [...] could be true. But not [...] a few kilometres... she [...] lying.*

Okay, so Isabella is only a few kilometres away. I try to ignore the smell of fried breakfast. It's getting harder to read Kurt. I need to make this last chance count. He'll truly be The Eraser after this. "Did you know Rick made a girl pregnant in his teenage years? She gave up their son for adoption. He can read minds too. Oh, you missed that?"

The hungry look on Kurt's face is almost funny. "Another one?"

"He's communicating with Isabella right now. He found her, he's just outside of her door."

Really? [...] bungalow park Loosduinen? Alert [...] need him [...]!

Aaron cheers. "Her signals are weakening. Go on!" He groans, and then crashes to the ground.

Kurt freezes, staring behind me with disbelief. A deafening noise ricochets off the walls, and Kurt slumps down. Cecilia springs forward and kicks his gun aside.

"It's okay now, Kathy." I feel a hand on my arm. Nicole. "I've switched off the machine. You're safe."

CHAPTER SIXTY-ONE

Cecilia runs to me and pulls at the straps around my hands.

Nicole holds up her hand. "As much as I hate to see Kathy tied up here, we might want to ensure she moves as little as possible until the electrodes are removed from her brain."

Cecilia opens her mouth, but before she can say anything, Nicole shakes her head. "I can't do it, too big a risk that I'll damage anything. I'll call the hospital. A neurosurgeon needs to remove these."

"Cecilia, I need you to find Isabella. I think Kurt's keeping her at bungalow park Loosduinen. Probably guarded by at least one of his goons."

Cecilia nods and retrieves her phone from her pocket. "I'll get right on it."

"Okay, thanks." Nicole hangs up and turns to me. "The neurosurgeon from the Erasmus hospital will be flown here asap." She checks my skull. "She'll remove the equipment and patch up your skull. We'll get you out soon."

"Uhm, ladies? Would you be willing to help me up?"

Nicole reddens. "I'm sorry. Yes, of course." She walks over to Schipper's bed. "I'll call my colleagues. They'll bring you to a hospital."

"No," says Schipper. "I stay here as long as Kathy's here." He shakily walks over and appears at my side.

I grin at his concerned face. "You remind me of a Greek statue now. With that sheet not quite covering everything."

Schipper blushes, shakes his head at me, and readjusts the sheet. He pulls up a chair and Nicole helps him sit.

After Cecilia finishes the call, she bends down. "Although Aaron is probably not going anywhere anytime soon, I'll cuff him, just in case." Her face softens. "Nicole, could you make sure the cops and paramedics can access this floor?"

From their facial expressions, it's clear the bond between them is strong. Nicole nods and exits the lab.

Cecilia takes my hand. "Nicole injected Aaron with a sedative. I was afraid we came too late. Nicole called me in the morning. She was told to stay away today, but when she checked Aaron's computer, she saw he was performing EEG tests." She glances at Schipper. "When you went missing, and I couldn't reach you both anymore, the task force started assembling a team, but Nicole and I didn't want to wait and came in."

Nicole enters the lab with a paramedic team and several cops, who stare at Schipper but then investigate the crime scene. Nicole moves close to Cecilia.

Cecilia steals a glance at her and smiles shyly. "We figured there was no time to lose. Nicole sneaked me in through the back." She radiates when Nicole smiles back at her.

"I'm so glad." I smile at both of them.

Cecilia holds up two phones. "Searched Kurt. Hope he didn't make back-ups."

I squeeze Cecilia's hand. "Right, I almost forgot. He did. I challenged Kurt to think about his back-ups. He's got two—one in a clock on a dresser, probably at his house. Another one at the back of a painting. I didn't get a clear view where, unfortunately."

Cecilia squeezes my hand back. "Good job, Kathy."

"Thanks. Same to you both. You make a great team together." I smile mischievously when they both blush. "The electricity in the air tells me you two will work it out on your own. But if you don't, I'll come after you."

Nicole stands up and puts an arm around Cecilia, whose neck and face flush.

One of the cops asks, "Cecilia, you have a minute?" They mumble to each other, Cecilia glancing at me. Once more I try to read their minds, but I only get a mixture of feelings. Too many people, and probably too few brain cells left. And I'm so, so tired.

Cecilia walks over to me. "They found Isabella. She's alive and well. They're taking her to the hospital to check her. Rick is on his way as well. But both seem physically unharmed."

Relieved, my eyes fill up. We're all still alive. This time, the hunt has not ended in someone in our family being killed. It just cost me some grey matter.

She glances over at the paramedics, who are still working on Kurt.

"Kurt will live. He'll be taken to a different hospital. We've taken several of his people into custody. You know a Jason? He already started to spill everything he claims he knows, without us even asking."

I grin. "He's probably just guilty of being a jerk. Nothing else. But let him feel the heat of the consequences of supporting a psychopath to power."

CHAPTER SIXTY-TWO

"Are you nervous, dear?" The nurse is friendly, unlike all the buzzing and whirling machines he hooked me up to. "There's no need. We just want you one night for observation. Dr. Visser says you're doing okay. She just wants to make sure."

The door opens, and Dr. Visser, the neurosurgeon who freed me at the Syndicate, walks in. She raises her eyebrows. She checks the monitors. In a fleeting moment, I see myself through her eyes, how she found me this afternoon. Bound, holes in my skull, hooked up to machines that had just fried away part of my brain.

"Nurse, I think we can unhook two of the three machines. And take them out of the room, please. I think Ms. Van der Laan has had enough of restraining machines for a while."

"Thanks," I say, grateful.

She nods. "You seem to be doing well. But we will check on you a couple of times during the night, measure your vitals. I will check in with you in the morning."

When she walks out of the room, she steps aside to let Nicole in, holding Isabella's hand. With her other hand, Nicole holds a balloon that says, 'You rock!'

Nicole shrugs. "It's a little corny, I know. Still, better than the 'Get well soon,' ones." She nods towards the balloon. "And I think you do." She ties the balloon to a cupboard handle.

Isabella beams at me, but soon her expression changes to confusion and then fright. Finally, she bursts into tears.

"You can't…hear me?" she hiccups.

I stretch my arms towards her, and she climbs onto my bed for a big hug. I bury my nose in her ear and whisper, "Not right now. You might have to teach me all over again. But I'm okay." I stroke her hair and back until her sobbing subsides. "How's your dad?"

"He's okay. He asked if we could go home, but the doctor wants to make sure all the sed… sleepy medicine is out of our system." She looks up at me, eyes wet. "I wish we could all be in one room."

"We're all okay. That is what matters."

Nicole takes Isabella's hand. "I'm sorry, Isabella, I have to take you back to your room now. The doctor said five minutes maximum to visit your aunt."

They stand up. While Isabella wipes her face dry with a tissue from my nightstand, Nicole leans over to me and whispers, "Cecilia says hi. She found the first back-up in the clock. She's still looking for the second one."

"I hope she finds it."

"She'll destroy them when she does. The information Kurt assembled is too explosive, even in the hands of good people."

When they walk through the door opening, Isabella turns around and waves. I smile.

I sink back into the pillows and stare out of the window. Between buildings, I can glimpse the Nieuwe Maas river, reflecting Rotterdam lighting up for the evening. The traffic outside is thinning, as are the sounds from the hospital hallways. Visiting hours are over, and patients and staff alike are gearing down for the night.

To my surprise, the door to my room opens once again. Schipper sticks his head through. When he sees I'm awake, he comes in and closes the door behind him.

"I'm so glad you are okay. Well, relatively." His eyes survey the bandages stuck to my head.

"Thanks."

"My apologies. I got you in danger way more than I could ever imagine."

"I'm fine. I never thought he would go this far." Kurt's pictures swim into my mind. I swallow and close my eyes. "What he did to you and Isabella…"

Schipper frowns and places his hand over mine. "Yeah. Even for

Kurt, that was..." He shakes his head. With his other hand, he wipes a tear from my cheek and touches my bandages. "You risked your brain, your life, bringing Kurt down. I don't think I'll ever forget that burning smell." He sits down. "But I understand the damage doesn't seem to be bad?"

I shrug. "Not for my normal functions. For my mind-reading, I'll have to see. I still get some emotions, but I hardly hear thoughts. Apparently, the brain can grow new cells and repair functionality. It might grow back, it might not. I'll know in a few months."

He studies me. *[...] weird [...]*.

I smile at him. "See, I got a bit of that. You feel sorry for me. It will be weird indeed. Now I just have to rely on what people actually say. Words usually cover less than forty percent of someone's actual meaning."

"Indeed. What handicapped people we are." He smiles wryly. "I like my 'handicap' as much as the next person. Someone else knowing everything you think...it's scary. Politicians spend most of their lives phrasing their words in an acceptable way to the public. To achieve maximum impact. To prevent upsetting people. To entice voters." He pats my hand. "That I didn't have to do that with you felt...unreal. Awkward. And, I have to admit, oddly liberating at the same time." He stares out of the window. He nods to himself, swallows, and looks me in the eye. "As you know, Kurt tried to establish a new role in the EU, that of EU President, restructuring the European Council and Commission into one organisation. Now that Kurt has been unmasked, the support from the people he blackmailed has disappeared, and that restructuring is off the table for now. Kurt's hold on people also emphasized the need of a strong anti-corruption EU committee. They've asked me to head that committee. I thought about refusing, but I've decided to do it."

"I'm glad. We need someone good. Someone fighting for the right reasons."

"I'd like you to work with me."

Open-mouthed, I stare at him. Not what I expected. So this is how other people feel all the time, when you don't know what's coming out of someone's mouth next.

"I like your style. You're direct. You will tell me when you don't like something. When you think I'm making a mistake." He leans over and says with emphasis, "If your mind-reading comes back to you, I swear I'll never ask you to read someone's mind for me. But it's okay to read mine. You might be the only one I can truly be myself with. I need someone to ground me. Please, come work with me."

While my reasoning brain heavily objects, thinking, 'I know nothing about politics,' I say, "I would love to."

And just like that, I accepted my sixth job in just over four years.

CHAPTER SIXTY-THREE

At the farmhouse, I first walk to the statue of Hekate. I place my left hand on the woman holding the torch and whisper, "Thanks, Mom."

Isabella and I are the third generation being chased, but partly thanks to the information my mother left me, we survived. Thanks to her information and her inheritance, my life is about to become a lot less solitary. Rick, Isabella, me—we all owe our lives to my mother. I kneel in front of the statue, the exquisitely carved stone that once frightened me, and place my arms around to give it a big hug.

With my right hand, I carefully touch the bandages on top of my head. They were renewed this morning, five days after the first bandages were placed. Five days, in which I've been planning and talking to the insurance broker as well as a contractor.

At the sound of gravel being crunched by car tires, I hoist myself up and walk around the house to greet Rick and Isabella.

"Kathy!" Isabella screams, running towards me.

I bend down so we can have a proper hug. "Hi, sweetheart."

"How's your head?" she asks, concerned, wiping a strand of my hair away.

"I'm okay."

In her eyes I can see she tries to read my mind, to know what is going on. But I learned at least something from Kurt and keep looking at Isabella, full attention on her, repressing any thoughts.

She gives me a funny look and then pirouettes 360 degrees around. "Is this where you live?" she asks. "What a big house. And the garden is huge."

Rick stands behind her, smiling.

I wave at him and take Isabella's hand. "This is where I'm going to live. First, the house needs to be repaired. Let's go inside." I open the door to let Isabella and Rick pass inside.

After showing them the house, I halt in the trashed living room, near the sliding doors to the terrace.

"Who did this?" Isabella asks, frowning.

"It doesn't matter. They can do no more harm. I'll rebuild it, much nicer than it was." I glance at Rick, who nods encouragingly.

I bend down. "Isabella, how would you like to move in here with me, together with your dad?"

Isabella's face breaks open in a big smile.

CHAPTER SIXTY-FOUR

"I still can't believe you want to live here. All those years you wanted nothing to do with the house." Dad surveys the room, now clear after the contractor worked hard for two days to remove the rubble.

I take his hand and lead him out through the glass doors onto the terrace, turning right on the path along the house, to the statue. I squeeze his hand, let go, and inhale deeply.

"Mom left something for me in the statue." I bend down to remove the slab from the base of the statue. This time, although still stubborn, I can remove it just with my hands.

Dad gasps, kneels next to me, and peers into the cavity.

I grab the keyring from my pocket, slip the small key in the metal plate, and remove the plate. "Last time when we were here, I discovered it. Mom communicated this hiding spot to me when I was young, but I never understood. When we came here, and I saw the statue, I remembered. She'd left me information. Because…" I swallow. "Because she knew I could read minds, just like her." I fiddle with the keyring, to avoid looking Dad in the eye.

Dad's trembling voice is so soft, I hardly hear him at first. "She tried to tell me something important. The day she died." He leans his elbows on his knees and lowers his head in his hands. "I'd been on her back for months. I knew she kept something from me. She said she wasn't ready to tell me, that her job didn't make her proud of who she was. She wanted to sort that out first. I was angry. Accused her of finding it more important to sort out her job than to be honest with me. She decided to quit her job straight away. She was on her way to Bernard to tell him that evening." He swallows audibly. "If I hadn't pushed her to tell me everything, she might not have died that evening."

I put an arm around his shoulder. "It wasn't your fault, Dad. Someone was after her and would have killed her, anyway." I clear my throat. "What she wanted to tell you was that she could read minds. Her father was a mind-reader as well, and he and her mother were killed because of it. She survived, together with her little brother. She didn't want to be pursued, like her parents. And be a danger to herself and you. But she knew I could mind-read as well. And she wanted to protect me." I glance up at him. "I tried to tell you as a child that I could mind-read."

He wraps his arms around me. "I know. And in a weird way, it made sense. But I pushed it away. I didn't want to hear it. Told myself it was the imagination of a little girl. I'm so sorry for not listening, Kath."

In my dad's mind, I feel his knees hurt from kneeling down. I pull him up and we walk to the house.

Inside, we sit down on two folding chairs the contractor left here, and I tell him about how my mother saved her brother, walking for a while, leaving him at a place where she thought he'd be safe. How she had looked him up later and paid for his treatment.

For a few minutes, we sit in silence, while my dad processes everything I said. He stares out of the window and twists his hands in his lap. "At first, I was surprised, well, angry, that you only called me after you left the hospital. That you didn't tell me anything about what was going on. I had a long talk with Alida. You both have been trying to spare me, because you both know I shy away from bad news. And you were both right. I pushed your mother to tell me something that was obviously bothering her, and it ruined us. I vowed to never push someone again. But I realise that's not the best solution, either." He grabs my hands. "I want you to feel safe with me, Kathy. I want to know about the important things. Your fears, your pain."

We sit until it's too dark to see each other's eyes, and talk about how I've feared being found out, how I yearned for more information about my mother, my loneliness. My anonymous calls to the police, and how it got me in trouble. I tell him about Kurt and the Syndicate. And then I tell him about my new friend Cecilia. About Paul and my new job. And last but not least, about Rick and Isabella moving in with me.

My father hugs me tight. "I'm so sorry you had to go through all this alone." He swallows. "Your mother was one of a kind. I never felt so understood and accepted by anyone. I love Alida, but I'll never forget your mom."

I squeeze him back.

He chuckles. "Your mom was right about the house being perfect for you. I'm so glad she left it to you."

I grab a flashlight out of my backpack and switch it on. "There's one more thing I'd like to do together, Dad."

We go outside and walk towards the statue. The cavity I showed Dad, where my mother hid the documents, is still open. I feel in my coat pocket for the memorial cube I brought from my apartment. I position it in the cavity, place the metal plate back, turn the lock, and replace the key in the knife blade.

My whisper "I love you Mom" seems to linger in the air, before being picked up by the gentle wind, travelling up towards the vast night sky.

CHAPTER SIXTY-FIVE

Despite the chilly spring breeze, the sun manages to bring some warmth to our faces.

"I love those early spring days," Cecilia says, stepping onto the ship. "The sun gaining strength, gearing up to bring life to nature once again."

I sniff at the cup in my hand. Coffee, hot and strong.

The bow wave of a big container ship hits our tourist boat, and Cecilia spills a little coffee on her jeans. She rubs it vigorously. "Nicole and I—two years ago, I didn't want it. I was so used to being alone. Besides, I didn't think my parents could handle me being in love with a woman." She notices the stain won't go and shrugs. "Anyway, I didn't want to lose her again."

"I think you two make a great couple."

"I hope so. We'll take baby steps." She nudges my shoulder and grins. "I mean, look at you. You're way more solitary than I am, and you're moving in with two people!"

I smile, happy. "They'll move into the front part of the house. I'll get a bedroom in the back, looking out onto the garden." And the statue. "We share the living room and kitchen in between, but we can be separate if we need to." I look up and admire the Erasmus bridge ahead of us.

Cecilia follows my gaze and grins. "You haven't left Rotterdam yet and you're already behaving like a tourist."

I smile. "Before I move, I wanted to do one of those river boat tours. I've lived in Rotterdam for years, but never explored the river this way." I'd been nervous about asking Cecilia. It had been the first time in years I asked a friend to do something together.

Cecilia points to an empty bench. "Shall we sit over there?"

We settle down. Cecilia offers to get snacks and walks away. I check out the people on the bench on the other side. Since I left the hospital two weeks ago, I've been practising mind-reading on strangers. I still can't follow entire sentences but I can hear some words again. Although I don't have to mind-read to know the couple on the opposite bench are in love. They sit close together, hold hands and talk as if they're telling their life stories.

Something about the guy looks familiar. I squint my eyes. I've seen her before, too.

He's [...] nice. [...] interview [...] Never thought [...]

The uncomfortable bench at the recruitment agency swirls into my mind. It's the nervous guy in the waiting room at the recruitment agency. And the recruiter who dismissed him even before she'd talked to him. I grin. So much for first impressions.

Cecilia returns and hands me an almond paste cookie, my favourite Dutch pastry. She sits down and retrieves a file folder from her backpack. "Here's the file Kurt had on you. Including the pictures."

I open the folder and study the picture on top, of Mom holding her baby brother. I swallow. "Thanks so much. It will get a prominent place in the living room." I can't wait to show it to Rick and my dad.

"We destroyed all his information, including what he collected on you and your uncle." She grabs a usb-stick from her backpack. "But it wasn't the only thing he collected. He managed to find the name of another family member of your grandfather. He suspected there were more mind-readers." She looks at me. "I made sure no one else has this information. Just you. It's up to you and only you to decide what you'd like to do with it."

I hold up my hand for the usb-stick. Cecilia places it in my palm and I close my fingers around it. "Wow. More family members..." Would there be more people like me after all? Like Isabella?

I glance at the couple. They met for the first time five weeks ago, but for me, a lifetime has passed since. I've got friends. Dad and I talked about Mom for longer than a minute. Several people know I'm a mind-reader and haven't rejected me. I'll move to the farmhouse, to live with two other mind-readers, and have the information to find even more potentially.

I stare into the water. "You know, I've always seen the river as a symbol of the division between me and the rest of the world. Often, I yearned to find a bridge to cross over to the other side. All the while retreating to the solitary riverbank on my side."

Cecilia places a hand on my shoulder. "And now you're in between."

I smile. "You know what, you're right. I'm no longer trying to find a bridge to the other side. I'm navigating the river."

ACKNOWLEDGEMENTS

After I completed my first full manuscript, which has been stowed away deep in the electronic jungle since, a brave friend read it. When we discussed the manuscript and books in general, she asked 'Why do authors write such agonisingly long acknowledgements? You're not going to, are you?' Yes, Irene, I am! Over the past years, I learned there are way more people influencing your book than can be named and no matter how long the acknowledgements are, it's never long enough.

The most influential are other writers I've shared parts of this book with. By sharing and critiquing each other's work, I've learned so much from you and I love the odd community we form. A warm hug to Tema, Belle, Carel, Robert, Krista, Laura, Judy, Yulia, Richard, CFK, numerous others, and Sisters in Crime Canada West, in particular Marcelle and Karen.

I'm also thankful for the Writers' Guild of Alberta and Edmonton Public Library, for giving the opportunity to discuss my work with writers in residence and for arranging blue pencil sessions with established authors. Without them, this book would not just be less interesting, but it would even miss the first two chapters.

You wouldn't hold this book in your hands if it wasn't for Netta Johnson and Stonehouse Publishing. Netta, I'll be eternally grateful for your enthusiasm and dedication to publish my book and make my dream come true!

I started writing in the first place because my parents taught me the love for (the Dutch) language. Our family tradition of writing long, funny, and silly Sinterklaas poems has sparked a life-long joy in playing around with words.

Invaluable as well is my first reader. Marike, I know you'd rather have me finishing the sequel than write these acknowledgements. I'm grateful for your comments and encouragement, and of course our forty-year friendship.

Last but not least, I wouldn't be who I am, and therefore not write what I write, without my family. Bob, Sofie, and Tim, I love you, you have enriched my life. Marcel, my supportive husband, I love you so much for being my adventurous companion on our discovery journey through life.

ABOUT THE AUTHOR

Mirjam Dikken was born and raised in The Netherlands. She has worked around the world through her jobs as a chemical engineer, recruiter, and HR manager. Besides moving around within The Netherlands, she lived in New Delhi, India, and Edmonton, Canada. As she and her family love living below sea level, they settled in the Hoeksche Waard, an inland island in The Netherlands. She now wanders around in the darker places of her imagination to write thrillers and other fiction. Her stories have appeared in anthologies and on the beer cans of her favourite coffee stout.